"I'll go down first and then you'll follow."

He made it sound so easy. With the torch in one hand, he reached out and grabbed a rope, then swung his body forward and wrapped his legs around it. She watched his technique as he worked his way down and leaned over when she couldn't see him anymore. When he reached the next level he threw the torch into the corridor. Using the slight slack of the rope Calum swung himself forward and jumped, landing on the dirt ground.

He leaned out and called up, "Are you ready?"

She swallowed loudly and replied, "I don't think I can do this."

"You'll be fine—"

A voice from above cut him off. "Is that a woman I hear? The men will have fun when they find you tomorrow." The voice laughed.

Straightening her spine and resolve, Alexandria yelled back, "They'll never find me." Without a second thought she swung herself out until she was wrapped around the rope. Now she just had to figure out how to get down. She wasn't as graceful or as quick as Calum, but she managed to shimmy down the rope.

He reached out a hand. "Take my hand and place your foot on the edge, and I'll pull you in."

Taking his hand she stretched out her leg as far as possible but could plant only the ball of her foot on the edge.

"Okay, now when I start to pull, let go."

Suddenly terrified, she nodded but didn't speak. When she felt him pulling her she let go of the rope, but at the same time her foot slipped on the dirt and she fell. She screamed until she slammed into the wall and lost her breath.

THE QUEEN'S NECKLACE

AMANDA SIMONI

Thank you, Mom, for all your support
and encouragement over the years.
I never would have finished this book
without you.

A portion of the proceeds earned from this book will be
donated to the Calgary Public Library Foundation.

For information on how
you can help please visit
http://www.addin.ca

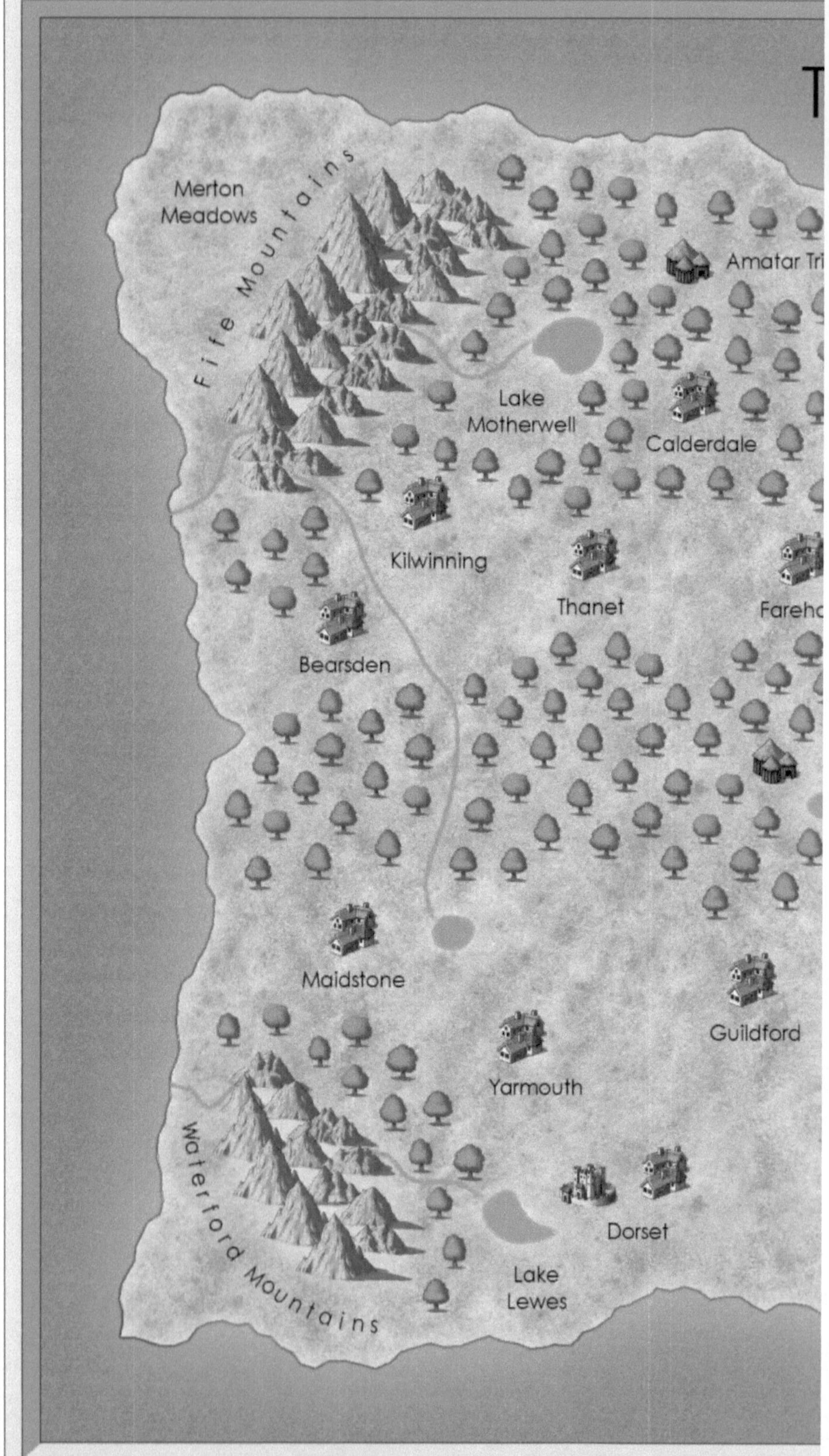

Merton Meadows
Fife Mountains
Amatar Tri
Lake Motherwell
Calderdale
Kilwinning
Thanet
Fareho
Bearsden
Maidstone
Guildford
Yarmouth
Dorset
Waterford Mountains
Lake Lewes
T

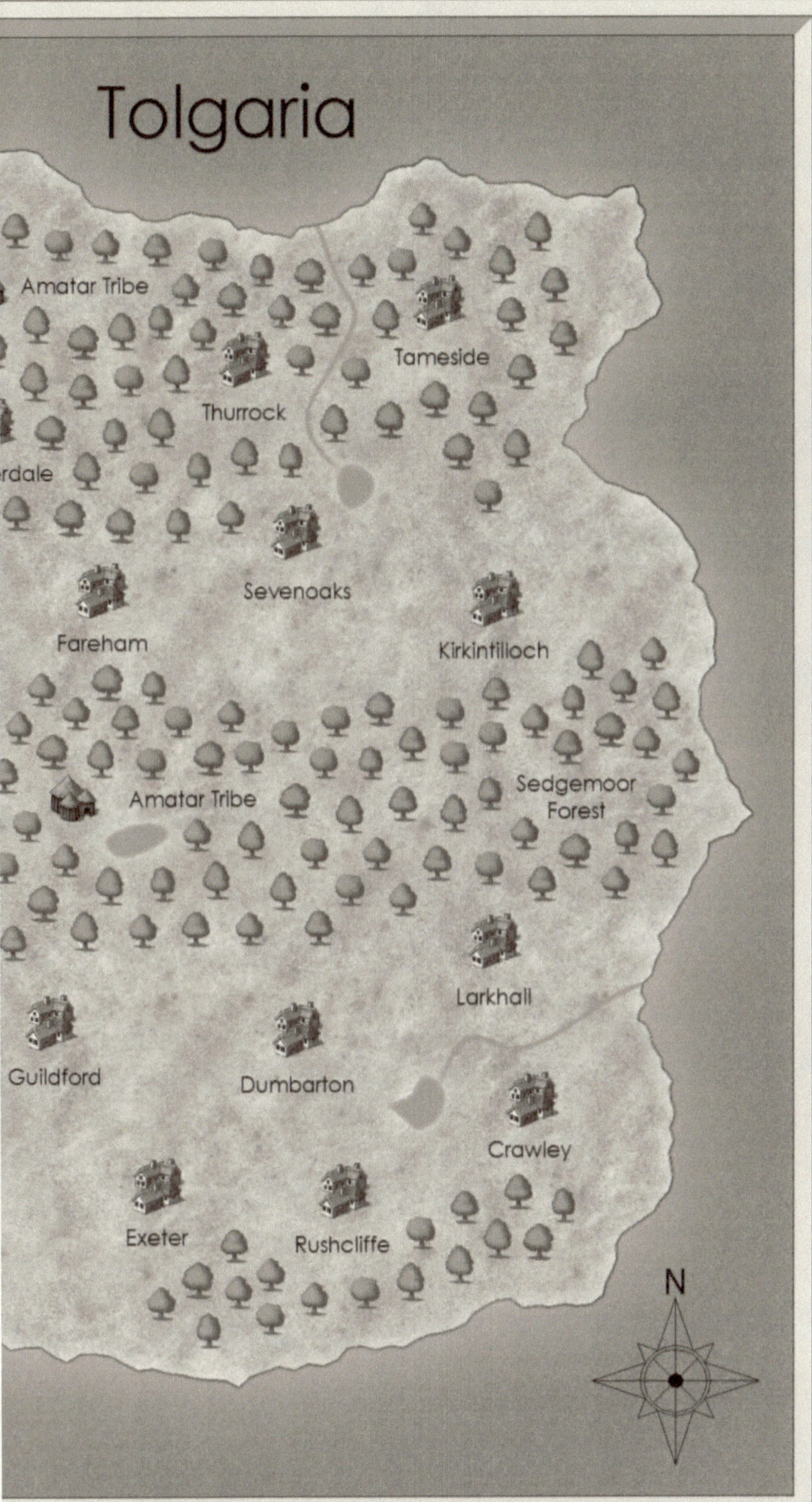

Tolgaria
Amatar Tribe
Tameside
Thurrock
...rdale
Sevenoaks
Fareham
Kirkintilloch
Amatar Tribe
Sedgemoor Forest
Larkhall
Guildford
Dumbarton
Crawley
Exeter
Rushcliffe
N

PROLOGUE

An elderly woman was sitting in a chair by the fire knitting. Her long white hair was pulled back in a bun and she was humming along to the song in her head.

Several children entered the room. "Grandma, grandma, tell us a story," they called as they ran to her side.

"Today I'm going to tell you a story about my great, great, great grandmother Alexandria, and how she changed Tolgaria forever." She continued to knit as the children settled at her feet.

"As you know, there are two very different races of people, the Tolgarians and the Amatarians, and they had been feuding since the beginning of time. The royal family of Dorset ruled the Tolgarians, while the Amatarians had their own leader, and their allegiance to him often caused conflict between the two races."

"Why?" one of her granddaughters asked.

"Because the king wanted to rule everyone, and the Amatarians refused to be ruled by the Tolgarians. Over the years several kings sent out soldiers to conquer the Amatarians, but they always failed. While the Amatarians had a smaller population, with one village in Sedgemoor Forest and another far north, near Lake Motherwell and the Fife Mountains, their men were stronger. Their style of fighting was also very different from the Tolgarians', and more effective, so they were often the victors."

"Cool," one boy exclaimed as he listened intently. He loved stories about fighting.

"One king finally realized he was never going to win and stopped the feud. The two races still didn't get along, but the fighting died down and the races began keeping their distance. The Amatarians were mostly left alone, for only some Tolgarian women have magick, but all Amatarians have magick, and the Tolgarians feared their powers."

The little boy let out a sigh of disappointment thinking this wasn't going to be a war story after all.

With an indulgent smile his grandmother continued. "As more villages appeared in Tolgaria, the Amatar tribe eventually had neighbors near their northern village, but they were still the only inhabitants of Sedgemoor Forest, a very large forest that separates the north and south regions. The northern villages became accustomed to seeing the Amatarians, and some of the animosity faded. It was different on the other side of Sedgemoor Forest. The Amatarians rarely traveled through the southern villages, so the Tolgarians in the south distrusted them and were known to attack. Long after the wars had ended, a Tolgarian healer was given a necklace promised to increase her powers, but she could feel its evil, so she asked a close friend with more magick than she possessed to help her hide it. They never told anyone its location, taking that knowledge to the grave. Perhaps they would have done things differently had they known what the future would hold."

Her grandsons all perked up. There was nothing they liked better than a battle story, while her girls liked romance. This was a story to satisfy both.

✠✠✠✠✠

Many years after the healer had died, a miner in Sevenoaks was chipping away at coal with his pickax when the area in front of him crumbled and a long, narrow, ornate wooden box rolled out. George looked around and saw that no one had noticed. Everyone was still hard at work.

Setting his pickax down, he lifted the box and studied the detailed carving on the lid. He'd never seen anything like it before. Flipping the silver latch, he opened it. The box was lined with black velvet. Inside lay a necklace comprised of thick links of silver. From the choker chain hung a thinner snake chain about two inches long, and attached to the end was a spider pendant.

It was the pendant that held his attention. The center of the spider's body was a large black stone. He didn't know much about jewels but thought he could probably get a good price for it. He decided to show it to his wife, Maggie, when he got home. She would have a better idea of its value.

George hid the necklace and got back to work. When it was time to go home he tucked the box into the back of his pants and covered it with his shirt and coat. Swinging the pickax over his shoulder, he chatted with the people he passed as he walked, just as he did every day.

He didn't feel guilty about taking the necklace. Whoever had owned it before had hidden it in the cave, he reasoned, and while he had no idea how it had gotten there, he was glad he had found it. His family could use the extra coins it would bring. He thought perhaps he should have turned it over to his boss, but as far as he was concerned, it was finders keepers.

When he arrived home, he leaned the pickax against his cabin and used the bucket of water left out for him to wash his hands and arms, his face and neck, before entering through the front door. His two girls were playing in front of the fire, and he could see that Maggie already had something simmering in a pot over the fire.

"Where's your mum?" he asked, placing the box on the table.

His eldest daughter, Grace, got up to stir the pot as she answered, "In the garden."

Sophia, his youngest daughter, skipped over and hugged his leg. "What's that?"

"Something for your mother," he said as he ruffled her hair.

"Can I see?" She stretched up on her toes, trying to see over the table.

"When your mum comes in." After giving Sophia a pat on the head, he headed back outside to the little garden behind their cabin, where his wife was picking vegetables.

While Sophia pouted, her sister ran over and took the box from the table. Opening it, she said, "Oh look. He got Mum a necklace." She held the box out so Sophia could see it.

"Pretty," Sophia said with a sigh, running her finger down the stone. All of a sudden she gasped, and her eyes grew wide before she collapsed to the ground.

"Sophia?" Grace dropped the box back on the table and knelt beside her sister. Shaking her she cried, "Sophia!" When her sister still didn't move she ran out the door, screaming for her parents.

They rushed in and fell to their knees beside her. Sophia's eyes were still wide open, and she wasn't breathing.

"What happened?" George asked.

"We . . . we were looking at the necklace . . . and then . . . and then she just fell," Grace cried.

Sitting back he whispered, "She's gone."

"No!" Maggie screamed, hugging her daughter to her chest as she cried.

"Can't Bethia make her better?" Grace asked, leaning against her father.

Maggie lifted her head, her tear-streaked face suddenly full of hope.

Bethia, the village's healer, lived just outside the village and had healed every ailment presented to her.

George scooped Sophia up and ran out the door, his wife and daughter behind him.

✠✠✠✠✠

Not so very far away another tragedy was unfolding.

Minerva and Henry were in their horse-drawn wagon heading to his cabin to start their life as husband and wife. In order to get married they'd had to travel to Sevenoaks and were now journeying through the forest back to Thurrock. They'd already had their wedding night at the inn in Sevenoaks and had spent the previous night in the back of their wagon in the forest. Now they were looking forward to spending the night in their new home. Because the road was narrow they were going slowly, laughing and kissing, thinking of the bliss to come.

As they bumped along, Minerva stared at her husband. *Husband*—how she loved that word. She'd waited so long for this. Leaning in to kiss his cheek she thought, *I may have waited years, but it was worth the wait.* Her friends had all gotten married a few years earlier, and most already had little ones. And even though she'd had offers from some good men, she knew Henry was the only man for her. She'd just had to wait until he'd realized she was the only one for him.

He turned and smiled at her with his brown eyes and she melted inside, as always. She could stare into his eyes for hours and never get tired of them, the gold in them captivating her. Minerva brushed his brown hair off his face while he talked, not really listening to what he was saying, just watching him.

His face was tanned from the many hours he'd spent outside. She loved that his hair was getting longer and she could run her fingers through it. Henry hated long hair, claiming it got in his face while he was working in the fields. Minerva wished he'd grow it out until he could pull it back like some of the other men he worked with, but knew he wouldn't wait that long. Soon it would bug him so much he'd chop it all off.

Hearing Minerva sigh, Henry glanced at her and once again couldn't believe his good luck, couldn't believe she'd waited for him. He didn't know why he'd taken so long to ask her, but at the last village dance he'd watched the men fighting to get to her side for a dance and realized he'd better make his move before he lost her. And now she was his wife.

He didn't blame his fellow villagers for wanting her. She was the most beautiful woman in Thurrock. Her long black hair was currently pulled back in a messy bun, and a few pieces blew in the wind around her heart-shaped face, highlighting her high cheekbones. She often wore her hair pulled back, but Henry loved it best when it fell in thick waves around her shoulders.

Her skin was as smooth and pale as marble, as though she never went outside, but he knew she spent hours tending her garden. She glanced his way again, her sky-blue eyes full of laughter and love, her naturally rosy lips curved up in a smile just for him. He knew from experience how soft they were and couldn't wait to feel that softness again.

Both of them were thinking about the wonderful life they had ahead of them when, out of nowhere, three men stepped in front of their wagon with their swords drawn.

All three were clean-shaven and wearing brown pants with white shirts. The man in the middle, who stood slightly in front of and slightly taller than the other two, was clearly the leader. His eyes were full of malice, and his mouth was set in an evil smirk.

Instantly Henry and Minerva were filled with fear.

The leader stepped forward. "Pay the toll and we'll let you pass."

Henry held up his hands. "We don't want any trouble."

"Neither do we. We just want your gold."

Henry untied the bag of coins from his hip and tossed it to the leader, who weighed the bag in his hand and shook his head. "Well this is disappointing. We might have to take something else to make up the difference."

Not liking the way the men were looking at his wife, Henry immediately said, "You can have the horses."

The two men behind the leader started to snicker as the leader looked over the pretty young woman in the wagon. "No, I think we'll just take your woman."

Minerva gripped Henry's arm and cowered against him with fear in her eyes.

Henry was a simple farmer and had nothing with which to defend himself against the swords, but he wasn't going to let them take his wife. Sitting up straighter he said, "You can't have her."

He picked up the reins, but the thieves had anticipated he would try to run them over and stepped forward, grabbing the horses before they could take off. The leader came around and grabbed Minerva, pulling her from the wagon.

She screamed and struggled against him.

"Let her go," Henry roared as he jumped from the wagon.

Immediately the other two grabbed him and held him back. He fought for all he was worth but in the end his struggles were in vain.

Minerva screamed Henry's name as one of the men stabbed him through his abdomen. She watched as he pulled his sword free and Henry fell to the ground. Focusing her attention on the one who'd killed him, she stopped struggling and gathered all her strength. She'd never used her magick to hurt someone before but knew it could be done. As her rage built, she felt power growing inside her and imagined her hands around his neck.

Henry's murderer suddenly grabbed his throat, gasping for air.

"What's wrong?" his friend asked. He turned around and screamed as he met Minerva's eyes, which were turning dark blue as magick filled her. "It's her! She's a witch."

The leader released her and she fell to her knees, never looking away from her target. The men tried to drag their friend away but couldn't move him. He dropped to his knees, still gasping. Fearing they would be next, the two thieves ran. It wasn't long before the friend they had abandoned fell back, as dead as Minerva's husband.

Crying, she crawled over to Henry and pulled him onto her lap. Her cries were full of pain and anger. She wished she'd had the power to kill the other two before they'd run off.

I can help you with that, a creepy voice whispered.

Minerva whipped her head around, looking for the owner of the voice. "Who's there?"

I'm not there. You'll have to come to me.

She continued to look around. "Who are you?"

You'll have to come to see.

It was as though someone were hiding behind the trees and speaking in a low hiss, even though Minerva could feel there was no one around. She thought it might be a trap, that this person must have strong magick to be able to talk to her from somewhere else.

You're right, I do have strong magick.

Minerva gasped. "You can read my mind."

Yes, and I can feel your pain.

Tears welled up in her eyes as she looked down at Henry and brushed his hair off his forehead.

I can give you what you want.

Full of hope, she asked, "You can bring him back?" She'd never heard of such magick.

No, but I can give you the men who took him from you.

Her eyes hardened as she thought of the two who had gotten away. "How?"

Come to me and I'll show you.

Minerva looked down at Henry. "I can't leave him," she said, stroking his cheek.

If you want to avenge him, you'll have to leave him.

"I can't."

He's not there anymore. He's gone.

"But to leave him here, in the middle of the road. Can't I take him home and bury him first?"

There's no time to for that. You'll have to decide. Do you want my help or not?

"Yes."

Then come to me, and I'll give you your vengeance.

Tears still streaming down her cheeks, she kissed Henry's lips for the last time and whispered, "I will avenge you." Standing, she asked in a clear voice, "How do I find you?"

You need to go back the way you came.

She walked through the night and for all of the next day, the voice directing her, until she was back in Sevenoaks in front of a cabin. Minerva stopped outside.

I'm inside, the voice said.

She hesitated and thought, *I can't just walk into a stranger's cabin.*

If you want to meet me, you have to come inside.

Taking a deep breath she opened the door, eager to meet the person behind the voice. It was dark inside, not a candle lit. She stepped in and saw the cabin was empty.

"Where are you?" she called.

Right here, the voice whispered.

She looked around again but still didn't see anyone. Minerva knew she wasn't alone though. She could feel power in the air, and it all seemed to be coming from the table. She saw a box on the table and reached for it. Just as her fingers were about to touch it, she hesitated.

Go on, the voice whispered seductively. *Open it.*

She still hesitated. It felt evil to her, as though it possessed the type of magick she'd been taught to stay away from.

Open it and you can have anything you want.

"I want Henry back."

I have a lot of power, but even I can't bring someone back from the dead.

"But you can find those who took him from me?"

Yes, and I can give you the power to destroy them.

She did want that—almost as much as she wanted Henry back. Determinedly, she opened the box. Minerva couldn't believe what she saw.

It was a necklace. The voice was coming from a necklace.

She could feel the power radiating from the spider pendant, and although she'd heard of objects that possessed magick, she'd never seen any before. And she was fairly certain they didn't talk.

That's right, there's nothing out there like me.

"How are you going to help me?"

Put me on.

She picked up the necklace and clasped it around her neck. Instantly she felt power flow through her body. It was like nothing she'd ever experienced before, like she could take on anything, and anyone.

Resting her hand on the pendant, Minerva asked with a strong voice, "How do we find them?"

Just beyond the village is a lake. Take me there.

As she walked through the village Minerva noticed people from all directions traveling north, and they looked forlorn. "What's going on?"

Nothing you need to worry about. The lake is through those trees.

The necklace knew that if Minerva found out the people were going to the miner's daughter's funeral, she might not take the next step, and the necklace needed a wearer.

Minerva walked through the trees and after a few minutes came upon the lake. As she approached the edge she asked, bewildered, "What are we doing here?"

I'm going to show you where they are.

"How? It's too dark."

In the lake a circle started to glow, and within that circle she saw several men in a tavern. Leaning forward, she recognized the two men who'd stopped her wagon. They were sitting at a table drinking. The leader pulled a barmaid into his lap as she served them a round of drinks. She didn't seem to be enjoying the attention.

I'd be doing the world a favor, she thought as she watched them.

That's right, the necklace whispered. *They don't deserve to live.*

"Where are they?"

The scene changed until she saw the tavern's name.

"I know that place. It's not far from where I live." Turning, she started walking back through the trees. "It'll take me days to get there," She said, discouraged.

I can get you there faster.

She stopped walking. "How?"

Just think about where you want to go and leave the rest to me.

Minerva thought about the tavern and felt a flood of energy flow through her body. Black smoke swirled around her until it was all she could see. Just as she started to fear what was happening, the smoke dissipated and she was standing in front of the tavern.

She wasn't sure if she could go through with it. She wasn't a murderer.

But think about what they did to Henry.

"Only one killed Henry, and I killed him," she said.

They would have killed him too. Look in the water.

In front of the tavern was a horse trough, and it started to glow. She walked over to it, and when she looked inside she saw Henry lying in the dirt, dead. Then she saw the moment of his death again. Crying, she covered her mouth with a hand. The final scene was of the two men in the tavern, laughing and drinking. Acting as though nothing had happened.

Rage filled her as she watched them, her hands clenched at her sides. She could picture herself choking the life from them as she had from their friend.

That's right, let the rage fill you. It will make you stronger.

Thinking she might need another push, the necklace showed her Henry lying in the dirt again, before the picture faded away and the water was back to normal. Feeling the hate within Minerva, the necklace knew it was time.

Now go inside.

Breathing heavily she stormed through the door, her hair flying around her, her eyes black as the night. All talk ceased. Everyone turned to stare at her, and they took in her wild hair and dirt-streaked clothing. Her skirt was stained with mud along the bottom. Everyone but two wondered what had happened to her. The two men from the woods recognized her and scrambled out of their seats.

Before anyone could step forward to offer her help, one of the thieves pointed a finger and yelled, "She's a witch."

She threw her hands forward and black smoke flew across the room, taking the thief with it. As the other tried to run for the back door she moved one hand in his direction until the smoke surrounded him and dragged him back.

People screamed and pushed each other as they tried to escape. A few tried to fight back. One broke a chair over her back, sending her flying, but the black smoke surrounded and protected her as it lifted her back to her feet.

Turning, Minerva confronted the man who'd hit her. "You dare to attack me?" She focused on him while the smoke held the other two prisoner. He started to choke, his hands clutching at his throat.

"Let him go," another man screamed, charging her.

She threw out her hand again and he stopped in his tracks. When he started to choke, she turned back to the first, wanting to make sure he didn't try to attack her again. She was surprised to see him on his knees, still gasping. She'd never been able to use her magick on more than one thing at a time before.

That's the power I can give you.

A few more men suddenly charged her. She turned her gaze to them and they all stopped, their hands clutching their throats.

Feeling the power flow through her, she walked towards them confidently. "You would try to stop me? You would try to save these murderers?" She waved her hand towards the two men still encircled within black smoke.

One tried to talk but couldn't get the words out. She eased the pressure on her hold so he could speak.

Gasping, he said, "They're not murderers. You are."

Leaning in she told him, "I'd never killed anyone before yesterday. Not until they killed my husband when he tried to protect me from them."

Looking around, she saw people cowering against the walls, watching her with terror in their eyes. Releasing all but the two she really wanted, she asked, "You would protect this scum?"

The one who'd spoken before separated himself from the group. "They're not scum."

Minerva turned back to him. As she moved forward, the smoke surrounding the men followed her, dragging them closer to the one who was speaking. "You know them, do you?"

"He's my brother," he answered, nodding towards the leader.

"Do you know what he was up to yesterday morning?" He didn't respond. "No? Well let me enlighten you. He and his two friends tried to rob me and my husband, and when they didn't like the amount of gold we had, your brother dragged me from our wagon saying I would make up the difference."

Looking around, she saw she had everyone's attention and continued. "Then your brother held me back while his friend killed my husband." Turning back to the man, she asked, "Do you know how long we'd been married? Two days." She spun around to face Henry's murderers. "We'd been married two days before you took him from me."

Minerva walked towards them. "Now your brother can watch you die like I watched my Henry." She felt her power growing as she prepared to end their lives.

"You're a liar," the man behind her called out.

Angry, she whirled around. "What did you say?"

"You're a liar. My brother would never kill anyone."

Screaming, Minerva threw her arms out wide and released the power she was feeling. Black smoke spread out from her in a circle, covering the room. When it faded, she saw the man lying on the ground, eyes open. Looking around she saw everyone was on the ground with their eyes and mouths open—the men who had attacked her, the people against the walls, everyone. She could tell by their vacant expressions that they were all dead.

She turned around frantically, hoping to find someone alive, and stopped when she recognized the barmaid she'd seen in the water. Minerva covered her mouth as horror filled her. She'd never planned on hurting anyone else, just the two who'd killed Henry.

"What have I done?" she whispered.

We've just started.

CHAPTER ONE

100 Years Later

Minerva stood on her balcony watching the sun rise over her lake, her long black hair blowing out behind her. Her blue eyes were no longer the color of the sky but darker, colder. She was wearing a hunter-green dress. The neckline and cinched waist showed off her curves before the garment flowed out into a full skirt. The spider necklace lay against her bare chest. It was the only necklace she ever wore, for she never took it off. Her lips were painted dark red, and her silver crown matched her necklace.

It's time, her necklace whispered.

She didn't need to ask what he meant. "Already?"

These last attacks have drained me faster than usual.

"Maybe this will teach them to stop attacking us." Turning, she called, "Alva." When no one appeared after a few seconds, she screamed, "*Alva!*"

A maid rushed into the room and stopped in the balcony's doorway.

Frowning, Minerva asked, "Where's Alva?"

"I haven't seen her yet today, Your Majesty."

"Find her and send her to me."

The maid curtsied and ran from the hall.

While she waited for her servant to answer her summons, Minerva turned back to the lake and thought about going for a ride later. One of her greatest pleasures was riding by the lake, the only place outside the castle where she was safe from attacks.

The balcony on which she stood was one of the two that flanked her throne room. Upon entering the room that had many years ago also served as a ballroom, one was greeted by five stone arches on either side, and they connected to form the soaring Gothic ceiling. Behind each of the arches were tall glass double doors that led to the balconies. Across from the entrance, at the other end of the long hall, three stairs led to the royal platform. On one side of the platform was a table that held her gold goblets and two jugs—one for water and one for wine—that she demanded always be full. It also held silver platters of fruit, cheese, and breads, from which her servants served her.

Two more stairs led to another small, round platform, on which sat her throne. It was carved out of white limestone and had a tall back that ended with a rounded arch. Ruby-red velvet cushions covered the seat and a portion of the back. Embedded in the stone were the bones of the former king and queen of Tolgaria. The longer arm and leg bones created a horrifying border around the edge of the back. Within that border were two arms, elbows to fingers, reaching for the sky. The space around them was filled with random bones. The skulls of the former king and queen rested at the end of the throne's arms. It had special meaning for the queen and served as a reminder to the people, whenever they stood before her, of her power.

Alva hurried into the room holding her long skirt out of her way. Wisps of hair flew out of her tight bun. She was a petite woman with a round face and tired eyes. When she saw the throne empty, Alva looked around nervously. She would be in big trouble if the queen had grown weary of waiting for her and left. When she saw her on the balcony she almost wept with relief.

Moving to the balcony door she took a deep breath to calm her nerves and curtsied, staying low. "You called for me, Your Majesty."

Minerva turned, her skirts swirling around her. "Alva, yes." Leaving the balcony she stalked to her throne and sat down before addressing her servant, who had followed and now stood before her on the royal platform. "I want you to go to one of the nearby villages and get me a child."

Alva stared at her in shock. "A child? But you just had one four months ago."

"Yes. Well, maybe you should remind the people that if they didn't constantly try to go against me, I wouldn't have to take more children," she said, checking her nails.

"But, Your Majesty, it's your taking more children that has them so upset," she said bravely.

Minerva turned her dark gaze to Alva. "As I said, I wouldn't have to take more children if they ceased their war against me. Now, go to a village and get me another child. This time make it a girl, around four or five. They're always purer than the boys."

Alva didn't move. She hated this duty and didn't think she could go through with it again so soon. For many years the queen had only sent someone every nine or ten months, but since Alva had taken over a few years ago, the time between had been growing shorter and shorter.

Raising her brow the queen said, "Maybe you don't want to go that far. You have a daughter that age, don't you?"

Terror filled her. "My baby? But . . . but you don't take children from the castle."

"No," the queen drawled, "that's your reward for your loyalty. But if you refuse to get me another child, I'll have to make an exception, won't I?"

She couldn't let her take her daughter, and would do anything to protect her. Curtsying, Alva said, "I'll leave immediately."

"Good. And Alva"—her servant turned back—"next time I won't give you a choice."

Alva nodded before rushing from the room. She ran all the way to her small cabin behind the castle and found her husband and two children inside. Immediately she scooped up her daughter and hugged her tight. Pressing a kiss to her head she squeezed her one more time before putting her down.

"I have to go, Rufus. I'll be back in a few days."

Her husband didn't need to hear any more to understand what was going on—only one thing caused her to leave Dorset. Motioning her to the corner, he whispered, "So soon? You just went a few months ago."

"I know, but all the recent attacks on the castle have drained her."

"You don't have to do this."

"I do, or else she'll take . . ." She couldn't finish, and her blue eyes welled up with tears as she looked at their daughter. She bit her full bottom lip to keep from crying out, not wanting to alarm her children.

Rufus turned as well, but his eyes filled with rage. "No. Not our girl." Rufus was a big man, muscular from his work as a blacksmith, but he was no match for the queen.

Alva nodded, tears falling down her cheeks. "If I don't get her a different one, she'll take ours."

He hugged his wife. "We could leave," he said. "We'll take our children and go." It was something they'd talked about since Alva took over as the queen's personal servant, but Alva had always been too afraid.

Pulling back, Alva whispered, "We can't. Remember what happened to the last family that tried. The queen will know."

One family had grown tired of the queen's demands a few months earlier and tried to escape in the middle of the night. Through ways unknown to the people of the castle, the queen found out what they were doing and sent her soldiers after them. She then executed the family and made everyone at the castle watch, reminding the people of what would happen if they crossed her.

Deciding not to argue with her, Rufus asked, "Where are you going?"

"I don't know. Everyone with young children has left the nearby villages. I don't know how far I'll have to go."

"Be safe," he told her with a kiss.

After kissing her children, Alva gathered several soldiers to travel with her, and they left the castle grounds. The villages nearest Dorset had no children, so they bypassed them and traveled farther. As the sun was setting on the fourth day of their journey, they reached Rushcliffe, a village that she knew still had children, but due to the late hour she didn't see any.

"We'll find a child in the morning," she said to the soldiers. "Let's make camp."

"Why don't you go through the homes?" one asked.

"The families will have a chance to hide their children before I can see them. No, we'll wait until the children are out and playing in the morning."

Once the sun was overhead the next day, Alva saw several young girls running around. One in particular had bouncing blonde curls, an angelic face, and looked to be around four years old. "Take her," she ordered the soldiers with a heavy heart.

As soon as the child began screaming, people started running over but stopped when they saw the soldiers, for they knew that interfering would mean their deaths. But that didn't stop the child's father, who charged forward with a pitchfork in his hands. He was easily knocked to the ground, and a few soldiers chuckled before heading for their horses. One soldier raised his sword to kill the man, but Alva stopped him. They were there for a child, not to kill.

Back at the castle, Alva took the little girl to the kitchen for a bath before dressing her in a pretty pink dress. The queen always insisted they be clean and nicely dressed before she saw them. The little girl wouldn't stop crying for her mum, so Alva rocked her as she did her own children, telling her everything would be alright, silently praying that God would forgive her.

She finally took her to the queen. Standing behind the girl, Alva rested her hands on her shaking shoulders.

Minerva looked the little girl over. "Good job, Alva. Leave us now."

Alva hurried from the room to wait until it was over.

The little girl started to whimper when she was alone with the queen. Even at her tender age she'd heard stories. She didn't understand what happened but knew the children the queen took never went home.

The queen crouched in front of her. "There's no need to be frightened. I'm not going to hurt you."

This is a good one, the necklace whispered. *She has power.*

The little girl's eyes went wide as the queen stroked a finger down her cheek. She suddenly stopped breathing and collapsed.

"See," the queen said, rising. "You didn't feel a thing." Calling Alva back in she said, "Take her away."

"Yes, Your Majesty." After curtsying, she picked up the little girl and carried her from the room.

✠✠✠✠

"This has to stop," Finnean stated with fire in his eyes as he slammed his fist on the table, causing his chin-length brown hair to swing forward. His face was set in anger, making his angular features seem even sharper. He was sitting at his parents' table with his family, sharing the news he'd just heard at the tavern.

The cabin wasn't very big, and the table took up most of the space. After the boys had moved out, their parents had removed their beds and gotten a bigger table to accommodate the whole family. Their sister's bed was on the other side of the room, along with a screen for privacy when changing. Beside the kitchen was a doorway leading to a small room that their parents used as a bedroom.

"What are we supposed to do?" Niall asked. He was the eldest, and the more levelheaded brother. He and Finnean looked a lot alike, with the same strong features and tanned skin. His hair was a little darker and longer, and he always wore it pulled back. The main difference was their eyes. He had serious brown eyes like their mother, while Finnean's blue eyes matched their father's.

Niall understood his brother's anger and wanted to go after the queen too, but what good would it do? Everyone who went after her died.

"We have to stop her," Finnean stated again, aggravated. "This is the second child already this year. And her soldiers are traveling further from Dorset. Who's to say they won't come here next time?"

His betrothed, Agnes, placed a hand on his arm, trying to calm him. Her eyes were the color of their lake, a warm, rich blue, and she had long black hair she wore in a braid. She was the perfect match for Finnean, not afraid to speak her mind and yet able to soothe him when he got upset.

"We're weeks from the castle," said Alexandria, the only daughter and the youngest sibling. "They've never come this far before." She was the complete opposite of her brothers. Those who didn't know them would never guess they were siblings. Whereas Alexandria was fair, her brothers were tanned from working outside, and she had a slim build, while they were muscular. She had an oval face with a full mouth, and her cheeks formed gentle curves that were always rosy. Her brothers claimed that the color in her cheeks came from the red in her blonde hair, which fell halfway down her back. She had dark brown eyes that could change from joyful to concerned and empathic in an instant.

Except for her hair, she looked just like her mother had when she was younger.

"That's not true," Niall told her. "Last year when she was traveling she took a child from Thanet, and that's only a day's ride from here."

"But that was the first time she'd been on this side of Sedgemoor Forest in what? Fifty years?" Alexandria asked.

"What difference does that make?" Finnean asked. "If families with kids move up here, then she'll send her soldiers up here."

"Most families feel safe in their villages. They're not moving up here," Alexandria countered.

"You've never been down south," Niall reminded her. "Families are moving away from Dorset, and eventually they'll be moving up here."

"Still," Agnes said, "it will take a long time for people to move up here. If she only comes this way every fifty years, our family will be safe."

Adella, their mother, spoke for the first time. "She was here sixteen years ago." Her long brown hair was pulled back in a bun, a few pieces escaping at the sides, softening her look. Her gaze passed over her children as she waited for their reaction.

"What?" Alexandria was shocked. She'd never heard this before, and being one of the healers, she heard every story.

"Here?" Niall asked.

"In Calderdale?" Finnean asked at the same time.

"She took a child."

Both brothers and their women looked at Alexandria. Then Niall's wife, Helen, placed a hand protectively on her swollen stomach, her shoulder-length light brown hair covering her face as she looked down upon her unborn child.

"Why are you all looking at me?"

"You're lucky she didn't take you," Agnes replied. "Everyone knows she likes girls with power."

"I wouldn't let her."

They all turned to Adella with questioning expressions on their faces, for they all knew any who tried to go against the queen were killed.

Alpin covered his wife's clenched hands with one of his and looked at her with concern. "I think it's time they knew." His blond hair was still pulled back from working in the fields. He watched his wife with concern. He knew she'd wished this day would never come, just as he always knew it would.

She nodded and took a deep breath. "When you were four, Alexandria, I heard she was in the area. I also knew she hadn't had a child in almost a year."

"Had? Do you know what she does to them?" Alexandria asked, leaning forward.

"Let your mother explain," Alpin said.

"I was afraid she'd take you, so I gave you a sleeping potion and hid you in an empty cabin for a few days. The Amatarians guarded you and made the cabin invisible, like their home."

The Amatar tribe lived in the forest just north of their village, not far from Lake Motherwell. Their home was invisible to Tolgarians, protected by their magick. Another reason the Tolgarians were afraid of them.

"But I didn't know about them then."

"You never saw them. You were asleep."

Alexandria couldn't believe what she was hearing. "How long was I there?"

"Four days."

Sitting back in her chair, she didn't know if she should be upset or not—not about the sleeping potion, as she knew her mother had been protecting her, but about the fact she'd never been told. "Why were you worried she'd take me?"

"Agnes is right. She likes girls with power, and even though you were so young, you were already showing signs of having magick."

"At four?"

Not all Tolgarian girls possessed magick, but those who did usually didn't show signs until around age five or six.

"I don't know why you're surprised. You come from a long line of healers."

Finnean looked at his mother suspiciously. "You know more than you're telling us."

Adella sighed. This was a difficult subject for her, but it was time her children knew the truth—at least some of it. "What do you want to know?"

"What does she do with the children?" Alexandria wanted to know. Everyone assumed that they were killed, as they were never seen again, but no one wanted to speculate about what the queen did to them first.

"She kills them."

Finnean rolled his eyes. "We know. Why is she killing them?"

Agnes slapped his hand, frowning at him. "Let your mother explain."

Adella sighed again. The moment she'd dreaded her entire life was here. "It's actually her necklace. That's where her powers come from. It's what keeps her young."

"So she kills children to keep her youth?" Niall asked, growing angry. His brother was right. She needed to be stopped.

"No. The necklace needs to rejuvenate itself. To do that, it needs the soul of someone pure. She used to take a child only once a year, but the more magick she uses the sooner she needs another child."

"Does she hurt them?" Alexandria asked, worry filling her eyes.

That was just like her daughter, wanting to know if anyone was in pain. "Not that I know of. The necklace doesn't hurt them. They're just alive one minute and dead the next."

"So if we destroy the necklace, we destroy her," Finnean stated, already planning how it could be done. "What does it look like?"

"It's a spider pendant with a black stone in the center. The stone is where all the magick is, and you can't destroy it. She never takes it off, and it always knows when someone's coming after her."

"That explains why she always wins," Niall said, sharing a look with Finnean.

Over the years many men had tried to end her reign, and none had ever come home.

"How do you know so much?" Alexandria asked, watching her mother. She had a feeling there was still more that their mother didn't want to tell them.

"Over the years, our family has followed everything she's done," Adella started to explain.

"Why?" Niall asked.

"Because we're the reason she has the necklace."

"*What!*" all three children cried at once. Agnes's jaw dropped while horror filled Helen's eyes.

"What do you mean?" Finnean asked.

"A long time ago, one of our ancestors was given the necklace as a thank-you. She was told it would increase her power so she could heal more people. She could feel it was evil and didn't like what it wanted her to do, so she took it off and—"

"Wait," Finnean interrupted. "What do you mean it wanted her to do things?"

"The story that's been passed down is that the necklace talks to you, tries to get you to use your magick in a different way. She asked a friend with more power to help her hide it, and then passed on the story to her children and grandchildren that not all magick is good. Our family has continued to pass on the story every generation."

"Then why did you never tell us?" Niall asked.

Sharing a look with her husband, Adella decided to tell them only part of the truth. "I didn't want you to carry that burden. It was so long ago it doesn't matter anymore."

Finnean leaned forward in his chair. "Tell us everything. How did she find the necklace? Did someone tell her where it was?"

Adella shook her head. "No one knew where it was. A hundred years ago, a miner in Sevenoaks found it in a cave and took it home. While his daughter was looking at it, it took her soul. Then it started looking for a new wearer."

"Did he know the necklace was evil?" Alexandria asked. "The miner, I mean."

"No, it wasn't until our ancestor heard the story and went to see the family that the miner and his wife realized the necklace was responsible for their daughter's death, and by that time the necklace was gone."

"But I thought you said the necklace could talk," Alexandria said. "Couldn't they hear it?"

"No, when the necklace talks it's like a whisper in your head. Not everyone hears it. In fact, only women can hear it because only women have magick, and it only talks to those who do."

"But Amatarian men have magick," Alexandria reminded her.

"True, but they're different from us. I don't know if they would be able to hear it. I don't know if the necklace would even try, as it's evil and they're pure good."

"So it found the queen," Finnean said. "It must have felt her evil."

"No," his mother corrected. "It felt her pain."

"Are you defending the queen?" Alexandria asked, shocked.

"The queen, no, but she wasn't always the queen, and she wasn't always evil." Adella's children watched her attentively as she told them the queen's story. "Her name is Minerva, and she's from Thurrock. On the same day the miner found the necklace, she was traveling home with her husband after getting married. On their way, they were robbed and her husband was killed. She was a witch, and she killed one thief while the others got away."

"So she was evil," Finnean declared.

"That doesn't make her evil," Alexandria told him.

"She killed someone," Finnean countered.

"She killed someone who attacked them and killed her husband. What would you have done?"

He kept his mouth shut, since he would have done the same if someone had attacked his family.

"That's what I thought," she said smugly. Turning back to her mother, she urged, "Go on."

"Feeling her pain and rage, the necklace called out to her, promising to help her. When she found the necklace, it gave her the power to find and kill the other men."

"How do you know all this?" Niall asked.

"When our ancestor found out Minerva had the necklace, she went to see her, to urge her to give it up. But Minerva liked the power too much. She had started ruling Thurrock and could have anything she wanted, and she wanted more. Tired of just ruling the north, she decided she wanted to rule the whole country. So she went to Dorset, killed the royal family, and took the throne. She's ruled ever since."

She glanced at her husband before adding, "Many have tried to stop her over the years, but they've all failed. She's too powerful."

Alpin took his wife's hand, offering comfort. He knew how hard it was for her to relive this, having mourned with her when her brothers hadn't come home. They'd been betrothed at the time and had postponed their wedding.

"Our ancestor must have been very strong to turn away from that power," Alexandria replied softly.

"But why didn't she destroy it?" Niall asked.

"I don't know. I can only assume her magick wasn't strong enough."

Alexandria figured that had to be the answer. While the women in her family had gifts beyond healing, these gifts had never been very powerful.

"So it's up to us," Finnean said with determination. "We have to destroy the necklace."

Agnes looked down at her lap. Knowing him as well as she did she'd known he was going to say that, but she didn't want him to go, afraid he would never come back. Helen was sitting beside her and took her hand, sharing her fear.

"No," Adella cried, standing. "Haven't you been listening? No one can kill her."

"That's the burden you were talking about, isn't it, Mum?" Alexandria remarked as it dawned on her. "This is the real reason you never told us."

Collapsing in her chair, Adella said, "Yes. Every generation the story is passed on, and the men always feel it's their duty to get the necklace back." Looking at her boys, she continued. "And they die. My brothers, my uncles, they never came back. I won't have the same happen to my sons."

Alexandria looked at her mother with sad eyes. She knew her two uncles had died before her birth but had never known how. Now she understood why her mother hadn't talked about their passing.

"But Mum, that's the reason the story is passed on," Finnean said. "It's our job to stop her."

"That's why I never told you. We *can't* stop her."

"I agree with Finn, Mum," Niall said. "We have to stop her."

"No," she said again, firmly. "You have a child on the way. Are you going to leave your wife to raise your baby on her own?" Turning to Finnean, she said, "And you, you're to be married in two days. Are you going to make her a widow so soon?"

"Now that we know the truth we can't just sit here," Finnean said.

"You'll have to. You're farmers, not soldiers. That's why I told you, to prove no man can kill her."

Maybe that's the problem, Alexandria thought. Since the necklace had magick and only women had magick, maybe only a woman could defeat it. She'd have to think about this, but quietly. Her family would never let her go.

CHAPTER TWO

A few days after Finnean's wedding, Alexandria had it all figured out. Since the necklace belonged to her family, and men couldn't destroy it, it was up to her to destroy it and kill the queen. None of her other gifts were as strong as her healing powers, and certainly not as strong as the queen's, but she figured she'd have time to practice on her way to Dorset.

She had determined it would take a week to get to Sedgemoor Forest, two weeks to get through it, then probably another week to reach Dorset. She wasn't entirely sure about the timing, having never been to Sedgemoor Forest or the southern region. Plus, she was planning on going to Thurrock first, which would likely add another week to her travels. She was confident she would have at least five weeks to improve her magick.

Alexandria was an expert rider but had decided not to take her horse, even though it would cut her travel time, knowing it would make her a target for thieves. Thanks to her brothers, she was also an excellent shot with a bow and arrow, so she'd be able to hunt for food and protect herself should anyone try to bother her. However, she planned to avoid people and travel at night, so she knew she'd have to find good hiding places where she could sleep during the day.

Out hunting in the forest, she tested her skills by throwing rocks to catch the rabbits in flight—and caught three out of four. Confident that she was a good shot and would be fine on her own, she rode home pleased, her hair flying out behind her, the rabbits tied to her saddle.

As she pulled up in front of her cabin, her mother was waiting for her, arms crossed over her tan vest, irritation bright in her eyes. The wind was blowing her burgundy skirt out around her.

Alexandria knew she was in trouble. Her mother hated when she wore pants, but it was such a pain wearing a skirt when riding. And she was still wearing her blouse and vest, so she was just as covered. In fact, on the horse, she was even more covered in pants, as her ankles didn't show and she didn't flash any leg when mounting or dismounting—so what was the big deal?

"Hi Mum," she called as she dismounted, a big smile on her face. "I caught three rabbits for supper." She hoped this would distract her mother from the lecture she knew was coming.

"Well, it's glad I am to have a third son to hunt for supper," Adella remarked, taking the rabbits.

"Come on, Mum. I've hunted before."

"Yes, and you know I've never approved," Adella said, following her daughter to the corral behind the cabin, where Alexandria took her horse's saddle off. "And where did you get those pants? I thought I threw them away."

Alexandria looked at her pants sheepishly. "You did. I took these from Finnean's old clothes."

Adella sighed. "How are we going to find you a husband if you continue to dress like a man?"

"I'm not that bad! I only wear pants when I'm riding. Or hunting," she added, closing the gate and heading back around to the front of the cabin.

Three women walked by, and when they saw Alexandria they giggled and started whispering behind their hands.

"See, people are laughing at you."

"Like I care what *they* think," Alexandria said, storming inside. "They're just a bunch of silly gossips."

"Two are married and the other just got engaged."

"I feel sorry for that man," Alexandria said, flopping into a chair at the table.

Laying a hand on her daughter's shoulder, Adella said softly, "It's Michael."

Shocked, Alexandria looked up at her mother. "Michael?"

Adella nodded, her irritation replaced by sympathy.

Alexandria had thought he was going to ask her parents for her hand. She didn't want to show she was hurt, so she shrugged and said casually, "I thought he had better taste."

Not wanting to sound cold but wanting to get her point across Adella said, "I'm sorry honey, but men don't want to marry girls who dress and act like men."

Offended, she stood up. "I don't act like a man."

With a raised brow Adella looked at her daughter's pants.

"That's different. I only wear them when I'm riding. A dress is too cumbersome." She stalked over to the screen in the corner beside her bed to change. The pants were big enough that she didn't need to take her boots off when removing them.

"No one else seems to have a problem," her mother countered.

Peeking her head out from behind the screen, Alexandria said, "Not many women actually ride, and they're not leaving the village to collect herbs or hunt." After sliding her brown skirt on, she tucked in her blouse and pulled her beige vest into place so it covered the seam.

"That's just it. Hunting's a man's job. You're not supposed to do it."

"Who's going to catch our food? Father's in the field all day and Niall and Finnean have their own families to hunt for now."

"Your father would find the time."

"But now he doesn't have to," Alexandria said, coming out from behind the screen. "Now he can spend more time with you. You're welcome."

Adella ignored that comment. "If you'd stop wearing pants and hunting, you could have a dozen men courting you."

"So you want me to act like those girls?" Alexandria asked, waving her hand towards the door.

"Yes!" More than anything, Adella wanted her daughter to act like a proper lady and find a husband.

"So you want me to get a job at the tavern and wear low-cut blouses and vests to show off my breasts?"

"No, that's not what I want."

"Well that's what they do, and since you made a point of telling me they're married, or about to be married, you must want me to be just like them."

Tired of arguing with her daughter, Adella waved her away and said, "Go see Helen. She's due any day now."

As if she needed to be told that. She'd been keeping an eye on her sister-in-law for months, and if Helen didn't have the baby that day, she was going to miss the birth, since she was planning on departing that night. The only way to pull this off was to leave in the middle of the night, while her family slept, so she'd be hours away before anyone even knew she was gone.

Alexandria knew her mother wanted her out of the cabin because she was annoyed with her, and because she wanted to throw away her pants—again. What her mother didn't know was that she had another pair hidden away. She'd actually tailored them so they'd fit her better for her journey.

Walking along the main road, Alexandria saw Michael in front of the tavern with a few of his friends. She stared straight ahead as she passed, refusing to acknowledge him.

Michael jogged to catch up. "Hey," he said awkwardly, "how's it goin'?"

"Good. I hear congratulations are in order."

He looked down at his feet as they walked. "You heard?"

"Did you think I wouldn't?"

"I was hoping to talk to you first," he answered with a sheepish smile.

"Since it's already going around, I guess you were a little slow, weren't you?" She refused to be swayed by his boyish charm, with his big puppy-dog baby-blue eyes. His light blond hair stopped at his ears, and his pale face was round with nondescript features.

"I'm sorry."

She stopped to look at him. They were the same height, so she didn't have to gaze up to look him in the eye. "For what?" she asked coolly. "For not telling me or for letting me think you were going to ask for me?"

"Both, I just . . ." He trailed off, not knowing how to continue.

"You just chickened out," she finished for him. "You told your mother you wanted to marry me and she was furious."

"Not exactly." He shifted his gaze away from hers.

"Oh no? We know she doesn't like me. That's why we never talked in public."

"She doesn't *dis*like you," he said, lying.

"She doesn't approve of me. She doesn't like that I'm a witch and she doesn't like that I wear pants when I ride." She would normally never call herself a witch, as she didn't think of herself that way, but she knew his mother did.

"You're a healer," he said, which was what he'd told his mother when she had called Alexandria a witch during their last argument.

People had been suspicious of witches ever since Minerva became queen. If a woman had powers she kept that information to herself, and most healers denied being witches, stating that their gifts were pure and used only for good.

She noticed he hadn't said anything about her wearing pants. When he didn't say anything else, she added, "So instead of standing up for yourself, you're going to marry a giggling simpleton barmaid who flirts with every man who buys a drink."

"Alex," he whispered, looking around, hoping no one could overhear them.

She didn't care if anyone heard her, and spoke clearly. "Well I hope you're happy Michael, and I wish you good luck. You're going to need it." She turned to continue on her way, but he grabbed her arm to stop her.

"What do you mean by that?"

With a pitying look, she said, "She's a barmaid. I may wear pants, but she shows a lot more skin than I do, and everyone knows barmaids sell more than just drinks."

"She's not like that," he said, defending his future wife.

Alexandria shrugged. "If you don't know that yet, you will soon." With that, she pulled her arm free and walked away.

When she reached Helen and Niall's cabin, she knocked briefly before walking in. Helen and Agnes were sitting at the table peeling potatoes. They both glanced over when Alexandria collapsed against the door.

"Are you alright?" Agnes asked, rushing over, her braid swinging.

"I just saw Michael."

Agnes led her to the table. "So he told you?"

"No," Alexandria answered, sitting down beside Helen. "Mum told me."

Helen's hair was pulled back to keep it off her face while she cooked. Her eyes full of concern, she rubbed Alexandria's arm and asked, "What did he say?"

She shrugged. "That he was sorry."

"Well I'm not sorry," Agnes stated, going back to peeling potatoes.

"Agnes," Helen hissed.

"What? We didn't like him," she reminded Helen. "And now that they're not marrying, we can say so."

Alexandria was shocked—she'd had no idea they didn't like him. "Why didn't you tell me?"

"It didn't matter how we felt," Helen said. "If you liked him, then we would try to get along with him."

"But you didn't like him," she said, clarifying.

"No, we didn't."

"Your brothers didn't like him either," Agnes told her.

Collapsing back in her chair, Alexandria said, "I can't believe no one told me. Maybe if I'd known I would have looked at him differently."

"If your brothers had told you, you would have run towards him," Agnes stated.

Alexandria couldn't argue that, as she often did the opposite of what her brothers said. "But I would have listened to you two. Why didn't you like him?"

"He's too weak," Agnes answered immediately.

"Michael's not weak." She paused, and wondered why she was defending him. He was marrying someone else. But he wasn't weak—he worked in his uncle's general store. He might not be as strong as her brothers, but she knew he helped unload new shipments and move things around in the store.

"I don't mean physically," Agnes replied. "I mean emotionally."

Thinking about it, Alexandria realized Agnes was right. He couldn't even stand up to his mother, the one person who'd love him no matter what he said or did.

"Are you hurt he's marrying someone else?" Helen asked softly.

"I was when Mum told me, but after talking to him, not as much. I don't think I want to marry a man who can't stand up for himself, and I'm definitely not upset that I won't have to deal with his mother." Alexandria hoped they bought her story. She was still hurt but didn't want to show it. She didn't like being pitied. Not wanting to talk about him anymore, she changed the subject. "Mum sent me to check on the baby."

"But she checked on me this morning," Helen said.

"She's mad at me and wanted me out of the cabin," Alexandria explained as she stood.

"What did you do?" Helen asked, scooting her chair back.

"I went riding this morning."

Helen and Agnes shared a grin.

"And what were you wearing?" Agnes asked sweetly.

"You know I was wearing pants. That's why I'm in trouble."

"You never know—with you it could be any number of things," Helen said with a laugh, smoothing her skirt.

Alexandria smiled sheepishly. "It could also be because I went hunting."

"There you go." Helen laughed again. "That must have set her off."

"I guess the fact that Michael's marrying someone else just proves her point." Before her sisters-in-law could respond, she added, "Let's see how Baby is doing." Placing her hands on Helen's stomach over her brown vest, Alexandria closed her eyes and opened herself up, allowing her magick to fill her until she could feel the baby. When she pulled back, she was smiling. "You're both good. Baby is happy and sleeping."

"Any signs that Baby is ready to come out?" Helen asked hopefully. She was feeling big and tired, and was ready to have her baby.

"Not yet, but Baby is sleeping. Things could change when Baby wakes up."

Agnes hated that no one was giving away if Baby was a boy or a girl. "And is Baby a he or a she?" Agnes asked craftily.

Smiling, Alexandria answered, "We'll have to wait for Baby to arrive to know."

"But you already know. Why won't you tell us?" Agnes whined.

"Because Baby's mum and dad don't want to know, so no one can know."

Agnes glared at Helen. "Why don't you want to know?"

"We want it to be a surprise," Helen said, rubbing circles on her stomach.

"When it's my turn I'm going to know." Smiling slyly, Agnes added, "But I'm going to make everyone else wait."

"Teasing us the whole time, no doubt," Alexandria said with a laugh.

"Of course."

"Do you want me to see if there's a baby yet?"

Agnes blushed. "Alex."

"What? It's what we do."

"I've only been married a few days," Agnes reminded her.

"Yes, and I'm sure you've been spending those days sewing by the fire."

"*Alex!*" Helen and Agnes cried in unison.

"What? You can't seriously think I don't know what goes on."

"You're not supposed to know what goes on," Helen said disapprovingly. "You're an innocent."

When Alexandria didn't say anything, Agnes grabbed her hand. "You are innocent, right?"

Insulted, she pulled her hand away. "Of course I am. How could you ask me that?"

"Well, we know you and Michael met in secret," Helen said hesitantly.

"To avoid his mother. We never did anything."

Both Agnes and Helen raised their brows.

"Really," she insisted. "We just talked." Seeing their disbelief, she added reluctantly, "The last couple of times, *after* we talked about marrying, he kissed me."

"That's what I thought," Agnes said, crossing her arms.

"Oh, don't be such a prude," Helen exclaimed, slapping Agnes's arm. "Like you and Finn didn't kiss before you were married."

"Really, the kisses weren't that special," Alexandria confessed. "They weren't that different from your wedding kiss."

Helen and Agnes shared another look. They'd been alone and he hadn't tried for more than a chaste kiss? Something must be wrong with him.

"That wasn't the only reason we were concerned," Helen admitted.

"You spend a lot of time with Demetrius too, and the Amatarians are known for their . . ." Agnes couldn't finish her sentence.

"Their passion? Their sexual ways?" Alexandria finished for her with a grin.

"Alex," Helen chided.

"I'm a healer," she said, leaning forward. "I know what happens between a man and a woman. People aren't as uptight as they used to be. Not all women are innocent when they wed anymore. I am," she said, before they could interrupt, "but as a woman I hear things. As a healer I know things."

"And Demetrius?" Helen asked.

"Is my best friend. He's like another brother to me. He's never tried anything," she assured them. "Although hanging around the tribe has taught me a lot."

"I'll bet," Agnes muttered. She was a good girl, so she never flirted with the Amatarians when they came through the village, but that didn't mean she was blind.

The tribe lived only a few hours away, so the Amatarians traveled through their village often. They didn't visit any establishments, but that didn't stop them from finding lovers. They were sensual people who didn't believe in staying pure until marriage, and they took their pleasure with anyone willing until they were ready to commit to one person—then they were true until death.

"You can tell my family that they have nothing to worry about. Should I marry, I'll enter it innocent." She got up to leave, a little insulted that her sisters-in-law thought she would go against how she'd been raised.

"You're going to marry," Agnes said, "and you're going to marry someone better than Michael."

"Really?" Alexandria asked, smiling sadly. "Michael was the only one to show interest in me, and he's marrying someone else." Turning to Helen, she said, "I'll check on you tomorrow. Send for us if you feel anything happening."

Instead of going home, Alexandria walked into the forest and paused to sit on a rock, not ready to see anyone. Thinking about

Michael, she was both hurt and angry. She didn't understand how Michael could have done this to her. Was there something wrong with her? If he'd truly wanted her, wouldn't he have fought for her?

On top of that, she couldn't believe her family thought she'd slept with Michael. Didn't they know her at all? If her parents had thought that then why hadn't her father forced marriage?

Maybe it was for the best. She was planning on leaving that night and was fairly confident she wouldn't be coming home. She only hoped that when she left this life, she'd be able to take the queen with her.

She heard rustling behind her and looked around, not worried. She knew all the villagers and Amatarians, and knew she was safe.

Her friend Demetrius walked through the trees. His skin was dark caramel, and his black hair was in a long braid that reached halfway down his back. He wore a loincloth and boots that laced up his calves. Bands circled his biceps, and a beaded necklace hung from his neck. The only thing covering his chest was the strap of his quiver, which held his bow at his back.

"What are you doing out here?" he asked in Amatarian, a smooth, lyrical language.

She shrugged and answered in his language, "I just wanted some time alone."

Grinning, he leaned against a tree. "What'd you do?"

She thought about playing it off and just telling him about how her mum was upset with her, but he was her best friend. He knew her better than anyone and would know something else was going on.

"Michael's getting married," Alexandria told him, switching to English.

Demetrius started to congratulate her and then realized she hadn't included herself in the statement. He leaned in to get a good look at her and saw the tears in her eyes. In his accented English he said, "He's marrying someone else."

She nodded, a tear spilling down her cheek.

He was comfortable with women and their emotions for the most part, but tears always made him feel weak and clumsy. So he tried to lighten the mood. "Do you want me to kill him?"

Alexandria laughed as she wiped her cheek. "Amatarians aren't killers."

"I've killed before," he reminded her.

"But only in self-defense," she reminded him.

With a shrug, he replied, "I'm sure your brothers and I can think of something."

She stood and started to walk away. "Thanks, but I don't think that will help me find a husband."

Falling in step beside her, he asked, "You aren't really upset about not marrying Michael, are you?"

"Of course I'm upset. He asked me to marry him. He was going to talk to my father this week, and instead he asked someone else, and a barmaid at that."

"But you don't love him." This was something Demetrius had never understood about the Tolgarians. His people didn't *mate*, which was their word for *marry*, unless they were in love, yet the Tolgarians tied themselves to people they didn't love, and sometimes barely knew.

"A lot of marriages start without love," Alex said defensively. "Love can grow between two people as they spend more time together."

"Or it can go the opposite way and they end up hating each other."

Stopping, she looked at her friend with curiosity. "Do you think that would have happened with me and Michael?"

"I don't know," he said, not looking her in the eye.

"Dem." She raised her hand to stop him before he could start walking again. "Please, tell me."

Sighing, he turned to face her. "I think that's what would have happened."

"Why?"

Demetrius decided to tell her exactly what he thought—maybe then she'd see it was a blessing Michael was marrying someone else. "He's weak and selfish. He'd resent the time you spent healing and would want you to take care of only him. He'd try to change you, and you'd start to resent him for that."

"Agnes and Helen didn't like him either, and they say my brothers didn't like him, and now I find out my best friend didn't like him. Why didn't anyone say anything?"

"I can't say for your family, but it wasn't my place to tell you."

"Why not? You're my friend, you're practically my brother, and you would've let me make a decision that would've made me miserable for the rest of my life?" She didn't understand why no one had talked to her about their thoughts of Michael. She couldn't believe they had all been willing to let her make such a big mistake.

Alexandria was also shocked that her sisters-in-law thought she and Demetrius had been together, which meant her brothers thought the same, which meant the town thought the same. *I guess the stares were for more than just wearing pants.*

She glanced his way as they walked. *I wonder if Dem knows what people are thinking about us*, she wondered. *Then again he probably wouldn't care. It's not like it would hurt his reputation.*

"I'm sorry I never said anything. Your rituals are very different from ours. Amatarians always seem happy to tie themselves to people they don't love. Next time I promise I'll tell you what I think."

"Good. Somebody has to be willing to tell me the truth."

Thinking over the last few days, he now wondered what was going on. Alexandria had been to the lake several times, and had been acting weird. He'd thought it had to do with becoming engaged to Michael, so if that wasn't the case then what was she up to?

They walked in silence for a few minutes before Demetrius asked, "Do you want to tell me what else is going on?"

Confused, she looked at him. "What do you mean?"

"I've noticed that you've been going to the lake every day."

For the first time in her life, Alexandria lied to her friend. "I didn't want to be around the cabin when Michael talked to my parents." In truth, she'd been going to the lake to collect extra herbs to make oil for her journey. She'd never been south and didn't know what she would find, should she need anything.

Before he could ask any more questions, she asked, "Do you want to join us for supper?"

He agreed, and they headed to her home.

As she entered the cabin she saw her whole family crammed around the table. They all looked at her with concerned expressions.

Not wanting them to bring up Michael, she smiled brightly and said, "Dem is joining us for supper."

Thankfully no one mentioned Michael and the evening flew by. That night Alexandria lay awake for hours, wanting to make sure her parents were in a deep sleep before she tried to leave. Just as she thought it was safe to get up, there was a pounding on the front door.

Her father rushed to the door and demanded to know who was there.

"It's Niall! Helen's having her baby!"

Alexandria hurried behind her screen to change, and when she emerged her parents were dressed and her mother was gathering what they needed. She helped her collect the last few items, then they all rushed out the door together. The men stayed outside the cabin with Finnean, pacing as they waited to hear Niall and Helen's child's first cry.

It was a long night. The sun was in the sky before the baby was born. Niall entered the cabin and went to his wife's side. The joy on his face as his child was placed in his arms brought tears to Alexandria's eyes. She was so happy she'd been around to witness this moment. Once mother and daughter were clean and resting, Alpin and Finnean headed for the fields and Adella and Alexandria headed home. Agnes stayed behind in case Helen needed anything.

On their way home, a young child stopped Alexandria and her mother, saying his father was hurt. Alexandria told her mother to go rest, that she would take care of it, but her mother wouldn't hear of it. She could see how tired her daughter was and knew she'd be no good to the villager, so she sent her on home.

Alexandria didn't argue. She knew she needed some sleep if she was going to leave that night. When she woke, her parents still weren't back. She started supper and it was almost done when her parents walked in, both exhausted. They went to bed as soon as they were done eating. After everything had been cleaned, Alexandria knew it was time to go. The timing had worked out perfectly, as though fate had intervened to give her a better chance.

She would be long gone before they woke and realized she was missing.

She changed into her brother's old dark-brown pants that she'd tailored and a blouse, and added her brown vest on top. After gathering her satchel, which she'd packed the day before, and her bow and arrows from under her bed, she wrote a note to her parents saying she'd gone to the lake. As she walked away, she turned back one last time to look at the cabin, certain this would be the last time she'd see her home.

CHAPTER THREE

When Finnean entered his parents' cabin, everyone was sitting around the table except his mother, who was pacing.

"Where's Alexandria?" Adella asked.

Instead of answering, he handed over the note he'd found at the lake.

Reading it, she gasped and grabbed the back of a chair for support. Finnean helped her into a seat.

"What is it?" Helen asked in a worried tone, rocking her daughter to sleep in her arms.

Niall picked up the note his mother had dropped and read it. "She's going after the queen."

"What?" Agnes asked, in shock. "What are we going to do?"

"We're going after her," Alpin stated.

"We'll leave now," Finnean said, placing a hand on his wife's shoulder.

"No," Adella said. "It's too dangerous to travel at night."

"But what about Alex?" Finnean asked. "She'll be out there at night."

"Your sister is smart. She'll be hiding somewhere until morning," Alpin said, agreeing with his wife.

"You can leave in the morning," Adella said.

Knowing not to argue anymore, Niall and Finnean left with their wives.

Once they were alone Adella turned to her husband. "What was she thinking?"

"She's just like her brothers," he answered, taking her hand. "She feels it's the family's responsibility, but unlike her brothers, she doesn't have a family to worry about."

"Then what are we?" she asked, offended.

He patted her hand. "You know what I mean. She's always been independent."

Adella leaned against her husband and rested her head on his shoulder as his arm went around her. "I pray our boys find her safe."

"They will," he assured her.

"And when she gets home, I'm going to kill her."

The next morning, Niall and Finnean were outside their parents' cabin getting ready to leave when Michael showed up.

"Is Alexandria around?"

Finnean gave him a stony stare. "Why?" Though glad Michael wasn't marrying his sister, he hadn't forgiven him for hurting her. Agnes had told him about their conversation and how his sister had tried to hide her feelings.

Looking down, Michael shifted uncomfortably. "I need to talk to her."

Raising his brows, Niall asked, "Don't you think you've said everything already?"

He shifted again. "I need to talk to her. I tried to find her yesterday."

Wanting to get going, Finnean turned to check his horse. "She's not here."

Michael knew they didn't like him and could understand why, but he wasn't about to give up. "When will she be back?"

Niall gave him an irked look before lying. "She's visiting our grandmother in Kilwinning. She won't be back for a few days." The family had decided that if anyone asked, this was the story they would provide. They didn't want anyone to know the truth.

Michael shook his head. He'd been worried about this. "She left because of me, didn't she? Because I'm marrying someone else."

Finnean spun around and stepped forward, wanting to hit him.

Niall stepped in front of his brother and said to Michael, "You really have a high opinion of yourself, but her leaving had absolutely nothing to do with you."

Seeing their angry expressions, he took a step back in fear but still asked, "Will you tell her I was looking for her?"

"No," Finnean answered shortly, stepping up beside his brother.

"You'd be better off focusing on your betrothed," Niall told him. "And forget about Alexandria, because I promise she's already forgotten about you."

Michael nodded and walked away. He'd just have to wait until she was back to talk to her.

✠✠✠✠✠

Walking through the forest, Alexandria smiled as she thought of her smooth progress. It had taken her a week on foot to get to Thurrock. She'd managed to find places to hide during the days, and hadn't run into anyone while traveling at night.

The one thing she hadn't considered was how she was going to get people in Thurrock to talk to her. No one would want to talk to a stranger, let alone an armed woman in pants. When she reached the edge of the town, she saw some clothes hanging to dry behind a cabin. After making sure no one was around, she grabbed a skirt as well as a blouse, since hers was dirty, and hoped no one would recognize the borrowed clothes.

Changing in the forest, she added her vest to the outfit, then pulled her hair into a bun. She hid her satchel and bow in a tree stump not far from the cabin before heading into town. Alexandria pretended her husband was getting supplies while she walked around trying to engage the villagers in conversation, and was overcome with disappointment when no one would talk about the queen.

I've wasted a week for nothing, she thought. *No one will even admit the queen was from Thurrock.*

She washed her borrowed clothes in a creek before hanging them back where she'd found them.

Alexandria traveled south for three days before coming across another creek. She nearly wept with pleasure, wanting a bath so badly. Biting her lip, she looked around. It was almost sunrise, but she hadn't seen anyone since she'd left Thurrock, and by her calculations she was still a day away from the next village.

She leaned her bow and quiver against a tree, then set her satchel down and dug through it until she found her homemade soap. After one last look around, she stripped and headed for the creek with her clothes. She washed them first before hanging them over a low branch to dry. Then she headed back to the creek and walked right in. The water only reached her knees, so she sat down to bathe.

Sighing with pleasure, she leaned back to let the water flow over her and wash the soap away. It had been over a week since she'd had a real bath. The last time she'd found water she'd been too close to Thurrock to risk indulging. When she was done, she used her blanket to dry off and then checked her clothes—her shirt was damp but dry enough to put on, but her pants needed more time. At least the shirt was long enough to cover her, hitting halfway down her thighs.

After retrieving her brush from her satchel, she sat crossed-legged by the creek and brushed her hair. The sun was higher now, and she could feel its warmth as it sparkled over the water.

"What do we have here?" a male voice asked from behind her.

Alexandria froze in alarm and wondered what to do. Should she try to run? She didn't know if she was in any danger. *He might just leave*, she thought. Standing, she turned to face the voice and saw two men in dirty clothes with grins on their faces. The one on the left had a scar running down his cheek, giving him a very menacing appearance, but it was the swords at their sides that concerned her the most.

Deciding to play it cool, she placed a hand over her heart and said with a little laugh, "You startled me. I thought you were my husband."

"Oh?" the man on the right said, "and where is he?"

"Hunting," she answered, praying that would send them on their way.

They both looked at her bow and arrows leaning against the tree, and she knew they didn't believe her. She had a feeling they weren't going to leave her alone.

The man on the left said, "It wasn't smart of him to leave a pretty little thing like yourself all alone. These woods aren't safe for a woman alone."

Trying to keep her composure, she smiled. "Thanks for the warning, but he should be back any minute."

The man on the left replied, "Oh, we wouldn't think of leaving you all alone. We'll just wait until he returns."

The other man chuckled, and she knew she was in trouble.

Turning, Alexandria rushed towards her satchel, where she kept her knife, only to stop when a third man, just as dirty as the other two, stepped out from behind the tree. He had a crooked nose and an evil smile. Without a second thought she turned and ran. The men let out a shout and started chasing after her. Thinking she could lose them in the forest, she veered away from the creek and into the trees.

It wasn't long before they caught up to her. One grabbed her around her waist, lifting her off her feet. She screamed until he cut her off by placing his hand over her mouth. Alexandria bit his hand, hard, and when her mouth was free she screamed again and started to struggle. Swinging her head back she smacked his nose, and he dropped her with a curse.

Before she could gain her feet another grabbed her, and the other approached her from the front with an ugly grin on his face. When he got close she brought her knee up into his groin, just as her brothers had taught her. He collapsed with a groan while she struggled against the one holding her, but his grip was too tight and she couldn't break free.

The first man came over and backhanded her across the face. "I'm going to teach you a lesson," he told her, unbuckling his sword belt.

Out of nowhere another man appeared; his dark brown pants, green shirt, and long brown coat blended well with the forest. The coat was open so his sword was visible. She also saw a knife strapped to his boot.

Now she was even more afraid. She knew what they wanted and there was no way she could fight off four men.

"Let her go," the newcomer demanded.

Her three attackers shared a look before two of the men stepped forward and spread out to attack the newcomer from either side. He pulled his sword just as they pulled theirs. These men were obviously not trained, as they nodded to each other before charging. He cut them down quickly before turning to the man who held Alexandria. Her captor threw her aside, pulled his sword, and charged, only to die as quickly as his friends.

Alexandria cowered against a tree, watching her rescuer with wide eyes as he cleaned his blade and sheathed it. She wondered what he was going to do next.

Her savior noticed her peaches-and-cream skin was flushed, and she was breathing heavily, whether from running or fear he didn't know. Based on her wet hair, bare feet, and lack of clothing, he assumed she'd been bathing by the creek. He tried to ignore her beauty, and nakedness, wanting her to feel safe.

After a few moments of silence he said, "Do you want to get your things?"

Straightening, Alexandria watched him warily, then turned and began walking away. When he touched her arm she jumped and spun around to face him, ready to defend herself.

"The creek's that way," he told her, pointing behind him. Seeing the fear in her warm brown eyes made him angry. *Why is she alone? Who's supposed to be protecting her?*

When she reached her things Alexandria grabbed her pants and noticed he'd turned away. She was grateful he was giving her some privacy. While he wasn't looking, she grabbed her knife from her satchel and tucked it into her waistband. The knife's sheath had a loop for a belt, but she didn't have one and silently cursed herself for not taking one of her brother's belts when she'd taken the pants. She hoped she wouldn't need to use her knife, but just because this stranger had saved her didn't mean he wasn't going to try to hurt her. He might have only saved her so he could have her to himself.

"Are you traveling alone?" he asked, his back still to her.

She didn't answer.

"Where are you going?"

When she didn't answer again, he turned to find her sitting, inspecting her feet. Moving forward he knelt in front of her to look, moving slowly so as not to scare her.

Her feet were covered in dirt and blood.

"You need to clean them before you put your boots back on," he told her.

Looking up, she noticed for the first time how handsome he was. His long blond hair was thick and luscious and had a little wave to it—the kind of hair every woman would want to run her fingers through, even though it was partly pulled back. He had a long face with sharp cheekbones and a cleft in his chin, and his eyes were a smoky gray. His jaw and mouth were strong and currently set in concern.

Speaking for the first time she said, "I know." She walked to the creek and sat down to let the water run over her feet. When they were clean, she inspected them again and was relieved to see there were only a few cuts. "Can you bring me my satchel?"

When he placed it beside her she searched inside for a small glass bottle, which contained oil extracted from many plants she used for healing. As she rubbed the oil into her feet, she opened herself up to make sure there wouldn't be any risk of infection, but she didn't heal the cuts because the stranger was watching, and she didn't want him to know she had power.

He set her boots down beside her. "Thank you." Alexandria knew she should thank him for saving her life as well but still wasn't sure what his intentions were. Once her boots were on, she stood and slung her satchel across her body so it rested on her hip.

He noticed her shirt pulling tightly across her body as her bag settled, accentuating her curves. Trying to avoid looking at her figure he lowered his eyes and took in her brown pants. Seeing how they hugged her hips and legs, he realized that wasn't a good place to look either. As he turned away, he caught sight of her knife at her waist.

Chuckling, he said, "That won't do you any good." When she looked at him with a confused expression, he pointed to her waist.

She placed her hand over her knife, and her eyes grew wary.

He held up his hands. "I'm not going to hurt you. I just meant you can't reach it quickly when it's under your shirt. Where's your belt?"

Still wary she answered, "I don't have one."

"You should get one in the next village. Where are you going?" he asked again.

"I'm meeting my brothers in Sevenoaks."

"I'm heading that way. I can take you."

Surprised, she wondered why he was offering. Was he being nice and offering to protect her, or was he trying to earn her trust so he could attack her later? She just wasn't sure.

Not wanting to take the chance, she said, "Thanks, but I'll be fine." She picked up her bow and quiver and prepared to leave.

He stepped in front of her to stop her. "As you just found out, it's not safe. You shouldn't be traveling on your own."

"That was my fault. I don't normally travel during the day. I just couldn't resist the water."

"What do you mean?"

"I've been traveling and wanted a bath," she started to explain, thinking it should have been obvious.

"No," he interrupted shaking his head. "I meant about traveling during the day."

"Oh, I hide during the day and sleep and travel at night."

He could understand her reasoning, but he knew from experience that the worst kind of men were out at night. "And you've never run into anyone?"

She shook her head. "This is the first time."

"We're about a two-day walk from Sevenoaks," he told her. "It's not a safe place, and there are all manner of men traveling day and night in this area. Let me take you to your brothers."

Alexandria had a feeling he wasn't going to let it go, so she agreed. *Stay on guard*, she told herself. *He might just be waiting for the right moment to attack.* Seeing her vest and blanket still on the branch, she took her satchel off. As she put on her vest and buttoned it up, she remembered what he'd said earlier and tucked her shirt behind her knife so it would be easier to grab should she need it. Then she rolled up her blanket and placed it in her satchel.

He noticed what she had done with the knife and was glad she was smart enough to take precautions.

They started walking, and after a few minutes the man said, "I'm Calum."

"Alexandria."

"You're not from Sevenoaks, are you?"

"Why do you say that?" she asked, facing ahead, her hand resting on her knife.

He ignored her defensive stance and said, "You look too soft to live there. Not to mention the women there don't wear pants."

"The women in my village don't wear pants either," she replied wryly.

"So you admit you're not from there."

Ignoring his last comment she asked, "What do you mean I'm too soft?"

Calum shrugged. "The women there are harder. They work the fields and raise their families."

Stopping to stare at him, she asked, "Are you saying you don't think I work?"

He took her hand and looked at her palm, feeling its softness before she pulled away. He started walking again and said over his shoulder, "You've never worked a hard day in your life."

She glared at his back, wanting to yell that she worked hard, that she'd like to see him deliver a baby or heal someone who was hurt, but she wasn't ready to tell him she was a healer, for fear he might be one of those people who thought healers were witches.

Looking around, she wondered if he'd come after her if she went in a different direction. She was still debating it when he called out, "I wouldn't if I were you. These woods are full of men like the ones you ran into earlier."

Alexandria continued to look around and finally decided it would better to deal with one man than to come across three again. She walked quickly to catch up with him.

Calum was glad she had chosen to join him, as he wasn't about to let her continue on her own and didn't relish the idea of secretly following her.

After they'd been walking for several minutes, Calum finally asked the question that had been burning in his mind. "Why did your brothers let you travel alone?"

She didn't answer right away, needing to think of another lie. "They thought I'd be fine if I traveled at night." It would be an easy lie to remember, since she believed she'd be fine traveling at night.

"And dressed like a man?" he asked, looking her over. Didn't they realize the pants were more enticing than a skirt?

Shrugging, she answered, "I wasn't supposed to run into anyone, and we thought the pants would be easier to travel in."

He could see how that would be true, but there was no way he would allow his sisters to travel alone. What kind of men were her brothers? He guessed he would find out when he met them.

"Since I know you're not from Sevenoaks, where are you from?"

"Up north," she answered, not wanting to tell him.

"So am I. What village?"

"Why does that matter?" Stories traveled like wildfire between the villages, and she didn't want any getting back to her family. If they heard about a woman wearing pants, they would know it was her. That was another reason she didn't want to run into anyone—she was sure people would talk about seeing a woman traveling by herself and wearing pants.

"Maybe we're from the same village," he suggested, not really believing this. He was pretty confident he would have noticed her around.

"We're not," she assured him.

Surprised by her definite response, he wondered how she could be so sure. "How do you know?"

She opened her mouth and paused, almost saying that she knew everyone in her village. Stopping, she looked at him. "Do you know me?"

"No."

"And I don't know you, so I think it's safe to say we don't live in the same village."

Raising his hands he said, "Okay, I get it, you don't want me to know where you're from." He'd just ask her brothers. Maybe they would tell him why she was being so secretive.

They walked in silence for hours, long after the sun had set. Finally Alexandria started yawning every few minutes, having missed her shut-eye during the day. She didn't say anything though because she didn't feel comfortable sleeping in front of him and wanted to wait until he needed to sleep too.

He finally stopped and said, "This looks good."

Looking around, she saw they were in a dense section of trees. "Good for what?" she asked with another yawn.

"To rest. You're asleep on your feet."

"I'm fine," she argued, fighting another yawn.

Having two sisters of his own, he knew better than to contradict her. "Well, I'm tired." He sat down, rested his back against the tree, and closed his eyes not quite all the way so he could watch her through a thin slit.

She looked around for a few minutes before picking a tree across from him. It was just the type of place she would have chosen to sleep—away from the beaten path with some tall bushes that would conceal her from anyone passing by.

Leaning her bow and quiver against the tree, she sat down and held her knife in her lap, one hand on the handle and the other on the sheath.

Calum shook his head. Did she really think she would be able to use the knife before he took it away from her if he were to attack? He didn't need to pretend to rest now, so he watched her. Her head kept falling forward, and she kept jerking it back as she struggled to stay awake. It wasn't long before sleep won and her head rested against the tree.

He had never seen anyone like her. Her pale skin suggested she'd never spent any time outdoors. Her long blonde hair with its strands of red looked so soft—he couldn't help but wonder what it felt like. She was so beautiful. Her brothers were idiots for letting her travel alone, and he planned on telling them.

When Alexandria woke up, she found herself on her back with something soft under her head. Sitting up, she looked down and saw a brown bundle. *That's not my satchel*, she thought. Shaking it out, she realized it was a man's coat. Remembering Calum, she quickly straightened and looked around. There were some logs and branches set up for a fire a few feet away, but no Calum. The sun was high, so she knew it was the middle of the day. Maybe he'd decided to leave her after all.

Just then Calum came out of the trees carrying a rabbit. "Good, you're up."

Brushing her hair off her face, she said, "You should have woken me sooner."

He shrugged as he put the rabbit down to start the fire. "You obviously needed the rest."

Nodding towards the rabbit, she asked, "Do you want me to clean it?"

"Do you know how?"

Offended she replied, "Of course I know how. What kind of life do you think I live?"

He was pleased to see a little fire in her brown eyes. He had been worried she was going to stay scared of him for the remainder of their time together, and he didn't want that, even if their journey was only going to last another day.

Standing she swiped the rabbit from the ground and stalked off.

"You'll need your knife," he called after her.

Her hand flew to her waist, and when she realized it wasn't there she swung around, alarmed. Calum was bent over the fire, his back to her. She didn't see her knife near him and then remembered that she'd been holding it when she fell asleep. Turning to the tree, she saw it leaning beside her bow and went back to grab it before stalking off into the trees again.

Calum chuckled after she was gone, thinking about how she was just like his sisters.

Alexandria found a long, thin branch with which she could skewer the rabbit before noticing a faint trickling sound. It took her a few minutes to find the source, but the beautiful sight was worth the search.

A few feet in front of her the ground changed from dirt to moss-covered rocks, and then dropped away. But she couldn't see the water she was hearing. Stepping forward she looked down and saw a clearing and a small pond. *How can I get down there?* she wondered. Off to her right she noticed a path and followed it. A minute later she was heading down a sloped trail between the trees. She broke through the trees to the small clearing and saw that the water was pouring out from between the rocks in a dozen little waterfalls, which cascaded into one pool. Walking to the water's edge she saw it wasn't very deep—certainly not deep enough to swim in.

Getting down to work she noticed the rabbit had already been gutted and bled. After cleaning the branch in the water she finished prepping the rabbit before skewering it. She was just washing her hands when she heard Calum yelling for her.

"I'm down here," she called back.

He moved to the cliff's edge and saw her. "What are you doing down there?"

"Enjoying the water. Come on down."

He found a way down and joined her by the water's edge.

She smiled at him for the first time as he approached. "Isn't it beautiful?"

Struck by the beauty of her smile, he nodded, having no breath with which to speak.

Turning back to the water she said, "We should eat here."

Calum looked around before answering. "That's not a good idea."

"Why not?"

"It's a popular place. Someone could come upon us."

She looked around as well but didn't see what he was seeing. "How do you know?"

He pointed to the grass around them. "See how it's flattened? That only happens when it's continually trampled."

Now she saw it. "Maybe it's only animals."

"Do you want to wait to find out?"

Thinking of the men who'd found her earlier, she answered, "No, let's go," and stood up. Before she could reach for the branch holding the rabbit, Calum picked it up.

They found the path they had come down, and Alexandria discovered it was harder going up than down. Her boots kept slipping on the loose dirt, causing her to grab trees for balance. Calum eventually held out his hand, and after she took it, he helped her the rest of the way up.

As they walked back to camp she cast sideway glances at him, trying to figure him out. Finally she asked, "Why'd you come looking for me?"

"You were gone awhile."

She looked at him with curiosity. "Were you worried about me?"

"I said I'd take you to your brothers," was all he said.

Alexandria smiled. He had been worried about her. It was a nice feeling, knowing someone outside her family cared about her. Not that she was deluding herself—she knew he'd leave as soon as they reached Sevenoaks.

Back at their camp the fire was going, and Calum cooked the rabbit. They ate in silence. "Are you ready to go?" he asked when they were done.

She adjusted her satchel and nodded. They walked for several hours in continued silence before taking a break to eat again. Calum built a fire after catching another rabbit. While it cooked, Alexandria sat by the fire across from him, feeling very awkward. She didn't know what to say to him.

He noticed her staring but didn't say anything, keeping his eyes focused on the rabbit. When he was finished eating he moved back to lean against a tree and waited for her.

"Do you need to sleep?" Alexandria finally asked, figuring he hadn't slept when she did.

"I'm fine." He was waiting for her, not resting.

They started on their way again. When the sun began to set they moved off the main path and into the trees. Their paced slowed a little as they maneuvered over the uneven terrain, avoiding the rocks and tree roots. A few hours later they came upon a smoother area and Calum stopped.

"We should camp here until sunrise," he said.

"Why are we stopping?"

"Sevenoaks is only about an hour away, but it's safer to go there during the day." He took off his belt and placed his sword against the tree before sitting down.

Taking off her satchel Alexandria kept her quiver on and placed her bow in her lap, thinking she would stand guard this time while he slept.

He hadn't planned on sleeping and thought he needed only a few minutes to rest, but his body disagreed, and he was asleep within minutes. He woke hours later when he heard a twig break. The first thing he saw when he opened his eyes was Alexandria staring into the trees with an arrow nocked. He grabbed his sword and stood.

"Stay here," he ordered.

Just as he started forward, a deer walked out of the trees. It lifted its head and sniffed the air. Alexandria and Calum didn't move, but it must have smelled them because it quickly turned and galloped back into the woods.

Alexandria laughed with relief as she lowered her bow. When she heard the twig break she'd been so scared but at the same time relieved that she wasn't alone. *It's amazing how fast things changed*, she thought as she looked at Calum with his sword drawn, ready to protect her. She'd been happy traveling alone, and now she was happy she wasn't. She wished he were traveling with her all the way to Dorset.

Sheathing his sword he asked, "Can you actually use that?" He nodded towards the bow and arrow in her hand.

Raising her brow, she replied, "Pick a target."

"Can you hit this tree?" he asked mockingly, pointing to the tree beside him.

She narrowed her eyes, marched over to him, and looked into the distance. "See that low branch?" she asked, indicating a tree in the distance.

"You can't hit that," he scoffed. The branch was barely wider than the arrow. He didn't know many men who could hit it—there was no way she could.

Flipping her hair over her shoulder, she took aim and released the arrow in the next breath. When it hit its mark, she smiled smugly. She went to retrieve it, and as she returned, he was still staring at the tree in amazement.

He looked at her expression and laughed. "Okay, so you can use it."

"My brothers taught me to hunt years ago," she explained. It was something their mother had never forgiven them for, but Alexandria had enjoyed going out with them and had been so proud when her aim eventually surpassed theirs.

Calum suddenly noticed how high the sun was and realized he'd slept the whole night. "We could have left a couple hours ago. Why didn't you wake me?"

Shrugging, she placed her bow against the tree. "Do you want to eat?"

"I'll wait for town. Your brothers are probably wondering where you are."

No, they're not, she thought. *At least not in the way you're thinking.* Not that she could tell him that. She wasn't sure what he would do if he found out her brothers weren't waiting for her.

In less than an hour, they were on the outskirts of Sevenoaks. The whole way, Alexandria had tried to think of excuses to leave Calum without going into the village. When she could see a few cottages, she stopped and turned to him. "Thanks for seeing me to Sevenoaks."

"I'll take you to your brothers. Where are they?"

"They're in town, but I have to change first," she told him, giving him the excuse she'd thought of.

He knew she was lying but just said, "I'll wait for you."

She'd been worried he'd say that and had another excuse ready. "No, that's okay, my brothers wouldn't like it if they found out I was traveling with a man."

"What would they do?" he asked, wondering how far she was going to take this charade.

"They'd demand you marry me," she told him, sure that would change his mind about taking her to her brothers.

He took a step closer. "Maybe I'm willing to take that risk."

Her eyes widened in surprise. She'd been so sure he wouldn't that she didn't have a backup.

Calum decided not to torture her anymore. "Look, I know you don't have to change. Do you want to tell me what's really going on?"

CHAPTER FOUR

"What makes you think I'm not going to change?" Alexandria asked innocently.

"You don't have a change of clothes in your satchel."

"What! You went through my satchel?"

"No, *you* went through your satchel beside me. There wasn't a change of clothes."

"Oh," she said, the anger leaving her. But what was she going to tell him now?

"Your brothers aren't here, are they."

Figuring he wouldn't give up, she sighed and told him the truth. "No."

"Where are they?"

"At home."

"Up north."

"Yes."

"And you're traveling south."

"Yes."

"Why?"

Looking away, she didn't answer.

He took another step forward and looked her in the eyes. "Why are you traveling south?"

"I'm going to Dorset." Seeing the question in his eyes, she straightened and added, "I'm going to kill the queen."

"What?" That was the last thing he had expected to hear.

"I'm going to kill the queen."

"Are you crazy?" he whispered. "You can't kill the queen."

"Why are you whispering?" she asked in a whisper of her own.

"I don't want anyone to hear your intentions."

"There's no one around to hear us," she told him, no longer whispering.

"Why do you want to kill her?"

Alexandria took a step back as horror entered her eyes. "You're on her side."

"No."

"Are you a solider?"

"No," he stated firmly, trying to reassure her. "I am not on her side, but that doesn't mean I'm going to commit suicide."

"What do you mean suicide?"

"Anyone who goes against the queen dies, so why are you going after her?"

"I have my reasons," she answered, raising her chin defiantly.

"How do you plan on killing a witch when you couldn't handle three guys?" He knew he was being mean but wanted to knock some sense into her.

"I can take care of myself," Alexandria stated, annoyed.

"Really?" He grabbed her arms. "Prove it."

She closed her eyes to center herself and focus. Calum was amazed to see her hair darken—the red seemed to come alive. Before he could say anything she opened her eyes and he saw flames flickering in them. Mesmerized, he stared into her eyes until the flames jumped out and his shirt caught on fire.

He flew backward and was smacking his arms and chest trying to put out the flames when they suddenly disappeared. He looked down at his shirt to find it intact. The fire hadn't been real. It had felt real, but he could see now it had all been in his mind.

Taking another step back, he said, "You're a witch."

"I'm a healer," she corrected, wondering what he'd do now that he knew.

After staring at her for a minute he asked, "Why are you watching me like that?"

She looked at him questioningly, and he looked pointedly at her hand, which had instinctively gone to her knife.

She lowered her hand before answering. "Not everyone likes healers. They think we're witches like the queen."

"Aren't you?"

Angry, she took a step forward. "I'm not a witch, I'm a healer."

"What do you call what you just did? Because I call it magick."

"Most healers have some magick," she countered defensively, "but that doesn't make us like the queen."

He disagreed—if you had power, then you were a witch, though he didn't think all witches were bad like some people did. He knew a few, and only a few of them were healers. Most of them kept their powers a secret, so he understood her fear.

After they had watched each other in silence for a minute, she said, "Now that you see I can take care of myself, you don't have to worry about me." Secretly she wished he'd continue to travel with her. She was surprised by how fast she'd come to trust him, especially since she knew nothing about him. There was just something in her gut telling her he'd never hurt her.

"Why didn't you use that trick when you were attacked?"

Flushing, Alexandria admitted, "I panicked. I need to focus and be calm when I use my powers. I wasn't calm, but it won't happen again."

He remembered her reaction—she'd been screaming and fighting. And he didn't think she'd be calm if she were attacked again. While he still felt it was a suicide mission, for some reason he felt responsible for her.

"I'll go with you," he said.

She stared at him in shock. She had assumed he would be glad to be rid of her. To clarify she asked, "Go with me where?"

"To Dorset. I'll help you kill the queen."

Alexandria threw her arms around him, happy and thankful. Suddenly realizing she was hugging a stranger, she pulled back and apologized, "I'm sorry, I . . ." She took a deep breath to calm herself, straightened, and looked him in the eyes. "Okay, let's go." She smiled brightly and turned away from the village.

"Go where?"

Looking back she said, "I thought you were coming with me to Dorset?"

"We need supplies first," he said, gesturing to Sevenoaks.

"Oh." Looking towards the village she said, "I'll wait for you here."

"I'm not leaving you alone."

"I can't go with you. I'm wearing pants."

I don't need the reminder, he thought. He'd been trying to avoid noticing how her pants hugged her slender frame, highlighting curves he shouldn't be aware of.

Calum understood her concern. People were going to stare and wonder about her, but it wasn't safe to leave her alone. "No one will bother you when you're with me." She looked uncertain, so he added, "It's not safe for you to stay here. This is a busy village, and men travel this road often."

"I'll hide in the trees."

"It's not a good idea. If someone finds you I won't be here to save you."

"I can take care of myself!"

Not wanting to argue with her, he decided to try a different tack. "Wouldn't you like a good meal at the inn?" She hesitated, so he continued. "We'll rent a room and you can have a bath and sleep in a bed while I get the supplies. Then we'll leave during the night."

The thought of a real bath and a real bed was too tempting to pass up. "Maybe you're right. I should come with you."

Calum smiled to himself. He untucked her shirt so it hid her knife. He knew people were going to stare, and not just because she was wearing pants. Women didn't travel armed, but he didn't think she would hand over her bow and quiver. And besides, he kind of liked how she looked with them.

"If anyone asks, you're my wife."

"What do I say if they ask where we're from or going?" She knew how nosy people could be.

"Don't say anything. They don't need to know."

As predicted, everyone stared at Alexandria as she and Calum walked through the village. She was uncomfortable with the attention but kept her composure. She felt better having Calum with her. He made her feel that everything was going to be all right.

She could see now what he'd been talking about. The men were rough and dangerous looking, and the woman looked just as rough, just as dangerous. It was a mining town, which meant the fields were left to be worked by the women, and their bodies showed it. They were stockier than the women in her village, and their skin was weathered from working under the hot sun every day. A few men covered with black dust carried pickaxes against their shoulders as they headed home.

"Wait here while I find out where the inn is," he said to her while staring at a group of men standing in front of the general store.

"I thought you'd been here before."

"I've never spent the night, and I usually eat at the tavern."

She wondered what else he usually did there but didn't ask; she could figure that out for herself. After all, she did have two brothers—not that they told her anything, but being a healer, she heard her patients talk, and they talked a lot.

"I'll be right back."

After Calum left, she noticed a few men watching her from the other side of the road. She did her best to ignore them but really didn't like how one was staring at her. Deliberately looking away as though he didn't concern her, she glanced down the street and prayed Calum was on his way back.

After a few moments the guy broke away from the group and came over to her. "Where are you from, sweetheart?"

With a cool glance she asked, "Why do you care?"

His eyes raked over her from top to bottom. "Do you always dress like a man?"

The look in his eyes made Alexandria extremely uncomfortable, but she refused to show it. "And if I do?"

"Then maybe you want to be treated like a man," he said, stepping closer.

Looking him in the eye she asked, "If I were a man, would you be over here bothering me?"

A hard look entered his eyes, but before he had a chance to say anything Calum was there.

"Is there a problem here?"

"Who are you?" the man asked, staring Calum down.

"Her husband," he said, stepping forward. "Is there a problem here?"

The man backed away with his hands up but sent Alexandria a wink before turning around.

Calum took another step forward but she grabbed his arm, stopping him.

"Where's the inn?"

Calum didn't answer and kept watching the man walk away.

"Where's the inn, Calum? I'm starving." As expected that got his attention.

He turned back to her. "Come on, it's around the corner."

After checking in as husband and wife, they went up to their room. Once inside Alexandria removed her satchel and said, "I hope my family doesn't hear about this, or they might really force you to marry me."

Considering their plans, that was the last thing he was worried about. "Do you want a bath first or food?"

She pressed a hand to her stomach. "Food, please."

"What do you want? I'll go down and bring it up."

"Whatever smells good."

Once he had left, she looked around the room. It wasn't large; the bed took up half the space. Across from it was a privacy screen against the wall and a small desk with a chair. She was relieved to see the chair as she didn't want to sit on the bed when Calum was in the room. She placed her knife on the desk and sat down, thinking about her next step.

Calum soon returned with a tray and set a full plate and tumbler down on the desk before sitting down on the bed to eat his food. Alexandria noted that he didn't seem bothered that they were alone in a room with a bed.

But then, why should it? she thought. *He's only thinking of me as a responsibility.*

"Why are you helping me?"

"What do you mean?" he asked, taking a bite of his biscuit.

"It's one thing to travel with me for a day when you think you're taking me to my brothers, but why are you coming with me to Dorset? Especially when you think it's suicide."

"Maybe I'm hoping to change your mind before we get there."

"You won't. I'm going to kill the queen."

"Or die trying."

"Or die trying," she agreed. "Do you still want to come with me?" She held her breath, waiting for his answer.

He thought about it again. If he went with her he was likely committing himself to his death. She was nothing to him, so why should he risk his life? But her anxious expression confirmed his decision. He had no love for the queen—in fact, he and his entire family wished her dead, and if he could contribute to her death in any way, then he was going to, even if it meant dying in the process.

And he didn't doubt he would die. Every man who went against the queen died. But he'd never heard of a woman going against the queen, so maybe Alexandria had a chance. She did have power—maybe that's what was needed to defeat the queen.

"Yes," he said finally. "I'm coming with you."

Alexandria let out a sigh of relief before turning back to her food.

When he was finished eating, Calum stood up and said, "I'll have them send up a tub for your bath while I get some supplies. Will an hour be enough time?"

"For what?"

"So I don't walk in on you."

She blushed and stuttered, "Yes, that's fine."

He nodded. "I have the key, so lock the door when you're alone."

A few minutes after he left, a man delivered a wooden tub, and a few women carried in buckets of water. After Alexandria had assured them the temperature was fine and they didn't need to boil more water, the women took the empty food tray and left, and Alexandria locked the door.

She let out a moan of pleasure as she slipped into the tub. She hadn't had hot water since she left home. Wanting to make sure she was done her bath before Calum got back, she didn't soak for too long. Using the soap she'd packed in her satchel, she washed her body and hair. An extra bucket of water had been left for her, and she poured it over her head to wash the soap away.

After drying off with the towels the women had left for her, she wrapped one around herself and then washed her clothes and draped them on the chair to dry. She moved the chair closer to the fire and hoped they would be dry before Calum returned.

Yawning, she decided to rest for a few minutes. She took off her wet towel before climbing under the sheets. Her family would be shocked and distressed to learn she was lying in a bed naked— even more so if they knew a man had the key to her room. She chuckled at the thought. Everyone in her village already thought she was scandalous for the way she dressed. If only they could see her now. She fell asleep with a smile on her face.

✠✠✠✠✠

Minerva was riding her horse by Lake Lewes. It was the only time she could be truly alone, as everyone else was forbidden from going near her lake.

Men are preparing to march on the castle, her necklace whispered.

Stopping her horse, Minerva looked towards the castle. There was no one in sight. Not that she had to worry, no one could kill her—but they could hurt her.

"Where are they?"

In Rushcliffe. The father of the little girl has found men to join him.

"So? Let them come. My men will cut them down before they even reach the castle walls."

One man from Rushcliffe is claiming to know a secret way in.

"What passageway?" Minerva knew of two secret passageways. Many years ago they had been used by soldiers who wanted to sneak away from their posts for a few hours. After making an example of the soldiers, she'd had the passageways sealed and then killed the men who'd sealed them so that she was the only living person to know about them.

He's not saying, but the others believe him and are going to follow him.

She dismounted and walked to the lake's edge. "Show me."

The water shimmered and created a picture in the middle of a circle. About twenty men were readying their horses. One man broke away from the group and walked to a family in front of a cabin.

That's the father.

She watched him cup the woman's face in his hands and kiss her before turning to hug the children—three boys of varying heights. Tears ran down the woman's cheeks as they said goodbye. He walked back to his horse and took the reins from another man.

He's the one claiming to know a secret passageway.

Minerva gasped upon seeing the man's face, and her hand shook as it stretched towards the water. He looked exactly like her late husband.

It's not Henry, her necklace told her.

"Is he a descendant?" she whispered with tears in her eyes.

Yes, through Henry's brother.

"I want him brought to me." Spinning around, she marched back to her horse and rode home.

As she approached the castle, a stable boy rushed forward to take her horse. "Find Brodrick and send him to me," she commanded.

"Yes, Your Majesty."

Sitting on her throne she waited impatiently, drumming her fingers on one of the skulls. Brodrick strode into the room. He stopped in front of the queen, went down to one knee, and bowed his head. His dark eyes and the dark stubble along his jaw matched his black uniform. A silver spider emblem was emblazoned across the breastplate. The only thing light about him was his silver sword, which was always at his side. He was an imposing figure who intimidated his men, making him Minerva's perfect head soldier.

"You wished to see me, Your Majesty."

"Yes. There are men in Rushcliffe planning on trying to kill me. I want you to take care of them."

Standing he said, "Of course, Your Majesty."

"But don't kill them all. One says he knows a secret passageway to the castle. Bring him to me."

He nodded. "Yes, Your Majesty."

✠✠✠✠✠

When Calum returned to the room he knocked. After a minute with no response, he angrily shoved the key in the door, expecting to find the room empty. Of course she had left—she felt she could take care of herself. He decided to drop off his purchases and go after her.

Entering the room, he stopped suddenly upon seeing the bed. Alexandria was asleep.

After locking the door behind him, Calum set his things down on the desk. The clothes on the chair were still damp, so he draped them over the screen to finish drying. He then shifted the chair until it was facing the bed before sitting down.

The room smelled of wildflowers, a scent that seemed to follow her. He knew it was from her soap and assumed she had made it. It was a nice change from the rose soap sold at every general store. Rose was the only scent he'd ever smelled on women, including his sisters. He thought about asking her for some wildflower soap for his sisters, certain that his brothers-in-law would appreciate the difference.

Calum knew she was naked under the sheets, as they weren't covering her completely. Her shoulders were bare except for a few strands of hair, and her left arm was exposed on top of the sheets, resting under her breasts. Her right leg was uncovered as well, and he couldn't help but admire it—smooth, supple, long. Her face was turned towards him and her lips, looking very soft and tempting, were curved in a slight smile. He wondered what they felt like.

Looking away, he told himself again that he would be better off not noticing how attractive she was, that it would be easier to travel with her if he didn't think of her like that. She wasn't a woman to dally with. He needed to think of her like one of his sisters—maybe that would help him control his thoughts.

When he saw the sky darkening through the windows, he wondered if he should wake her for supper but decided to let her sleep awhile longer as she obviously needed it. He lit candles around the room while he waited for her to stir.

Sighing in her sleep Alexandria rolled onto her right side, causing the sheets to slip a little lower. Calum was relieved that her arm held them in place so she was still covered. The last thing he needed while trying to keep himself under control was more temptation. He turned his chair to face the fire, unable to continue staring at her and keep his thoughts platonic.

After an hour Calum felt it was time they had supper, since he knew the kitchen wouldn't be open much longer and they should eat again before leaving. Kneeling beside the bed, he brushed her hair off her cheek so that it fell over her shoulder.

It's even softer than I imagined, he thought as the strands slipped through his fingers.

She sighed again and snuggled into her pillow. He forced himself to ignore her soft skin as he gently touched her shoulder and shook her. He said her name softly so as not to startle her.

Her eyes opened slowly, and she smiled at him. When she tried to sit up, he kept his hand on her shoulder to hold her down.

"I'm going to get us some food while you get dressed," he said.

Her eyes widened as she realized what she was wearing, or more accurately, wasn't wearing. Clutching the sheets to her chest she sank back into the bed and nodded.

After closing the door behind him, Calum paused and listened to Alexandria scramble across the room, presumably gathering her clothes. He chuckled as he headed downstairs to order them a meal. When he returned she was dressed and sitting at the desk.

He sat down on the bed again to eat. "I got you something." He nodded towards the parcel on the desk.

Intrigued, she turned away from her food to unwrap it. It was a belt—a dark brown leather belt that would fit through the loop on the back of her knife's sheath. "Thank you," she said, running it through her fingers.

Calum shrugged as though it wasn't a big deal before changing the subject. "I think we should wait a few hours before leaving, unless you're willing to wait until morning. It will look less suspicious if we leave then."

"Can we go by the mine before we leave?" she asked, putting her belt aside to continue eating.

Surprised he asked, "Why do you want to go there?"

"Can we go?" she asked again without offering an explanation.

"Not if we leave in the morning. The men would never allow it."

"What if we went tonight and then came back here? Then we could leave in the morning."

"Will you tell me why you want to go to the mine?" If he was going to help her then she needed to trust him.

"I'm not sure how to explain it. It's something my mother can do, but since I'm here, I want to try it."

"Try what?" When she hesitated, he added, "If you trust me to get you to Dorset, can't you trust me with this?"

Staring at him seriously she said, "I shouldn't trust you, since I don't know you, but I do. I don't know why but I do." And she did trust him—with her life. She hadn't known him long, but somehow she knew he would never do anything to hurt her.

"Then tell me why you want to go to the mine."

"Well . . . when my mother touches things, she learns about their past. I want to try at the mine, to see if I can learn anything."

"About what?"

"The necklace."

"What necklace?" he asked, exasperated that she was making him drag the information out of her bit by bit.

Alexandria realized that of course he wouldn't have a clue what she was talking about—and how could he? She'd only found out about the necklace a few weeks before. As far as she knew, only her family knew about its existence; otherwise, she imagined there would have been a lot of talk about it in the past when men were planning their attacks.

"The queen's necklace is what she gets her power from," Alexandria explained. "And the necklace was in the mine before she found it."

Calum put his food aside and stared at her intently. "What do you know about this necklace? And how do you know about it?"

Praying he would still help her after hearing the truth, she said, "It used to belong to my family." Seeing his expression she quickly added, "We're not evil. Like I've told you, we're healers and have been forever. Someone gave the necklace to one of my ancestors, saying it would help her heal, but she knew it was evil so she hid it in the mine."

"And the queen found it there."

"A miner found it a hundred years ago and took it home. The queen found it there, but she wasn't the queen yet. A few years after she found the necklace, she killed the royal family and took over."

"How is it I've never heard of her necklace?" he wondered out loud.

"I don't know. The story's been passed down to every generation in my family, and the men always end up going after her, but I didn't know about the necklace until my mother told us."

"It sounds like you only just found out."

Alexandria nodded. "After the last child was taken, my brothers said they wanted to go after the queen, and that's when my mother told us."

"And yet you're here without your brothers."

"My mother convinced my brothers there was nothing they could do. The men in my family go after the queen but never come back, and my mother wasn't going to let that happen to her sons."

"But she let her daughter go."

Flushing, Alexandria looked down at her lap. "I didn't tell her. I wrote a note and left during the night. I think the reason the men always fail is because they don't have magick, and that's what the necklace is—magick."

He continued to question her until she had told him everything she knew. Finally he asked, not really wanting to know, "What does she do with . . . the children?"

"The necklace takes their souls. That's how it rejuvenates itself."

"Does it hurt them?"

"Not that I know of."

Relieved with that answer, he moved on to what he really wanted to know. "So if you destroy the necklace you kill the queen."

"If I destroy the necklace I'll be able to kill the queen," she said, correcting him.

"How are you going to destroy it?"

"I don't know, but I believe the only way to do it is with magick—that's why I planned to practice while traveling." And she had been practicing, until she'd met Calum. Now that he knew the truth about her she could start again.

Leaning forward, he rested his elbows on his knees and asked, "Do you really think you can kill her?"

Letting out a sigh she answered honestly, "No. I'm just praying I can improve my powers enough to destroy the necklace. Then she won't be immortal the next time she's attacked."

"And you think going to the mine will help?"

"I don't know, but I want to try."

"We'll wait a few hours and then go," he told her. If there was any way seeing the mine could help her, then he was willing to make the dangerous trip.

CHAPTER FIVE

Calum left the room first and listened for any sounds from downstairs. He didn't hear anything but thought it would be better to go down the back stairs. He'd checked them out earlier and discovered that they led to the kitchen and then outside.

There was a dog curled up sleeping in front of the last step. Calum stepped over him before turning and taking Alexandria by the waist to lift her off the last step and over the dog. The kitchen was pitch-black so they walked slowly, not wanting to bump into anything and wake the owners. Thankfully the door was well oiled, so it didn't squeak as Calum eased it open.

He took Alexandria's hand and led her behind the cabins, feeling this route was safer than the main road. Calum led the way through the dark as the moon cast little light. Pausing between two cabins he made sure the road was clear before crossing. He then led them behind more buildings until they were at the edge of town. Thirty minutes later they reached the mine.

Hiding in the trees behind some bushes they saw two men blocking the entrance. One left but Calum didn't know if it was to relieve himself or to do a patrol. When the man didn't return after a few minutes Calum whispered, "Wait here."

"Where are you going?" Alexandria whispered to his retreating back. He didn't answer and she was soon alone. Sinking lower into the bushes she watched the guard. Suddenly there was a noise in the trees near the mine. *Where's Calum? The other guard is coming back*, she thought, wishing she hadn't left her bow and arrow at the inn.

The guard also heard the noise and looked around. When it sounded again he went into the trees to investigate.

A few seconds later Calum emerged from the same section of trees and waved her over. He grabbed a torch from the stack near the mine's entrance and used a flint from the box beside the torches to light it.

"What did you do?" she whispered.

"Nothing, he'll be back any second. We'd better hurry."

Inside, to the left of the entrance, was a wooden elevator. Alexandria held the torch while Calum untied the rope that locked it in place. Then they stepped on the platform, and he used the pulley system to lower the elevator into the tunnel.

It made so much noise she was sure they were going to get caught. When they had gone down a few levels, she told him to stop.

"It goes down further," he told her.

"But this is the level where the necklace was found," she replied, sensing it.

As they stepped off the platform onto the dirt ground, Calum took the torch back and held it out to light their way. They walked down a long, cold corridor, the dark walls absorbing the light so they could see only a few feet in front of them. They passed several tunnels that branched off the corridor before she stopped.

"It's this one." Alexandria pointed to the tunnel on their left. "It was found in this one."

Turning back he asked, "How do you know?"

"I can feel its evil."

Suddenly a voice echoed through the corridor. "Who's down there?"

Alexandria clutched his arm and asked in a whisper, "What do we do?"

"Down here." Calum led her into the tunnel at which she had pointed as they heard the elevator start squeaking.

He started to put out the torch, but Alexandria stopped him.

"We have to put it out," he told her. "They'll see it."

The squeaking continued as the elevator came down the shaft.

"Let me." Her eyes brightened, and she stared at the torch until it produced nothing more than a dim glow, barely noticeable.

Calum could see light coming from another torch as someone walked through the corridor. From the sound of footsteps he could tell there was more than one man—probably the two who'd been guarding the entrance. He pulled Alexandria further down into the tunnel, then pressed her into a crevice and stood in front of her.

"Who's there?" the voice called again.

"Are you sure someone's down here?" another voice asked.

"You saw the elevator. Do you suppose it went down on its own?" the first voice asked sarcastically.

"There've been tales of ghosts down here."

The first man laughed. "You're new to the night watch, so you'll have to believe me when I say there are no ghosts, just trespassers."

"Well I don't see anyone."

As the man holding the torch waved it in front of their tunnel, Calum pressed himself further into the wall, shielding Alexandria.

"They've put out their torch, so we can't find them. Let's head back. They'll either die stumbling around in the dark or the miners will find them in the morning."

"What happens if the miners find them?"

"I don't know, but there are many places down here for them to dispose of a body."

Alexandria gripped the back of Calum's shirt as the men talked about what they thought the miners did to trespassers. The voices faded, and soon the elevator started squeaking again, indicating they were alone once more.

"They're gone," Calum said, stepping away from the wall.

Alexandria focused on the torch until it burned as brightly as before.

"Can you create fire as well?" he asked.

"Yes."

"Then you could have lit the torch instead of letting me do it?"

"It would have taken me longer than it did you," Alexandria answered with a smile. Getting back to business she glanced around. "We have to go further."

As they continued walking down the tunnel, Alexandria paused often to press her hand against the wall. Finally she said,

"We're close, I can feel it." She picked up her pace, then suddenly stopped and pressed both hands to the wall. "This is it. This is where he found the necklace." Keeping her hands on the wall, she closed her eyes and focused all her power on trying to see within. "I can see the tunnel," she said after a few minutes. "It was smaller, narrower then." With a sigh of disappointment she lowered her hands and opened her eyes. "We should go."

"Did you learn anything?"

She shook her head. "No."

"But you saw the tunnel."

"Yes, and I saw the miner find the necklace. I also saw the necklace being placed in the cave, but my ancestor didn't know anything about it, let alone about how to destroy it."

"What about the necklace itself? Can you still feel it?"

"Yes, I feel its evil. I can feel that for all the years it was here it was waiting, almost as though it knew it would be found one day." Taking a step away from the wall, she sighed again. "But I can't feel how to destroy it."

"I guess that would be too easy," Calum said jokingly, trying to cheer her up. He didn't like seeing her so upset with herself.

"This is the second time I've tried to get some information and have come up with nothing."

"When was the first time?"

"After leaving home I went to Thurrock, where the queen is from, but no one would talk about her. I guess after a hundred years it's too much to expect that anyone would know anything useful."

"At least you know there isn't some information out there you don't know." He brushed her hair over her shoulder and placed a finger under her chin to raise her gaze to his. "Don't worry, we'll find a way to defeat her. But first we need to get out of this mine."

Smiling, she followed him out of the tunnel. When they reached the elevator he pulled on the ropes, but as he suspected, the miners had tied them back up.

"We won't be getting out this way," he said.

Pressing her hand to the wall, Alexandria said, "There's another way out."

"Great. Where?"

With a wry smile, she answered, "Down one level."

"There's no other way?"

"Not on this level. How are we going to get down?"

He tugged on the ropes. If they were secure enough to hold the elevator, they should be secure enough to climb down. "We'll go down these ropes."

She raised her brows and clarified, "You want us to climb down the ropes?"

"Do you have a better idea?"

She laid her hand on the wall again and saw there was no other way to get down. "If we're going to use the ropes, why don't we go up?"

He didn't think she'd be able to pull herself up that far but didn't say so. "That's not a good idea. The guards will hear us and be ready to take us out before I can gain my footing."

That sounded reasonable to her and she nodded. "Down it is." Looking at the ropes in the middle of the giant hole, she asked, "Exactly how are we going to do this?"

"I'll go down first and then you'll follow."

He made it sound so easy. With the torch in one hand, he reached out and grabbed a rope, then swung his body forward and wrapped his legs around it. She watched his technique as he worked his way down and leaned over when she couldn't see him anymore. When he reached the next level he threw the torch into the corridor. Using the slight slack of the rope Calum swung himself forward and jumped, landing on the dirt ground.

He leaned out and called up, "Are you ready?"

She swallowed loudly and replied, "I don't think I can do this."

"You'll be fine—"

A voice from above cut him off. "Is that a woman I hear? The men will have fun when they find you tomorrow." The voice laughed.

Straightening her spine and resolve, Alexandria yelled back, "They'll never find me." Without a second thought she swung herself out until she was wrapped around the rope. Now she just had to figure out how to get down. She wasn't as graceful or as quick as Calum, but she managed to shimmy down the rope.

He reached out a hand. "Take my hand and place your foot on the edge, and I'll pull you in."

Taking his hand she stretched out her leg as far as possible but could plant only the ball of her foot on the edge.

"Okay, now when I start to pull, let go."

Suddenly terrified, she nodded but didn't speak. When she felt him pulling her she let go of the rope, but at the same time her foot slipped on the dirt and she fell. She screamed until she slammed into the wall and lost her breath.

"Give me your other hand," Calum demanded urgently. He braced himself with his legs apart as he held on to her. When he had both of her hands, he leaned forward and pulled her up, wrapping her arms around his neck. "Hold on to me." Then he wrapped his arms around her waist and pulled her the rest of the way up.

Even though she was now safe, she didn't let go.

He held on too, relieved that she was okay. He was amazed by how quickly he'd come to care for her.

"That's the second time you've saved me," she said, pulling back. Their eyes locked. She could have sworn she saw desire in his eyes and thought he might kiss her. But he didn't.

With a smile he let her go and replied, "Let's not make it a habit."

She laughed. "I can live with that."

Calum picked up the torch and looked around. "So how do we get out of here?"

Placing her hand on the wall again she closed her eyes. After a minute she took the torch and said, "Follow me."

She led them through a maze of tunnels, stopping every once in a while to touch the walls. Eventually they found a tunnel that was boarded off.

"This is it. This is where they used to take their loads up." She grabbed a board and started pulling, but it wouldn't budge.

"Allow me." Calum grabbed a board and pulled it free with a few tugs. He removed a few more until they were able to get through.

The tunnel was narrow, just wide enough for them to crawl. They made their way through until they reached more boards, which Calum also removed. After climbing out he turned to help Alexandria. Not wanting the guards to catch them, he quickly put out the torch. Leaving it beside the opening they hurried across the small clearing to the trees.

"I never thanked you for saving my life," Alexandria said as they walked back to the inn.

"Don't worry about it. You weren't in any danger. I had you the whole time."

"I know. I mean the other day, with those guys. Thank you."

He glanced over and saw her staring at the ground. "No problem."

They didn't speak again until they reached the inn. Calum motioned for her to be quiet while he eased the door open. Once he was certain no one was around, he waved her on in front of him. The dog was still sleeping in front of the stairs, so Calum lifted Alexandria to the next step and followed her up.

Back in their room, Calum lit the candles, and Alexandria gasped when she saw her reflection in the mirror. Her face and hair were streaked with soot, and her clothes and hands were black. Looking at Calum, she saw he was just as dirty.

"I guess we shouldn't have let them take the bath away," Calum said jokingly.

"What do we do?" she asked. "If anyone sees us they'll know it was us in the mine."

Picking up a candle, he said, "Don't worry, I'll get us some water," and headed back downstairs, where he found two buckets in the kitchen. He filled them at the well behind the inn and took them back to the room. They used a cloth to wash their faces, hands, and hair. When they were done he took the buckets back downstairs and dumped the water outside before returning them to the kitchen.

"What about our clothes?" Alexandria asked.

"I'll order another bath tomorrow and we can wash them then."

Looking around awkwardly, she asked, "What do we do now?"

"We should try and get some sleep."

Laughing she said, "I slept all day, you go ahead."

"Do you want to lie down?"

"No, you take the bed. I'm going to meditate and see if I learn anything new."

She sat cross-legged in front of the fire with her back to the bed. Taking advantage of the situation, Calum stripped out of his dirty clothes and slipped under the sheets that smelled like Alexandria. Taking a deep breath he fell asleep thinking of her.

While he slept, Alexandria closed her eyes, breathing evenly. She went over everything she knew and had learned, everything her mother had told her, and tried to determine if she was missing something—something that could help her destroy the necklace.

Opening her eyes she sighed. Based on everything she knew, she had no chance of winning.

✠✠✠✠

The pair left Sevenoaks the next morning after another bath and washing and drying their clothes. Alexandria was wearing her new belt over her vest with her knife resting on her hip for all to see. They headed north towards Thurrock for an hour, just in case anyone was watching them. Then they cut through the trees and headed back south. Calum took them further into the woods, between Sevenoaks and Kirkintilloch, thinking there would be less chance of running into anyone there.

A few hours later, they were out of the forest. Alexandria stopped and looked around at the grassland.

"What's wrong?" Calum asked when he noticed she'd stopped.

"I didn't know the forest ended," she explained. Glancing around again she asked, "Where are we?"

Pointing, Calum answered, "Sevenoaks is about two hours that way." Then he pointed the other way. "And Kirkintilloch is about a day's ride that way."

"I thought Sevenoaks was surrounded by the forest."

"No, just the north side."

Shaking her head, Alexandria marveled at her naivety. "I guess it was pretty stupid to think I could do this alone. I thought the trees would protect me all the way to Sedgemoor Forest."

Calum didn't say anything but agreed that her decision to travel alone had been foolish.

"How long before we reach the forest?" she asked, turning to him.

"It's a three-day ride so it'll probably take us four or five days, though we could make it faster if we don't sleep much."

"I'd rather get there faster. I don't like being in the open."

While he didn't want to be in the open either, he had a feeling she had a different motivation for getting there faster.

They walked until the moon was high in the sky. Calum stopped when he noticed Alexandria stumbling, clearly exhausted.

"I think we should rest for a few hours," he said, setting the satchel he'd bought in Sevenoaks down.

"I'm fine," she told him with a yawn. "We should keep going."

She looked as though she were about to topple over. Knowing she would stop if he said he needed to, Calum lied and said, "I'm tired. I need to rest for a while."

"Okay." She took off her satchel and quiver. Pulling her blanket out, she lay down and tucked her satchel under her head like a pillow. Within seconds she was asleep.

He shook his head, not understanding why she wouldn't admit to being tired. His sisters were like that too—even though they were smaller than he was they wouldn't stop until he did. He'd never claimed to understand a woman's mind, but he'd always thought it was foolish that they wouldn't admit when they needed a break. Lying down he closed his eyes to rest, knowing if anyone tried to sneak up on them he would hear the grass.

He woke a few hours later to a rustling. The sun was just starting to rise. He lay still but didn't sense any danger. It was quiet for a moment. When the rustling started again, he turned his head to see a rabbit hop through the grass and sniff at his satchel.

Slowly sitting up, he reached over and picked up the rabbit by its ears. "Looks like I've caught breakfast," he said to the rabbit. It wrinkled its nose at him in response.

By the time Alexandria woke, the rabbit was cleaned, skewered, and ready to be cooked. Calum had stacked branches under it for a fire but hadn't lit it yet.

"Good morning," he said when she sat up.

Pushing her hair off her face, she sat cross-legged and asked, "Did you sleep at all?"

"A few hours, until this little guy woke me when he came sniffing around our things," he answered, gesturing towards the rabbit. Reaching in his satchel, he took out one of the canteens he'd bought and tossed it her way, impressed when she caught it.

Grateful, she unscrewed the lid and drank the water. When she held it out to him, he shook his head.

"I have my own."

Smiling sheepishly, she figured he probably thought she was stupid for not having her own. "I always managed to find water in the forest."

"We'll have to be careful. I don't know if we'll find water before we reach Sedgemoor," was all he said about the matter. "I thought I'd let you light the fire so we can save our matches." In truth he wanted to see what she could do. She'd claimed to be not very talented, but he wondered if she was just hiding her true power from him.

"It may take a minute," she warned.

Calum shrugged. "We're not in a hurry."

"I thought we wanted to get to the forest quickly."

"We can spare a few minutes. There's no one around."

Resting her hands on her knees, she closed her eyes. Where the air had been still there was now a breeze blowing her long strands behind her. Calum watched her hair get darker, redder, as it blew in the wind. When her eyes opened, he could see the flames as he had before, dancing in her brown eyes, but this time she was staring at the wood. All of a sudden the wood started to smoke, and then spark, and then a small flame erupted and the wood caught fire. The wind died as the flames left her eyes and her hair fell back to her shoulders.

She moved a few branches into the flames, making a nice campfire. Smiling warily, she said, "Not very impressive, is it?"

"Considering I can only make fire with a match, I'd say it's damn impressive."

"But it's not a great weapon."

"If you practice, though, you can make it stronger?"

"I should be able to. That's how it's worked with my other gifts."

Calum looked up sharply. "You have other powers?"

Knowing what he was thinking, she smiled. "Nothing that can be used in a fight. My other gifts all deal with healing."

"But what else can you do?"

Turning her gaze to her satchel, she held out her hand. Suddenly the flap opened and a small bottle floated through the air and landed in her hand.

Looking at Calum, she said, "That's my only gift other than the ability to heal and create fire, but I don't see how it's of any use."

"I don't see how that helps with healing."

"Oh but it does. When I'm healing I connect with the person, feel what they're feeling—that's what helps me heal them on the inside. But I also use herbs to prevent infections and help heal externally. If I need an herb and it's not within reach, I don't have to break the connection to retrieve it. I can think of what I need and summon it while still healing."

"Have you summoned anything bigger than a bottle?"

"Some bottles bigger than this one, and bowls of water." She laughed. "They were tricky. It took time to learn to move them without spilling the water."

Being able to control the movement would be useful if she could lift a weapon, Calum thought. "You got that bottle very quickly."

"I've been doing it for years, so it's easier than creating fire."

"Do you think you could learn to lift a sword?"

"I don't know. I don't see why not, but what good would that do?"

Calum's mind spun with possibilities. "The queen is heavily guarded, but if we distracted the guards with weapons, we could slip past them."

Alexandria nodded, thinking it was a good plan. She hadn't known how she was going to get around them and had hoped the fact she didn't have an army would allow her to slip past the queen's soldiers and into the castle. If she could just improve her magick enough to destroy the necklace she knew someone else— maybe even Calum—would kill the queen.

"What about that trick you played on me?" he asked.

She looked down at her lap. "I'm sorry about that."

He waved her apology away. "I felt the fire. I could smell my clothes and skin burning."

Feeling even more ashamed she apologized again. "I'm so sorry. I shouldn't have done that. I was angry."

"I don't care about that. Can you make the flames real?"

"I don't know. I've never tried." Tilting her head slightly, she thought about it. "I don't see why not, but right now the only fire I can make is what you just saw."

"How did you learn that trick?"

"My mum taught me. My father wanted me to be able to defend myself, but I'm a healer—I don't hurt people. My mum and I call it a mind trick because I make you think something is happening that isn't."

"Can you make them think anything else is happening?"

"I don't know. Since fire is my gift, that's what I've used."

Excited, Calum thought about it as he checked the rabbit. This could be it—if she could strengthen her powers, she could defeat the queen. He'd never seen magick like hers. None of the healers and witches he knew had this kind of power. Well, that wasn't entirely true. He knew one healer who had strong magick, but she was too old to ask to fight.

"What are your mother's powers?"

"Well you already know about when she touches something."

"Yeah." *But that wasn't helpful*, he thought.

"She can also control water."

Now that sounded interesting. "Can you do that too?"

"No."

"But you just learned you have your mother's other power," he reminded her. "Maybe you can do this too."

"When I was younger and we were figuring out what my gifts were she tried to teach me but I couldn't do it. I didn't find her other gifts interesting, so I never tried to use one—until the mine."

"Are all healers so powerful?"

"No. Some don't have any powers and just know how to set bones and sew cuts and prevent infections. I don't know many healers like the ones in my family—we've always had extra gifts."

"I know some healers and witches but not any with powers like yours," he told her.

"They're out there, but they keep their gifts quiet because of the queen. And I'm not even that powerful. My grandmother is really powerful. She can do all the things my mum and I can do, and probably more."

"Where's your grandmother?" he asked, thinking maybe they should take a trip there and get her help with increasing Alexandria's powers.

"She lives in Kilwinning."

Calum paused—that's where the healer he knew lived. "Is her name Phoebe?"

"How did you know?"

"I know her. I knew she had strong magick, but I didn't know exactly what she could do."

"How do you know her? Are you from Kilwinning?"

"No, I'm from Thanet."

"My grandmother never leaves her village. How'd you meet?"

"She came to our village last year."

This surprised Alexandria. As far as she knew, her grandmother hadn't traveled anywhere for years. "Why?"

"She came after the queen took a girl from our village."

"So how'd you meet her?" she asked, now understanding why her grandmother had gone there. "Did you know the girl?"

"She was my niece."

CHAPTER SIX

Alexandria gasped. "I'm so sorry." Now it made sense. He wasn't staying with her for her sake—he wanted revenge on the queen for his niece's death.

"I came back just in time for her funeral. Your grandmother was there." He stabbed the rabbit with his knife, but it wasn't cooked through yet. "My sister told me the queen's servant took her, and they found her dead in the fields hours later." He looked directly at Alexandria, his gaze intense. "We knew the queen killed the children she took, but we didn't know how, or why. Why didn't your grandmother say anything?"

"I don't know. My family believes no one can beat her. They've seen too many loved ones die. Maybe she was worried that if you had that knowledge in your grief and anger, you and other men would go after her, and die."

He smiled, thinking she was probably right. "She told me not to despair, that one day I would have my revenge. I didn't remember that until now. I wonder if she knew we'd meet."

"She says she can't see the future, but I swear she can sense things. She always told me my day would come." She laughed. "I always thought she meant marriage, as all the girls around me were getting married but I had no prospects. Now I wonder if she meant this."

Calum raised his brows. "*You* have no prospects?" He didn't believe that. She was the most beautiful woman he'd ever seen.

Maybe her brothers were scaring the men away. He'd scared away most of the men who'd come sniffing around his sisters. In fact, the only two he hadn't been able to scare away were the ones his sisters had married.

She flushed. "Men don't want to marry a woman as independent as I am."

"Describe this independence."

She gave him an exasperated look. "I'm traveling to Dorset alone to kill the queen. Wouldn't you call that being independent?"

"Yes, but since you came up with that plan right before you left, I doubt it's the reason you have no suitors. Are you sure your brothers aren't scaring them away?"

With sadness in her voice, she said, "I'm sure. Everyone says I'm independent because I wear pants when I ride . . . and hunt."

"That's it? No one wants to marry you because you wear pants and hunt?" he asked with a laugh in his voice.

She lifted her chin. "It's not funny."

"Yes, it is. If that's the reason, then you should visit my village."

"Oh? Do women wear pants in your Thanet?"

"No, but the men there wouldn't let a beautiful woman like you get away for such a stupid reason."

She didn't know how to respond to that. *He thinks I'm beautiful.* She smiled and lowered her eyes as warmth spread through her.

"There must have been someone who saw past it," he insisted. He just couldn't believe all the men in her village were idiots.

The smile left her face as she thought of Michael. "There was one. He was my friend, and we used to meet in secret."

Calum wasn't sure he liked where this was going.

"He said he wanted to marry me, but he recently became betrothed to someone else."

"Is he the reason you decided to go after the queen?"

"No, I'd already decided to go."

"If he let you go he must be very stupid."

Smiling at him she said, "Thank you. He is, but I'm not upset about it."

Calum didn't believe that. Having two sisters, he knew how emotional women could be.

Seeing his expression, she laughed. "I'm really not upset. He did me a favor."

"How so?" The rabbit was finally cooked, and he sliced off some meat for her.

"My whole family hated him but never told me, and I'd hate being married to a weak man." After a few bites, she added, "He asked the other girl instead of me because his mother freaked out when he told her he wanted to marry me. Since his mother and I didn't get along, I can say I'm delightfully pleased I don't have to deal with her."

"Then I guess he did do you a favor." He handed her another piece of meat.

She stared off into the distance wistfully. "Although I would have loved to dance at our wedding."

"Is he a good dancer?"

"I don't know. I've never danced."

Now that really surprised him. He could picture her twirling around, her blonde hair flying, her dark brown eyes twinkling, a smile on her lips. "Doesn't your village have dances?"

"Sure, but the men only dance with the women they're interested in, or married to. And since no one outside my family knew Michael was interested in me, and no one else was interested in me, I've never danced."

"I'll tell you what—when we defeat the queen, there will be a huge party. We'll dance then." He held his canteen out. "Deal?"

She tapped her canteen to his and grinned. "Deal."

✠✠✠✠✠

Back in Calderdale, Niall and Finnean dismounted their horses and led them around back to the corral, where they fed and watered them before entering their parent's cabin. They were sorry to see the hope leave their mother's eyes when she saw they were alone.

Niall kissed his wife, who was sitting at the table with Agnes, Adella, and Alpin, and ran a hand down her hair before kissing his daughter's head.

Finnean sat down beside Agnes and took her hand. Letting out a tired sigh he said, "She wasn't in Kilwinning."

"Where could she be?" Adella whispered. Her eyes were full of worry, and her face looked tired. She hadn't had a decent night's sleep since her daughter left.

Niall placed his hand on his mother's shoulder as he sat down. "Grandmother says she hasn't seen her."

"You don't believe her?" Alpin asked as he took his wife's hand.

"I don't know." Niall rubbed a hand across his face. "She seemed to know more than she was telling us."

"We've checked Fareham, Sevenoaks, and Thanet," Finnean said. "Wherever she is, she's staying out of the villages."

"It's been two weeks," Niall added. "She could be anywhere."

"Why do you think my mother's lying?" Adella asked.

"She told us not to worry, that we'd be getting news of Alex soon," Finnean answered.

"And that's all she said?"

"Yes."

"Then that's all she knows. She wouldn't let us worry like this if she knew more."

"I know, but it really felt as though she knew something more," Finnean stated.

"Didn't you tell me that's one of her gifts?" Agnes asked. "The ability to see the future?"

"Contrary to what my sons think, she can't see the future," Adella said, smiling at her children. "She can sense things but doesn't know where or when they'll happen."

"So she must sense Alexandria is okay," Helen said as she rocked her sleeping daughter in her arms.

"Yes," Adella agreed. "We must pray she's right and that we'll hear from her soon."

"Don't worry, Mum," Niall said. "We *will* find her. We'll bring her home."

✠✠✠✠✠

For the next few days, Alexandria and Calum traveled while the sun was out, pausing for meals and to practice her powers, and made camp at night. On the fourth day they made camp as the sun was setting. Calum collected several logs and set them out so Alexandria could practice. He was impressed by her determination to improve her powers, knowing she wanted to be as strong as she could when they went against the queen's soldiers. After she had lit a log, he would put out the fire while she worked on lighting another.

"You're getting faster," he remarked after she had ignited a few.

She sighed, not as pleased with her progress. "It's because I'm warmed up. It's still taking too long to light the first one, and the flames still aren't very big."

"Can't you do what you did in the mine?" he asked. "When you lit the torch?"

Focusing on the fire she'd just started, she used her gift to make it bigger, until it covered the whole log.

"That's great!"

"Not if we want it to be a weapon," she countered. "I need to make it big from the start, so they can't put it out before it spreads."

"We'll keep working on it. I want to work on something else for now. Come over here."

When she was standing in front of him, away from the flaming log, Calum pulled his sword and held it in front of him, the blade vertical in the air.

"Take my sword."

She reached out her hand.

"Not like that," he said, stepping back.

Understanding what he meant, she focused on the sword, calling it towards her as she did her herbs. It was heavier than anything she'd tried to move before. The sword started shaking in his hand, and when he let go, it stayed in the air and then slowly started to move towards Alexandria. All of a sudden the sword swung downward. Gasping, she lost her hold and it crashed into the grass.

"Not bad for your first try," he said. "Shall we try it again?"

She nodded, taking a deep breath to center herself.

Each time they tried she got better, and since this was a gift she used frequently, she found it easier to improve on than the fire gift. Finally she pulled it from his hand straight into hers.

Excited, she let out a triumphant cry, raising her arm in the air. In her excitement she forgot to keep her focus on the sword, and it plummeted to the ground, taking her with it.

She lifted herself onto her elbows as Calum knelt before her. She spit out grass as he helped her up. Laughing, she brushed herself off. "Well, I guess I need to remember to focus after I have it too."

He picked up his sword and held it out to her. "You should get used to its weight."

Taking it with both hands, she found it wasn't as heavy as she had thought and assumed it must have been the suddenness of the weight that had taken her by surprise. She swung it a few times.

Calum shook his head. "I see we need to work on that as well." He showed her a few moves, and they practiced until she was too tired to continue.

The next day they reached Sedgemoor Forest just as the sun was fading. Alexandria summoned some logs together and lit them but was still not pleased with how long it took. Then they practiced using her gifts in different ways. Before Calum had explained it, she hadn't known how her gifts could be used during a fight, and she now realized she'd been naive in the ways of war and was lucky to have someone with that knowledge helping her.

Alexandria was grateful to have the protection of the trees again, and she slept as peacefully that night as she had at the inn. But it wasn't just the trees that made her feel protected—Calum did too. She was so thankful he was traveling with her, realizing now that she'd never have made it on her own.

When she woke the sun was high, but she couldn't see it through the trees. Sitting up she didn't see Calum and looked around for him. Hearing twigs snap, she placed her hand on her knife and sighed with relief when Calum came into view.

"Good morning," he said, noticing her hand leaving her knife. He was sorry he'd startled her but glad she was prepared. He didn't think she would be an easy target if she was attacked again.

They traveled for a few hours before stopping to hunt for some food. Alexandria displayed her bow and arrow skills and caught some birds for supper.

While they were eating, she asked Calum, "What do you do that you know so much about fighting?"

"I'm a horse breeder in Thanet," he answered. "When I take horses to other villages to sell, I'd better be able to protect them."

"Is that what you were doing when you met me?"

He nodded. "I was traveling back from Tameside."

"How come you don't have a horse?"

"I sold him in Thurrock."

"You sold your horse?"

"That's what I do."

Shaking her head, Alexandria said, "I could never sell my horse."

"I don't travel with one I wouldn't be willing to sell," he explained. "It happens too often that someone wants the one I'm riding."

"That makes sense. Are you the only breeder there?"

"Along with my family. Why do you ask?"

"My brothers always go to Thanet when they want a new horse," she explained.

"What are their names? Maybe I know them."

"Niall and Finnean."

"From Calderdale," he said with a nod. "They've bought a few horses from me over the years. I didn't know they had a sister."

She laughed. "I doubt you talk about women or family while they look at your horses."

He didn't think she'd be impressed by what they talked, and joked, about while going over the horses, so he kept his mouth shut.

"They bought a horse a couple years ago for Alex, who I thought was another brother. I assume now that was you."

"Yeah, she was for my eighteenth birthday. I named her Buttercup. She's a great horse."

Calum smirked. His sisters always gave their horses cutesy names too. "Knowing your brothers, I'm surprised they didn't go after you when you left."

Picking at her food, she said, "They probably did, but I didn't head south, as they would have thought. They would have been on their way home before you and I met."

"How do you know?"

"I'd already been gone a week when we met. They would have been to Fareham and back within that time. Do you have anyone waiting for your return?" she asked suddenly. What she really wanted to know was if he was married. Just because he wasn't wearing a ring didn't mean he didn't have a wife back home. A lot of men who worked in the fields didn't wear rings—maybe it was the same for horse breeders.

"My family will be wondering where I am. I was heading home when we met."

That didn't answer her question. "Will they come looking for you?"

"No. They'll think something happened to me."

"I'm sorry. Is there any way we can send word to them?"

"Not until we reach another village."

"How long will it take us to get through Sedgemoor?"

"It takes me about two weeks by horse, so I'd say at least three weeks walking."

"Three weeks? Really?" She'd hoped to make it in two.

"If we don't rush. I think we should use this time to strengthen your powers."

"You're probably right. I'm not improving as fast as I'd hoped."

Calum shook his head. "You're being too hard on yourself. You're getting stronger every day."

"But I'm nowhere near where I need to be to destroy the necklace," she reminded him.

"You'll get there," he assured her.

She turned the subject back to his family. "Can you wait three weeks to get word to your family?"

"It'll be fine. My brothers-in-law will be upset that I left them with the horses, but they'll forget it when they hear why."

She nodded, knowing his family would forgive him anything when they heard he was avenging his niece. She just hoped her family would forgive her.

"What about your parents?" she asked, still wondering if he was married or not.

"It's just my father. My mum died a few years ago. I'm glad she wasn't there to bury her grandchild. I think it would have killed her. It nearly killed my sister."

"How is she now?"

"Better. She had her husband, Eadan, and our sister, Una. I think if she hadn't needed Eadan so much he would have gone after the queen then and there. I don't think Clara could have handled two funerals."

"Does she have other children?"

"No. She had been carrying her second child but lost him due to the stress." Yet another death he blamed on the queen.

"I'm so sorry," she said softly, feeling bad that she had brought up such painful memories for him.

"It's been a tough year for my family, but ever since Una announced she was pregnant a few months ago, Clara's been wanting another of her own." Looking up, he added, "I know she'd feel much better about having a child if the queen were dead."

"So would every other mother," she added.

He smiled slightly and nodded, but was more concerned about his own family than anyone else.

Alexandria didn't notice his lack of concern, having other thoughts on her mind. It didn't sound as though he was married, but she still wasn't sure. Maybe he had a betrothed. Should she bring it up again? Should she just ask him outright?

Finally she blurted, "Do you have anyone else waiting for you?"

Grinning, Calum finally understood what she was after. "Do you mean a wife?"

"Or someone who's waiting to become your wife."

"Does it matter?" he asked, enjoying how she was trying to act uninterested.

Staring into the fire, she said neutrally, "No, I'm just wondering who I'd have to send word to if you died."

"If *I* died? You think I'm going to die but you're going to make it?"

"You're the one who calls it a suicide mission," she reminded him.

"You don't think you're going to live through this either," he reminded her.

Raising her chin, Alexandria said, "I've changed my mind."

"Really?" Did she feel she was going to be strong enough to defeat the queen by the time they reached her? "What's made you change your mind?"

"I was thinking about what my mother always says. When she heals people, she tells them to think positive, that positive thoughts help them heal faster."

He raised his brows with skepticism. "Does that actually work?"

"I don't know," she said with a shrug. "But we have this one cranky man in the village, and when he gets hurt, it always takes him longer to heal. So I'm going to believe it's true and that I'm going to win and go home." Looking at him, she said, "Are you going to believe you're going home?"

"Not yet, but I do believe you have a better chance than anyone else to defeat her." Standing, he picked up their empty canteens and headed into the trees. Just before he was out of sight, he said over his shoulder, "There's no one else waiting for me back home."

She smiled after him, wondering why he'd finally told her. *If he thinks I have feelings for him and he doesn't return them, then he could have said someone was waiting for him. Maybe because he thinks we're going to die, he didn't see any reason to lie. Or maybe he thinks because we're going to die, he can dally with me and it won't cost him anything.* She still didn't know him well, but she didn't think it was the last reason, certain he was an honorable man. They'd been traveling together for over a week and he hadn't tried anything. Maybe he did have feelings for her and wasn't just there for his niece. She just wished she knew what his feelings were.

Alexandria brought herself back to reality. She shouldn't be thinking about this. They had bigger things to worry about and she needed to focus on how to kill the queen, not whether or not he liked her.

While Calum was looking for water, she worked on her fire gift, putting it out before lighting it again. She was getting a little faster at starting the fires, but the flames still weren't very big.

Calum returned with the water, and they took a break before putting in some more practice with the sword, both with her gift and without. She was light on her feet and able to move quickly when he came at her—she just needed to increase her arm strength so she could swing the sword more easily.

After practicing for a few hours, her arms were aching so much she could barely lift it. Going into the woods, she looked for some herbs to help her muscles, and after finding what she needed, she returned to camp and placed her herbs beside the fire. Straightening she looked around.

"What are you looking for?" Calum asked.

"I need to boil some water."

Calum found a rock with a dip in it, and he used his knife to chip out a larger hole.

"Is this deep enough?" he asked, handing it to her.

"Can you go a little deeper in the center?"

He did as she asked to make it perfect, and after rinsing it, he filled it with water and put it in the fire. Alexandria chopped the herbs, added them to the water, and stirred them with a stick. While they boiled, she took a bottle of oil out of her satchel and rubbed it into her arms.

"What is that?" he asked, gesturing to the bottle.

"Arnica oil. It helps relieve muscle pain, and I'm boiling rosemary in the water, which will help too, so I won't be as sore tomorrow."

"Can't you just heal yourself?"

"That's not how it works," she explained. "I can only heal a physical wound, like a cut or broken bone. Herbs help take away the pain or prevent infections, but to answer your question, I can heal myself if I break a bone or get cut."

Thinking back he asked, "So you could have healed your feet when we first met?"

"Yes."

"Why didn't you?"

"I was afraid," Alexandria admitted. "Not everyone likes healers. I thought it was better to keep it to myself."

He nodded, understanding. These days people were very suspicious of power, including healing.

She took her rock bowl from the fire and let it cool for a few minutes before drinking it. Then she lay down and closed her eyes.

Calum watched her sleep for a while, wondering how they were going to get through this. He was more worried about getting past the queen's soldiers than dealing with the queen herself. Half the battle would be getting to her, and they hadn't yet discussed how that was going to happen.

✠✠✠✠✠

Brodrick dragged a man into the throne room and threw him to the ground a few feet from the throne.

Minerva lost her breath at the sight of him. It was as though her Henry were in front of her. His hair was longer than Henry's had been, but his eyes were the same shade of golden brown.

On his knees he glared at the queen, not concerned about his safety as he assumed he was about to die anyway.

"Leave us."

Brodrick didn't move. He'd never left her alone with someone from outside the castle before—especially not with someone he knew wanted to kill her.

Turning to him with eyes hard as stone, she demanded, "Leave us."

Brodrick obeyed but stayed near the door in case she needed him. He tried to listen but was too far away and she wasn't yelling . . . yet.

Minerva walked down the few steps in front of her throne and stopped before him. "What's your name?"

He didn't answer.

Running a finger down his cheek, she said, "You look just like a man I once knew."

"What'd you do to him? Kill him?" he asked insolently.

"I married him," she answered with a smile. Stepping back, she said, "Tell me about this secret passage you know of."

"Is that why I was brought here?" he asked. "So you can find out about the passage and then kill me?"

She brushed his hair off his forehead. "I'm not going to kill you. I want you to stay with me."

He looked at her as though she were crazy. "What happened to your husband?" She was so close. He was sure this was the closest anyone had ever gotten to her. He could kill her now. There was a small knife in his boot that the soldiers hadn't found when they'd disarmed him.

"He was murdered." Touching his face again, she whispered seductively, "I can give you anything, everything you want." She leaned in to kiss him.

In a swift motion, he pulled out his knife and stabbed her in the stomach. As her eyes widened with pain, he twisted the knife and said, "I want you to die."

She fell back against the steps, her mouth open in a silent gasp, staring at him in disbelief.

He rose to his feet, but didn't flee. He knew he wasn't going to escape with his life, but if she died, it would all be worth it.

Her dark blue eyes hardened as she got to her feet. Black smoke swirled around her. He watched in amazement as the knife disappeared along with her wound.

"You would try to kill me?" she asked, her voice hard as steel. "I'm offering you everything."

"There's nothing you could give me that would make me stay with you, and I'll try to kill you every chance I get."

Rage filled her, and she threw her hands out, sending black smoke to circle him, her eyes growing dark as night. He started to gasp for air, grabbing at his throat. After a minute his hands fell to his sides and his eyes rolled back. As she lowered her hands he collapsed to the floor.

When he lay dead at her feet, she stumbled back a few steps. "What have I done?" she whispered, horrified.

He's not Henry.

Leaning down, she touched his cheek. "He looks just like him."

That doesn't make him your husband. Would your Henry have treated you the way he did?

She straightened, her face turning to stone. "No. He loved me. He died protecting me. He would never hurt me."

Hold on to your memories. They're all you have of him. You won't find him in another man.

Looking down at the man at her feet, who looked so much like her husband, she sighed. "I thought I could pretend Henry was with me."

He's not. Just because this man looked like him doesn't make him Henry.

Sighing again, she said, "I know." After one last look she climbed the stairs to her throne and composed herself before yelling, "Brodrick." When he was before her, she gestured to the body on the ground. "Get rid of him."

Brodrick bowed before picking up the dead body and throwing it over his shoulder. Turning, he left the hall.

✠✠✠✠✠

Alexandria and Calum had fallen into a routine. They traveled during the day, stopped to practice her powers and have supper, practiced some more, then slept. She liked that they took turns hunting—he didn't seem to mind that she had skills, and even complimented her on being a better shot.

Ten days later they were about halfway through Sedgemoor Forest and still hadn't come across anyone else. They spent a few hours training with the sword before taking a break, deciding it was time for some food. Alexandria was resting by the campfire when she heard someone approaching.

Assuming it was Calum returning from hunting she called out, "Back already?" and smiled in the direction of the noise.

But it wasn't Calum who stepped through the trees. It was a tall man with short brown hair and a brown goatee wearing all black and carrying a sword. She could tell by the quality of his clothes that he had money. *Probably a business owner. What's he doing in the forest?* she wondered.

"Expecting someone?" he asked with a wicked smile.

"My husband," she answered, standing. It didn't matter why he was there—she didn't like the look in his dark eyes. This time she was prepared to defend herself. Her bow and arrow were leaning against a tree across from the fire, but she had her knife.

Hearing someone else coming, she was filled with relief, thinking it had to be Calum. Unfortunately it wasn't. Two men with thick beards stepped into view and joined the first. One had long blond hair and the other had long black hair. They were also dressed in black and carried swords. She knew it would be difficult to beat these large men, but she had a few tricks up her sleeve. She just needed to stay calm.

"I heard there was a woman traveling these parts in pants but didn't believe it," the first man said as his eyes roamed her body. "My wife wouldn't dare leave our home in pants."

"Then maybe you should get back to her," Alexandria said. She kept her hand loose by her side but was ready to grab her knife if they tried anything.

All three men moved forward, but she refused to move back. To do so would show she was afraid.

"Maybe we'd rather stay here with you."

"My husband won't like it," she warned them.

He looked around and said casually with his arms extended, palms facing upward, "He's not here to object, is he?" Looking at their fire, he asked, "Got anything to drink?"

"No," she answered firmly.

Another man asked, "Where's your hospitality?"

Raising her brow insolently, she replied, "My hospitality is reserved for gentlemen."

He pressed his hands to his chest. "We're gentlemen."

Suddenly they looked over her shoulder and grinned. She heard something behind her but was afraid to turn her back on the men in front of her.

"I send you hunting and look what you find," a voice behind her said.

Spinning around to face the new threat, Alexandria saw two more men. One was clearly their leader. He was dressed in black pants and a dark green coat and wore a bejeweled ring on the hand that was resting on the hilt of his sword. His clothes looked to be of the same quality as the first man's. Perhaps they were related. The man with him looked like the other two—servants, she assumed.

"The best kind of catch if you ask me," the well-dressed man behind her answered.

The leader shook his head. "I hope my men didn't scare you," he said with a charming smile. "They were taking my son hunting."

She didn't lower her guard. There was something in his eyes she didn't trust. "They startled me," she admitted. "I was expecting my husband."

"And where is your husband?" he asked, stepping forward, his hands clasped behind his back.

She knew his pose was supposed to inspire trust, but she didn't buy it, sure he'd be fast enough to grab his sword, or her, before she could do anything.

"He's hunting. He should be back soon."

Hearing the men behind her move, she glanced over her shoulder and saw they had come closer.

Turning back to the leader, she said, "I think you'd better go."

He smiled again, this time less charmingly. "Now why would I want to do that? Even if he comes back before we're gone, he's only one man to my four."

Straightening, she placed her hand on her knife. "He can easily take four men, and you're forgetting me."

He threw his head back and laughed. "You may dress like a man and carry a knife, but I doubt you know how to use it."

Alexandria centered herself, preparing to showcase everything she'd been practicing. *I'll show you I'm not as weak as I look.*

CHAPTER SEVEN

Calum was coming back from hunting when he heard male voices in their camp. He stopped before they saw him, so he could assess the situation. Hearing the last part of the conversation, he knew trouble was brewing and stepped through the trees.

"Ah," the leader exclaimed. "This must be the husband now."

"That's right," Calum answered, setting down the rabbit. "And who are you?"

The leader waved the question aside. "Oh, you don't need to know my name. You won't be alive long enough to use it." He nodded at his men.

They pulled their swords and approached Calum from both sides.

Drawing his own sword, Calum glanced at Alexandria. She had pulled her knife and was staring at the leader. Calum could see her hair darkening and knew she was gathering her powers. Turning back to the men, he blocked the first attack and knocked his attacker down. The other three charged. Calum blocked their swords and kicked out, hitting one in the stomach and sending him to the ground. Another swung at his legs. Calum jumped back, but the sword caught his left thigh.

The leader suddenly screamed as he burst into flames. His men turned to see what was wrong, making it easy for Calum to quickly kill two. He then killed the son as he was raising his sword towards Alexandria. The last one standing had more skill than his friends, and was in fact the one who'd struck Calum's leg.

Alexandria summoned her bow and an arrow, which she quickly shot straight into the leader's heart. Gasping, she dropped her bow and placed her hands on her knees, trying not to be sick. She'd never killed a man before and wished she didn't have to again, even though she knew she would to get to the queen.

The lone survivor's and Calum's swords clashed. Just when it seemed like the stranger was gaining the advantage, Calum suddenly stabbed him through the chest. Resting on his sword, he saw Alexandria still leaning over and ran to her side.

Running a hand down her hair he asked, "Are you okay?"

Nodding, she leaned against him and rested her cheek on his chest. "I've never killed anyone before," she whispered. "I don't like it."

He wrapped one arm around her. His other hand still held his sword, in case anyone else approached. "You're not supposed to like it," he told her. "Only evil people enjoy killing."

"Like the queen and her men."

"Yes."

She leaned back until her eyes met his. "And to stop her I'm going to have to kill again."

"Yes."

"Then let's hope I'm strong enough to get through this."

He cupped the side of her face with his free hand. "You *are* strong enough," he assured her. "You got through this."

Taking a step back, she smiled, not wanting to admit she'd nearly been sick. She noticed him leaning on his sword and gasped when she looked down and saw the blood.

"You're hurt. Why didn't you say so?"

"I'm fine." He pulled her up when she tried to kneel down and inspect the injury. "We have to get out of here. They might not have been alone."

"It can wait a few minutes. Let me heal your leg."

"How long will that take?"

"I need to collect some herbs," she said, kneeling again to see how deep the wound was.

"We don't have time for that, Alex."

She looked up sharply.

"Sorry, Alexandria."

Shaking her head, she smiled. "My family calls me Alex, usually in the same exasperated tone you just used."

"I'm sorry, but we really need to get out of here."

"If there were men with them they would have heard the fighting and have been here by now. We aren't leaving until I at least put a compress on your leg to stop an infection." Standing, she said, "Sit down. You need to take the weight off your leg. I'll be back in a few minutes."

She searched the area until she found chamomile. As she knelt to pick some, someone stepped in front of her. Her surprise quickly turned to relief when she saw it was an Amatarian—she had nothing to fear. She was even more surprised when she looked up and realized it was her friend. As usual he had his bow and quiver strapped to his back, but for the first time she saw a sword at his hip.

"Demetrius! What are you doing here?"

"Looking for you." He helped her to her feet. "We have to get out of here. There were sounds of a fight, and men are searching for its location."

"I can't go. My friend was hurt in the fight. I need to get back to him." She turned and hurried back thought the trees.

"What do you mean 'him'?" he called after her. Not liking the sound of that he followed her.

She knelt beside Calum and stilled him when he tried to stand upon seeing her friend. "It's okay," she said. "He's my friend."

"He's an Amatarian warrior," he whispered, watching the man behind her warily.

Alexandria smiled. "They're peaceful people. We have nothing to fear."

Tired of waiting for her answer, Demetrius asked in Amatarian, "What's going on?"

She lifted the torn pieces of Calum's pants away from his wound and pushed on the skin, making him bleed so she could clean his blood. In English, she said, "Don't be rude, Dem, speak English."

"Who is this man to you?" he asked, still speaking Amatarian.

After a glance at Calum she turned to face Demetrius and answered in Amatarian. "He's my friend. He saved me from some men a few weeks ago." Looking at the fallen men around them, she added, "And again today."

"Which wouldn't have happened if you'd stayed home where you belong."

Turning back to Calum, she dampened the bottom of her shirt with water and cleaned his wound. In English she said, "If you're here to criticize me instead of help you can leave."

She placed the chamomile in the rock bowl with a little water and used another rock to grind it into a paste.

Demetrius placed a hand on her shoulder. Speaking in English for the first time he said, "I'm sorry. We can discuss this later. Right now we need to leave before the other men find us."

Calum sat up. "There are other men?" Looking at Alexandria, he said, "I told you we needed to leave."

Once again she stopped him from getting up. "It can wait a few more minutes." She rubbed the salve into his leg and opened herself to see how bad it was, knowing there wasn't time to do a full healing. Thankfully nothing was torn on the inside and he wasn't in danger of dying. Alexandria placed a clean leaf over the salve and bound the wound with a strip of cloth she had cut from the bottom of her shirt. It would have to do until they were somewhere safe.

"We're not far from my tribe," Demetrius said as Calum stood.

"We're not going with you," Calum stated firmly.

"We'll be safe there," Alexandria said. "You can trust them."

Calum pulled her a few feet away and whispered harshly, "We *can't* trust them. They kill Tolgarians, not help them."

"They're not killers. They only harm those who try to harm them."

"I don't trust him."

"Trust me," she whispered back. "They won't hurt us, we're friends. My family has always been friends with them."

"And him?" he asked, looking at Demetrius over her shoulder.

"His name is Demetrius and he's my best friend—has been for a long time." Packing their things, she added, "He taught me to ride bareback and hunt better than my brothers. He was even my first—"

"I get it." Calum cut her off. Here he'd been thinking she was innocent. He hadn't known she was so close with the Amatarians, known for being fearsome warriors and unfaithful lovers, sleeping with any willing person.

Alexandria handed Demetrius Calum's satchel before putting on her own and then her bow and quiver. "Can you walk?" she asked Calum.

"I'm fine," he replied, still eyeing Demetrius.

She wasn't surprised. Her brothers would never admit it when they were in pain, especially in front of other men. "Then let's go."

Demetrius grabbed the rabbit as they were leaving and shrugged when he saw Alexandria's expression. "There's no reason he should go to waste."

She rolled her eyes as they headed into the trees.

"Where's your tribe?" Calum asked.

"Our village is just a few minutes away."

Calum glanced at Alexandria before turning back to her friend. "I've traveled these woods many times and have never seen a village."

"Of course you haven't," Demetrius replied.

Smiling, Alexandria explained, "Their home is protected by magick. People can't see it unless they're from the Amatar tribe."

"Are you trying to tell me someone could just walk through their village and not see anything?"

"No one walks through their village. Have you ever traveled south from Fareham and gone through the center of the forest?"

"Of course."

Glancing at him sideways, she asked, "Are you sure? Think carefully. Did you start to go south but for one reason or another end up going east or west instead?"

Most of the time he came straight down from Thanet but realized when he came from Fareham he always seemed to veer towards the west, and he couldn't remember why.

Seeing his frown, she explained, "It's their magick. It sends you around the village and you don't even notice."

"How are you two such good friends if he lives way down here?"

"He actually lives with the tribe a few hours north of me, but the Amatarians do travel between the tribes."

"I'm down here looking for you," Demetrius said. "I've been looking for you since your mother told me you disappeared."

"I thought you left your family a note," Calum interjected.

"I did. I told them I was at the lake, and I hid a note at the lake a few days before I left that explained where I was going."

"Your brothers left the next morning to try to catch you. I found out after they were gone, when your mother came to our tribe to ask if I knew anything."

"Did you know anything?" Calum asked, thinking that he wasn't a very good friend if he'd known and hadn't tried to stop her, or at least go with her if he hadn't been able to stop her.

"No, I didn't," Demetrius answered coldly. Turning to Alexandria, he added, "And as her friend and confidant, I'd like to know why I wasn't told."

"Because you would have tried to talk me out of it," she answered.

"Damn right I would have!" he burst. "What were you thinking? Of all the stupid ideas you've had, this one's the worst."

Straightening, she said, "I didn't ask your opinion."

He sighed. "Don't get your nose out of joint. If I couldn't have stopped you, I would have come with you."

Stopping, she turned to him. "You can't Dem, you know that, and I would never have asked it of you."

They stared at each other until Calum asked, "Would one of you like to clue me in?"

Alexandria started walking again. "The Amatarians and the queen have a truce. I wouldn't ask him to break that."

"We're here," Demetrius said, stopping.

Calum looked around. "There's nothing but forest here."

Alexandria laughed. "You can't see it, remember?"

"Can you?"

"No, but I can feel it. I know how to find their village."

She took Calum's hand and laced their fingers together. Glancing down, Calum saw she was also holding Demetrius's hand. Demetrius stepped forward and disappeared, followed by Alexandria, who pulled Calum along after her.

Suddenly there were people walking in front of him and huts in the distance, where a moment earlier there had been only trees. He hadn't believed them, but couldn't deny what was before his eyes.

Demetrius stepped away to speak with a few Amatarian men.

The thatched-roof huts were round and made from small trees and large branches woven together. Several huts were joined together, and Calum figured they belonged to larger families. He'd come across a few Amatarian men before, so he wasn't surprised by their caramel skin color, dark hair, or lack of clothing—only loincloths covered them.

What did surprise him was the beauty of their women and what they wore. Instead of skirts and blouses like the Tolgarian women, they were robed in sleeveless dresses with plunging necklines and slits in the skirts up to the thighs. He couldn't help but watch them—every step they took showed off their curves and long legs.

Still holding his hand, Alexandria gave it a tug to get him moving again. She noticed his stunned expression and assumed he'd never seen an Amatarian woman before. As they walked through the village, Alexandria noticed the interested looks Calum was getting from the women and grew annoyed. *How am I supposed to compete with them?*

The Amatarian women didn't wait until they were married to have sex. They believed if you felt desire, you should explore it. That way, you would be certain of compatibility when you mated. They only mated for love, and if they didn't fall in love, they were happy to stay single and explore their passions with other single men—for once Amatarians mated, they were faithful for life.

Demetrius led them to a large hut and told them to wait before pushing aside the curtain door and going inside. After a few minutes, he held the curtain back and ushered them in.

Inside the hut, which was the largest in the village, the branches were covered with tapestries, making the room warm and cozy. There were a few chairs near the walls for the elders, but most people, a few women and many men, stood. Across from the door was a long table, behind which several men were seated. In the center, in the largest chair, sat Genesis, the leader of the Amatar tribe. Like all the others he was bare chested and wore bands around his biceps and his hair in a braid down his back. The only thing different about him was that he wore several beaded necklaces around his neck instead of one.

Letting go of Calum's hand, Alexandria stepped forward and bowed her head.

Genesis leaned forward and folded his hands on the table. "I hear you've got your family worried about you. Would you care to explain what's going on?"

Raising her head, she said, "I will, but my friend was hurt." She gestured towards Calum. "If it's alright with you, I'd like to take him to the healer's hut first."

"Fine," Genesis said, taking note of Calum's leg. "But after he's healed, we'd like to hear what you're up to."

She bowed her head again then rushed back to Calum's side and took his hand. Demetrius led them to a healer's hut.

At the door, Alexandria said to the female Amatarian inside, "My friend has hurt his leg. Will you heal it please?"

"Of course, I would be pleased to." Holding the curtain back she waved her arm and said, "Come in."

Demetrius waited outside while Alexandria and Calum entered. Looking around, Calum saw a small fire with a pot boiling over it and two small tables covered with bowls and jars full of oils and powders. In the center of the hut was a long, high table, on which Calum assumed people were treated.

"You need to lie down," Alexandria told him.

Looking at table again, he asked, "Do I have to?"

Men, she thought. *They're always the most difficult patients.* "No, but you do have to sit there so we can see your leg."

Once he was sitting, Alexandria unwrapped his leg and peeled back the leaf. After checking Calum's leg, the healer turned to one of the tables that held her herbs and started picking the ones she wanted.

"Wait, you're doing the healing, right?" Calum asked Alexandria as he watched the healer mix some powders in a bowl.

"She's more gifted than I. You're in good hands," she assured him. "Trust me."

"I do. I trust *you*. Not anyone else."

In Amatarian, the healer said, "It's alright. You can do it. Most men only want their women to heal them."

Alexandria smiled, not wanting to tell the healer she wasn't his woman, that Calum simply didn't trust Amatarians.

The healer passed her bowls and cloths. Alexandria thanked her in Amatarian as she set them on the table beside Calum. After soaking both cloths, she cleaned his leg with one before folding the other and resting it on his wound. Placing both hands over it, she closed her eyes and opened herself to him.

Warmth spread through his thigh as the pain faded. When she removed her hands and the cloth, he was amazed to see only a thin red line.

Running her thumb across the line she said, "If you'd let her heal you, you wouldn't have this."

"I don't mind a scar."

She took some cream from the healer and massaged it into his leg. "Hopefully it won't scar."

He watched the healer shake several powders into a goblet before pouring boiling water in. After stirring it, the healer handed it to Alexandria, who turned to hand it to Calum.

"What is it? I thought you were healing me."

"I did. This will help ensure you don't get an infection." He was looking at it so suspiciously that she took a drink to show him it was fine. "She might have used a little more lavender than I would have, but otherwise it's just as I'd make it."

Taking the goblet, he sniffed it and frowned. "It smells like flowers."

"It is. Along with other plants and herbs." She nudged it towards his mouth. "Drink it while it's still warm."

After a sip he discovered it tasted like flowers too. Wanting to get it over with, he downed it.

"Now that wasn't so bad, was it?" Alexandria ignored his glare while taking the goblet from him. Handing it back to the healer she thanked her for the use of her herbs.

The healer nodded and left them alone.

"Did you ask her to leave?"

"No, I thanked her for the herbs. She's probably going to give Genesis a report."

"Who's he?"

"He's the leader of the Amatar tribe. You could say he's like their king, but they don't call him that."

"What do they call him?"

"Genesis. The Amatarians have no need for labels, just as he sees no need to separate himself from his people. He lives and acts like one of them." Heading towards the door she said, "We'd better get back. He'll be waiting to hear from me."

"Who were the men sitting with him?"

"His council. He always meets with them before making a decision."

"So they help him decide."

"You could say that. He always makes the final decisions, but to do what's best for his people, he wants to hear all thoughts."

Demetrius was waiting to take them back to Genesis's hut. Once inside, Alexandria stepped forward to the center of the room and bowed her head again.

"Now you may explain what's going on. Your mother is very worried," Genesis said in English.

"You've seen her?" Alexandria asked, straightening.

"She came to see me after you disappeared, wanting to speak with Demetrius. It's my understanding Demetrius knew nothing to tell her," he remarked with a raised brow.

Shaking her head Alexandria confirmed, "I didn't tell him anything."

"I went searching for her as soon as I found out," Demetrius said. Turning to Alexandria he added, "During my trip here, I looked for signs of you but didn't find any."

"I stayed off the main paths," she explained.

Genesis thought that was smart of her but wasn't willing to say so, not yet sure her journey as a whole was smart. "And this man?" he asked, nodding towards Calum.

"I met him outside Thurrock. He saved me from some men who were chasing me."

"Why were they chasing you?"

"Why do you think?" Calum called out, moving to step forward, but Demetrius placed a hand on his shoulder to hold him in place.

"Ah," Genesis drawled. "I sometimes forget the extent of evil that Tolgarian men are capable of. So this man saved you, and then?"

"I told him I was meeting my brothers in Sevenoaks. He agreed to take me, and when we arrived, I admitted that I had lied and told him I was actually going to Dorset."

Genesis leaned forward, his eyes watching her intently. "Why are you going to Dorset?"

Standing tall she announced, "I'm going to kill the queen."

The room broke out in murmurs and whispers while Genesis stared at her.

Calum moved forward to stand beside her and took her hand, lacing their fingers together to show he was with her.

When Genesis spoke again, the room instantly quieted. "And he agreed to help you?"

"Yes."

"Why?"

"The queen killed his niece last year. After he heard my plan, he thought that I would have a better chance of defeating her than others who've tried."

"Why do you think you can win when so many have lost over the years?"

"Because of my gifts. The queen's necklace is magick, and I think only someone with magick can destroy it. Calum has been helping me strengthen my powers during our journey."

"How do you plan on destroying the necklace?" he asked curiously.

"I don't know, but I believe when the time comes, I'll know what to do."

Nodding, he said, "You've given me much to think about. Tomorrow you'll show me your talents. Maybe we can help you with them."

Alexandria bowed her head in gratitude.

In Amatarian, Genesis asked, "Are you sleeping together?"

Blushing, she answered in his language. "No."

"There's no need to blush. You know our feeling about this."

"Yes, and you know my family's feelings about this."

He nodded. "Yes, yet another of your customs we don't understand. Well, I didn't mean to embarrass you. I just want to know if you wish to share a hut."

"Yes, please. A *hut*, not a bed."

Seeing Calum's frustration, Genesis apologized in English. "Forgive my rudeness. We just had something to clear up. Demetrius will take you to get something to eat while I have a hut prepared for you."

CHAPTER EIGHT

Demetrius led them to the clearing with communal tables, where the Amatarians ate. Unlike the Tolgarians', their homes had no kitchens. A few cooking huts surrounded the tables. They were worked by both male and female Amatarians, who took turns preparing the meals.

Calum sat down on a bench beside Alexandria with Demetrius across from them, a few places down from the other Amatarians. It didn't surprise Calum to hear them greet Demetrius, but he was surprised they knew Alexandria. She was leaning forward to look past him and speaking Amatarian. He had no idea what she was saying but their language sounded so beautiful coming from her.

Another Amatarian sat down beside Demetrius and, after a greeting, turned to Calum and said in English, "So you're the one who saved Alex."

Alexandria groaned. "How did you hear about that already?"

He grinned and answered, "News travels fast."

Wanting to change the subject she turned to Calum. "This is Thaddeus. He's from the north tribe with Dem." Looking at Thaddeus again she asked, "How have you been? I haven't seen you much lately."

"I've been staying here more."

Grinning, Demetrius asked, "Any reason for that?"

"The food's better," was his answer.

Two Amatarian women appeared and placed several platters of food, plus a stack of plates and utensils, in front of them. One smiled intimately at Thaddeus before walking away. He continued to stare after her while the others filled their plates.

Alexandria shared a smile with Demetrius before saying, "Right. It's the food that keeps him here."

After supper, Demetrius showed Alexandria and Calum to their hut. Inside were two pallets, one on either side, and a small table between that held a jug of water and a lit candle. Evening sunlight shone through the small gaps in the woven branches.

In Amatarian, he asked, "Are you sure you want to stay here? You can stay with me."

She knew he wasn't suggesting anything. They were just friends and he was protective of her like a brother. "I'm fine here," she assured him.

Demetrius glared at Calum before leaving.

"What was that about?" Calum asked.

"He's not happy I'm staying here. He thinks I should stay with him," she explained.

Calum figured it was because Demetrius wanted her. He'd seen the way he watched her, and since they'd already been lovers, Demetrius probably didn't want to share. Calum might want her too but he'd never dishonor her that way. It didn't matter that she wasn't innocent—she was the kind of woman you married. Not wanting her to see the desire that entered his eyes at the thought of bedding her, he turned around.

A woman stood so close he needed to step back.

She had long, flowing black hair and warm hazel eyes—eyes full of appreciation. In her arms were a few blankets. Calum did his best to keep his eyes on hers, but her deep neckline was offering a tantalizing view.

Her eyes not leaving Calum's, Talora asked Alexandria in Amatarian, "Are you staying here tonight?"

"Yes."

"Pity, but you've always had good taste."

What did she mean by that? Alexandria wondered. It was rumored that Talora had slept with one of Alexandria's brothers, but she'd never asked them if it was true. But what did that have to do with her taste? They were her brothers. Was she referring to

Michael? She didn't consider her attraction to him good taste, especially now that she knew everyone hated him. *And why am I worrying about this? He's marrying someone else, so what do I care who he's slept with.*

Talora handed Calum the blankets and said to Alexandria, "If you change your mind let me know. I wouldn't mind keeping him company." With one last sultry look, she left the hut.

"What was *that* about?" Calum asked.

Taking a blanket from his pile, Alexandria answered, "She wanted to know if I was staying here, because if I wasn't, she would be willing to stay with you."

He went to the door and held the curtain open to watch Talora walk away. Her hips swayed seductively, as though she knew he was watching.

Alexandria was hurt by the interest in his expression. She knew they weren't together but had really started liking him. And she'd been sure that he wasn't traveling with her only to avenge his niece's death. *I guess I shouldn't be surprised*, she thought. *I was wrong about Michael too.*

Turning away, she asked, "Would you like me to find somewhere else to sleep?"

Even though Calum found the thought of being with the other woman pleasant, he knew Alexandria would stay with Demetrius, and he really didn't like that thought.

"No, you should stay here. You may have been with him before, but I don't trust him or the others. I don't think we should be separated."

Confused, Alexandria said, "I've never slept in their village before, but you don't have to worry. They won't hurt us."

She spread her blanket out on the pallets and sat down.

"Then where do you . . . ? Never mind, it's none of my business." Turning away, he shook out his blanket before sitting.

"What are you talking about?"

"It's none of my business," he said again. In truth he really didn't want to know. Maybe because she was around the Amatarians so much, her view on things was different. Maybe she also felt one didn't have to wait for marriage. He knew it was a double standard—he was no innocent, but he fully expected his wife to be—and he didn't care.

"What's none of your business?" she asked, exasperated. She had no idea what he was talking about.

Since she wasn't going to let it go he answered, "Where the two of you go to be together."

With a furrowed brow, she asked, "You mean where we hang out? Why is that such a big deal to ask? We hang out with his tribe, or with my family, or in the woods or at the lake."

Raking his hand through his hair, he blurted, "No, I mean where you have sex."

Her eyes widened. "We don't . . . we've never . . ."

"You told me he was your first lover," he reminded her.

"I never said that."

"You were about to, in the woods."

She suddenly remembered their conversation and when he'd cut her off. Laughing, she said, "That's *not* what I was going to say. I was going to say he was my first patient."

Calum stared at her in shock. "What?"

"When I was eight, I went to the lake to collect some herbs for my mother. That was my only job back then. I saw him playing in the water. A man came out of nowhere and attacked him, trying to kill him. So I threw a rock and hit the man to distract him, then Demetrius killed him."

"How could you do that? You put yourself in danger."

She shook her head. "I may not have known any Amatarians yet, but my mother had told me about them. There was no reason for that man to attack. He just didn't like the Amatarians. Demetrius was hurt, and I tried to take him home so my mother could heal him, but he wouldn't move, and he wouldn't speak English. I didn't know how to speak Amatarian yet. I thought he didn't understand me and motioned him to stay put while I went back for my herbs. Thankfully it wasn't a bad wound, but it had gotten dirty during the fight."

"And you healed him."

Nodding she said, "Yes. He took me back to his tribe, and I met Genesis's father, who was their leader at the time. He and Demetrius spoke, and then he spoke to me in English." She smiled. "He said Demetrius wanted to keep me. He told me only one other Tolgarian came on their land and asked me to whom I belonged. It turns out my mother was that one person. They took me home and Demetrius and I became friends."

"Why is your mother allowed?"

"I don't know how it started, but the women in my family have always been allowed—the healers, that is. My grandmother used to visit them often before she moved to Kilwinning."

"Are all the women in your family healers?" he asked.

"Most of them. It's been a long time since there wasn't a healer in the family."

"What happens if there's no daughter?"

She frowned, thinking about it. "I don't think that's happened. The story of the necklace is passed down to every generation, and all the sons go off to fight the queen and die. If there were no daughters to pass on the story, we wouldn't know it today."

The grandmother could have passed on the story, but that would only work for so long, he thought, but didn't say anything.

"How does your leg feel?" she asked suddenly.

Moving it, he said, "I don't feel a thing."

"Good. I'll ask if we can take some herbs with us. I should have brought some from home."

"Can't you find them in the woods?"

"Not the one in particular I need. It grows in the mountains. The Amatarians harvest it and give some to my mother. It helps speed up healing."

"What does your mother give them?"

She frowned. "I have no idea. I don't have any money." Pausing, she added, "I don't think they even use money here."

"I have money if you need it," he offered.

She smiled her thanks. Since she'd planned on staying away from villages and hadn't wanted to steal from her parents, she hadn't taken any coins with her.

"Alexandria, are you inside?"

"Come in," she called out.

Genesis pushed aside the curtain and walked in. He looked at both of them sitting on separate pallets before turning to Alexandria. Holding out a dress, he said, "I brought you something to sleep in."

Standing, she took it from him. "Thank you." She could see it was one of their revealing dresses and wondered how Calum would react to seeing her in it. *Will he look at me the same way he looked at Talora?*

Looking at her bloodstained shirt, Genesis said, "Leave your clothing outside and we'll see what we can do with it."

Nodding, she thanked him again, and he left. She raised her brow at Calum as she held the dress out.

Calum tried not to picture her in the dress. She didn't need anything to make her more enticing—he was already having a hard time keeping those thoughts in check. "I'm going to sleep," he told her. Climbing under the blanket, he faced the wall so he couldn't see her.

I guess that's my answer, she thought ruefully. Changing quickly, she put her shirt outside then blew out the candle and climbed under her blanket to sleep.

✠✠✠✠✠

Back in Calderdale, Niall and Finnean were on a mission to find their parents. There was no one at the cabin, so Niall went home to see if his mother was visiting his family but found only his wife and sister-in-law. After telling them he had news about Alexandria, they said they'd go to his parents' cabin and wait.

Finnean found his father in the fields and told him what was going on.

"Adella is healing," Alpin replied. "Go find her, and I'll meet you at home."

Leaving the fields Finnean crossed paths with his mother, on her way home. "Niall has news of Alexandria," he said.

Dropping her bag of supplies she picked up her green skirt and ran. She burst through her front door with Finnean right behind her. "What did you hear?"

"Sit down, Mum," Niall said, gesturing to the empty chair beside his father.

Sinking into the chair, her eyes filled with worry. "It's not bad news, is it?"

When the family was settled, Niall said, "There was a miner here from Sevenoaks selling coal to the general store. He was talking about a strange couple who'd passed through last week. A women wearing pants and carrying a bow."

Adella gasped and took her husband's hand. "It's her."

"I don't know." Niall hesitated. "I didn't get to question the miner. He was already gone by the time I got the news."

"Why don't you think it's your sister?" Agnes asked.

"Did you say a couple?" Finnean asked at the same time.

Niall nodded. "They were a couple claiming to be married."

"*What?*" Finnean roared.

"Calm down," Helen said. "I don't believe Alexandria would get married without her family there."

"Of course not," Adella agreed. "There has to be another explanation."

Finnean stood and slammed his fist on the table. "We're going to get her right now."

"She was there a week ago," Niall said. "She'll be gone by now."

"We're not even sure it's your sister," Helen added.

"Who else could it be?" Finnean asked forcefully. "No other woman wears pants."

"They might not really be married," Agnes suggested. She tugged on her husband's arm until he sat again.

"What do you mean?" Helen asked, rocking her daughter in her arms.

"She and the man could have just said they were married so no one would question them about why they were traveling together."

"If she's traveling with a man, then she damn well better be married," Finnean stated, his blue eyes flashing.

"Do you know where the miner went?" Alpin asked. "Can we catch up to him and question him?"

"The store owner might know," Niall answered.

"We should go back to Sevenoaks and ask around," Finnean said.

"That might be best," Helen agreed. "Ask around and see if anyone heard about her plans."

"And who she was traveling with," their father added. He was not happy to hear his daughter was traveling with some man but was calmer than his son and willing to wait until he had the whole story before reacting.

"And ask what she looked like to make sure it was Alexandria," Agnes said.

There was a knock at the door. Niall answered it to find an Amatarian and invited him in.

Upon seeing him Adella stood up. "Semja, is everything alright?"

"We just received word from Genesis," the Amatarian answered.

Placing one hand over her heart, Adella reached for her husband with her other hand. "Is it about Alexandria?"

Semja nodded. "She's with him."

"Oh, thank God." She exhaled and sank back into her seat.

"When will she be here?" Niall asked.

"She's not here," Semja explained. "She's at our village in Sedgemoor Forest." Turning back to Adella he added, "She plans on killing the queen."

Alpin nodded. "We know that's her plan. We were hoping to bring her home before the queen finds out."

"Would you like me to send a message back to Genesis?"

"Thank him for me," Adella answered.

Semja nodded and turned for the door.

"Wait," Alpin called. "Did he say anything about her traveling with someone?"

He shook his head. "I only know that Demetrius found her."

After he was gone, Niall asked, "What are we going to do?"

"Why didn't you tell him to have Genesis send her home?" Finnean asked at the same time.

"Do you think your sister would listen?" Alpin asked.

"Then what are we going to do?" Niall asked again.

"You're going to ride to Sedgemoor Forest and bring your sister home," his father answered.

✠✠✠✠✠

After breakfast, Alexandria and Calum left the meal area and headed off to meet with Genesis. Someone had managed to get the blood out of her shirt and had hemmed the torn bottom. It now stopped at her hip so she wore it tucked into her pants. Calum was fully dressed—he even wore his sword, despite Alexandria's protests. She felt it was an insult to the Amatarians, but he had refused to leave it in their hut.

"Genesis lives in a pretty luxurious hut compared to the others," Calum remarked as they walked.

"He doesn't live there," she explained. "It's the meeting hut. He lives in one like everyone else's."

Pushing the curtain aside, they entered the hut and found Genesis and the council sitting behind the table. Others were present as well, including Demetrius and his friend Thaddeus. Positioned behind Genesis was Cristian, the Amatarian in charge of training.

Standing before Genesis, Alexandria waited to be addressed.

"You mentioned yesterday you've been practicing your talents. Please show us," Genesis requested, waving his arm.

"My gift is fire, so it would be better if we went outside," she said.

"Then let's go." Genesis led them to the training field, where other Amatarians were practicing their skills with swords and bow and arrows.

"So what can you do?" one of the councilmen asked.

"She can make a man think he's on fire," Calum told them.

"Really?" the councilman asked. He'd never heard of this trick before. Even the Amatarians couldn't control the mind.

"It's my strongest gift with fire. My mum taught me a long time ago so I could protect myself."

Genesis knew of this gift but had never seen her use it.

"If someone is attacking you, why don't you just set him on fire?" Thaddeus asked. He'd also never heard of such a gift.

"Because I heal people. I don't hurt them."

"And yet you want to go after the queen? You really thought this through, didn't you," Demetrius said sarcastically.

She shot him a dirty look before answering, "That's different. You know I don't want to hurt anyone, but someone has to stop her, and I think that person has to have magick."

"You said it's your strongest gift with fire. What do you mean by that?" the councilman asked.

"When I was young, my father worried about me, so my mum taught me how to make people think they were on fire so I could run away. She made me practice until that power was strong and I could call upon it quickly. I've never had to use it before yesterday, when I used it to kill a man."

"You set him on fire?" Cristian asked.

"I made him think he was on fire while I summoned my bow and arrow. Then I shot him." Shrugging she added, "It's not much of a weapon though. I need to make it stronger, but I don't like the idea of making the fire real."

"You killed a man yesterday," Calum said, stepping forward. "I think that makes it a weapon."

"Yeah, I killed one while you killed four."

"I killed three while they were distracted by your fire."

Genesis cut in. "Can we see it?"

"I can only do it to someone," she said, looking at Calum.

Having been through it already, he wasn't eager to volunteer, but he knew she needed to show them what she could do.

Demetrius stepped forward and said, "You can do it to me."

"It's going to hurt," she warned him, not liking the idea of hurting her best friend. Not that she wanted to hurt Calum again, but at least he knew what to expect.

"It's fine. Just don't really set me on fire," he said jokingly.

Smiling slightly she stepped forward. Everyone else created a circle around them. Closing her eyes she focused. Everyone but Calum and Genesis started to whisper when her hair darkened and the wind picked up to blow it out behind her. When she opened her eyes, a few people gasped at the sight of the flames flickering in her brown irises.

Then the fire seemed to jump from her eyes and land on Demetrius, who, though expecting it, still let out a shout and tried to put out the flames. In seconds they were gone, and when everyone turned to Alexandria, she was back to normal.

"That was amazing," Thaddeus exclaimed. "If you could make that fire real, you would have a powerful weapon to use against the queen."

The Amatarians had no love for the queen and in fact prayed the Tolgarians would find a way to defeat her, but due to their truce, and the fact that they didn't get along with most Tolgarians, they had never helped anyone try to defeat her.

"Can you make real fire?" another councilman asked. The Amatarians couldn't do this, but he'd heard of some Tolgarians who could.

"Yes, she can," Calum answered.

"I can make a small fire," she said. "That's one of the gifts I've been working on. It still takes longer than I'd like to start it, but I'm faster than I was a week ago." Looking around, she said, "I need something to light."

One man left the circle and came back with a small log.

Thanking him she sat down beside the log and closed her eyes. She heard whispers again as her hair darkened. When she opened her eyes, everyone stared at the log, waiting for it to explode. There was smoke, and then a small flame burst onto the wood. Staring at the fire, she made it bigger until it covered the whole log.

Standing, she turned to Genesis. "Not very impressive, is it?"

Moving beside her, he placed a hand on her shoulder and said, "It's very impressive when your main talent is healing."

Calum also moved forward. "Once she's warmed up she can light them much faster."

"You mentioned this was only one of the talents you've been working on," Genesis said. "What else can you do?"

Taking a step back she looked at Calum, who'd also taken a few steps back to put some distance between them. Genesis moved back to stand with the others circling them.

Alexandria and Calum faced each other, and he clasped his hands behind his back. As she threw out her hand his sword flew out of its sheath and into her grasp. She swung it around a few times as he'd shown her before letting go and allowing her magick to hold it. It stayed in the air and swung a few more times before landing with its tip in the dirt in front of Calum.

Grasping the hilt, he pulled it from the ground and sheathed it. Then he left the circle to grab another log, and when he was back within the circle he held it above his head.

Seeing that one of the Amatarians was wearing a full quiver, she summoned three arrows. Once they were hovering in front of her, she sent them one at a time into the log, which Calum moved after each arrow strike.

Alexandria turned back to Genesis. "That's it."

Stepping forward again he remarked, "You don't look very impressed with yourself."

"I'm not. It takes all my focus to use my gifts, making me an easy target for someone else to take out."

"We'll work on it," he assured her. "Can you send two arrows at the same time?"

Nodding she answered, "Yes, but I can only aim one. The other just goes flying."

"It's an improvement," Calum said. "A few days ago she couldn't send two at the same time. Give her time and she'll be able to aim both."

"You have a lot of faith in her," Genesis said.

Calum shook his head. "It's not faith. I've watched her improve every day. Give her enough time and I think she could aim a fleet of arrows."

"And what do you do?" Genesis asked Calum.

"I'm a horse breeder."

Genesis looked at the sword at Calum's side. "Can you use that?"

"Would you like to see?"

Alexandria gave him a nudge and a disapproving look. She knew he didn't trust them, but that didn't mean he could be disrespectful.

Genesis turned to Cristian, who nodded, agreeing to fight him.

"I would be glad to fight him," Demetrius offered, relishing the idea of knocking Calum on his ass and giving him a taste of what would happen if he hurt Alexandria.

"The pleasure would be mine," Calum said. Demetrius might be her friend but he didn't like the way he stared at her and would love to knock him on his ass.

Genesis nodded his consent. He wanted to see how well Alexandria's new friend could handle himself—for her safety would be in his hands.

Alexandria laid a hand on Calum's arm. "You aren't really going to fight, are you?"

"When the Amatarians train, do they go all out?" Calum asked.

"Yes."

"Then so will I." Seeing her worried expression, he said, "Don't worry, I won't hurt him." *Too much*, he added to himself.

Alexandria went to Demetrius's side as he chose a sword from a rack of weapons. "You're going to be careful, right?"

Lifting a sword he asked, "Are you worried about me or him?"

"Both. But I *need* him. I can't do this on my own."

Seeing her anxious eyes he sighed. "Don't worry, it's not a real fight. We just want to see what he can do. Who knows, maybe we can teach him a few things." With his arm around her shoulder, he led her back to the circle thinking, *If this guy's going to take care of her, I'm going to make sure he knows how.*

Alexandria stood off to the side and watched as Demetrius and Calum squared off in the center of the circle. She bit her lip until Genesis moved beside her and put his hand on her shoulder.

"Don't worry so. We just want to observe his skills."

"I have a feeling Calum and Demetrius have other plans."

Noticing the way the two men were staring each other down he agreed, but only said, "It'll be fine. Should one, or both, get hurt, we have many excellent healers, including yourself, who can take care of them."

"If they get hurt I might just let them both suffer," she muttered, knowing she was telling a lie. She wouldn't be able to watch either of them in pain.

After a signal from Genesis, Calum pulled his sword and the battle began. At first they played with each other, moving slowly, testing. One would strike, the other would block, and then both would back off until one moved forward to strike again. Then as if by silent agreement, they were done playing. Both jumped forward to strike. They moved around each other, swinging, jumping, striking in what looked to be a choreographed dance.

Alexandria held her breath, her hands over her heart. They were equally matched, and the spectators cheered them on. Then Calum swung his sword downward, and even though Demetrius blocked it, the force sent him to the ground. Alexandria gasped, and her hand flew to her mouth. Before Calum could strike again, Demetrius rolled away and jumped to his feet.

Just when it looked as though one had gained the advantage, the other struck back. Alexandria didn't know how much longer she could watch this. Glancing away she noticed a few women watching with great appreciation, including Talora, and didn't know how much longer she could watch that either.

The fight went on for several minutes and neither of them showed signs of tiring. Finally Genesis raised his hand and stepped forward, calling a halt to the fight. "That was impressive," he said. "You're welcome to practice with us while you're here."

"I wouldn't mind having another go," Demetrius admitted with a grin. "I haven't had that much fun in ages."

Grinning back, Calum said, "Next time we should try hand to hand."

A few other men stepped forward, wanting a chance to face off against Calum. None had met a Tolgarian with that much skill before.

Alexandria shook her head in disgust as she walked away. *Men*, she thought. Before the fight they seemed to hate each other, and now they looked like the best of friends.

CHAPTER NINE

Genesis found Alexandria behind some huts, walking along the trees. He stopped and watched an array of emotions cross her face, and wondered if she was thinking about the queen or her family.

As she walked closer she noticed Genesis and stopped. "Have you sent word to my mother?"

"Last night. She knows you're here and safe."

She started walking again and Genesis fell in step beside her. "Did she send a message back?" she asked.

"No, but knowing your mother as I do, I would imagine your brothers are on their way to retrieve you."

Glancing at him she asked, "Is there any point in asking you to send a message to her telling her not to send my brothers?"

"I doubt she would listen. And I'm sure they've already left," he told her.

"I should leave. Make my way to Dorset before my brothers find me."

"Don't be hasty," Genesis warned her. "You're not ready to face the queen. It will take two weeks at a hard ride for your brothers to get here. You have time yet."

"Can you spare a few herbs when I do leave? I have no gold to pay you."

He waved his hand. "We have no use for gold."

"Then how does my mother pay you?" Alexandria asked.

"She doesn't. Our alliance goes back a very long time—to when our tribe and the Tolgarians were at war."

She listened attentively, having never heard the story before.

"Your ancestor was traveling through the Fife Mountains to Merton Meadows, the valley where all the best herbs grow. As you know, the journey to the valley is difficult and dangerous, for Tolgarians, and can take over a week, but we're able to travel there easily. Along the way she met one of our men, who'd been attacked by a mountain lion. Without hesitation she healed him. We didn't speak English then, but the two managed to communicate. He was impressed that she'd helped him without asking for anything in return. That was the first friendship between our two people," he said with a smile. "She taught us English and we taught her Amatarian. That friendship between our people has lasted ever since, and now we collect extra herbs from the valley for your family."

They stopped and sat on a large boulder.

"Did you know the necklace was given to my family then?" she asked, staring down at her hands.

"Yes. Your ancestor feared its evil but couldn't destroy it, so she brought it to us and we hid it."

"Why didn't you destroy it?" she asked.

"We couldn't. Several tried but nothing worked. Your family hoped it would never be found, but we always knew it would be. Evil never stays hidden for long. We prayed that a future generation would be strong enough to do what couldn't be done then." Taking a deep breath, he added, "And I believe that time has come."

She looked up at him. "You think I can do this?"

He took her hand and said, "I *know* you can do this, with a little help."

"What kind of help?"

Patting her hand, he stood. "We'll discuss that later. Right now, your man is coming."

Alexandria couldn't see him but didn't question Genesis. If he said Calum was coming, then he was. A moment later he came around one of the huts, glancing this way and that way until his eyes landed on her.

He lengthened his stride to reach her. "I've been looking all over for you."

She raised a brow in disbelief. "Really? I thought you and Dem were going to fight without swords."

"He was too tired, wanted something to eat first. I thought you'd want to join us but I couldn't find you," he said admonishingly. He still didn't know these people, and given their sexual attitudes, he didn't like not knowing where she was. Didn't she see how the men watched her?

"I didn't think you'd notice, the way you and Dem were carrying on."

"Are you hungry?" he asked, ignoring her comment.

"No," she said, just to be obstinate.

"I could use something," Genesis chimed in. Looking at Alexandria, he added, "You should eat. You'll need your strength for this afternoon."

"What's going to happen this afternoon?" she asked.

"We're going to practice your magick."

"Will you still send my mum the message?" she called after him as he walked away.

Genesis turned back. "I'll send it, but I'm sure they've already left."

"Thank you."

"What message?" Calum asked when they were alone.

"I don't want my parents sending my brothers after me," she explained. "But he thinks they've probably already left."

"How could he possibly get a message to her before your brothers leave?"

Alexandria smiled. "They have a different way of sending messages. When an Amatarian meditates, he can send a message to another Amatarian, no matter where he is."

"What if the other isn't meditating?"

"He doesn't have to be. Only the one sending the message has to meditate." She started walking, and he fell into step beside her. "I do hope my family gets the message before my brothers leave. I don't want them involved. They have families to take care of."

✠✠✠✠✠

Calum and Alexandria stood on the sidelines of the training field watching Demetrius and Thaddeus practice.

"Who's that?" Calum asked, gesturing towards Cristian, who was walking around the field. He looked like all the other Amatarian men, but there was an air of authority about him that drew attention.

"That's Cristian. He's in charge of training."

"So he's like the head warrior."

She shrugged. "I guess you could say that, but they're not warriors."

Calum didn't argue with her, but they all looked like warriors to him. What she didn't understand was that being a warrior wasn't a bad thing. Being a warrior didn't make you a killer—it just meant you were strong and skilled.

She turned back to watch her friends. "You're lucky Dem didn't use his gifts against you."

"He has power?"

"All Amatarians have magick of some kind. Some gifts are small and gentle, and some can be used as weapons."

"What's Demetrius's power?" he asked, watching them.

Thaddeus suddenly threw out his hands, and Demetrius went flying.

"Hey, he can move things like you." Calum looked at her. "Do you think you can throw a man like that?"

"I don't know, but that's not Thaddeus's gift," she said. "He can control the wind, creating big gusts to throw a person."

Still on the ground, Demetrius placed his hand flat on the dirt until the ground began to shake. Thaddeus looked around as though he was waiting for something. Suddenly a vine burst from the ground and wrapped around his leg. Another wrapped around his wrist, making him drop the sword he was holding. Three more burst from the ground, the first two capturing his other arm and leg, the last one circling his waist. They held him in the air while Demetrius laughed.

"That's cheating," Thaddeus called out.

"You used your talent first," Demetrius reminded him.

"As you can see, Demetrius can control vines," Alexandria drawled, waving her hand towards them.

"Can he do that anywhere?" Calum's mind was racing. The possibilities for their powers in battle were endless.

"No, only where there's earth. Sometimes he can call them through wood but never through stone."

Genesis approached them from behind. "Alexandria."

She and Calum turned around.

"Can you come with me, please?"

When they both stepped forward, Genesis held up his hand. "Just Alexandria."

Before Calum could argue, she placed a hand on his arm. "It's alright. Why don't you join Dem and Thad—just don't let them gang up on you. I don't want to come back and find you wrapped in vines and blowing in the wind." She hoped her insult would distract him.

He gave her a disgusted look before going to join the other men.

Turning back to Genesis, she caught his knowing smile. "What?"

"You know him well."

She laughed and walked towards him. "I have three brothers. I know *men* well."

They walked to the main hut, where two of the councilmen were waiting. On the table was a box.

Picking it up Genesis said, "I have what you need to strengthen your powers." He opened the box and held it in front of him.

Stepping forward she peered in. It was a necklace. Attached to the woven gold chain was a large oval stone the color of pale honey. A thin gold band wrapped around the stone and created a loop for the chain. Gasping, she took a step back and looked at him with horrified eyes.

"It's okay," he assured her. "It's nothing like her necklace."

Nodding, she stepped forward to peer at it again. "Where'd you get it?"

"We made it many years ago. It has no power of its own."

Alexandria glanced up, wondering why he was showing it to her. "I don't understand. How does this help me? I need something to make me more powerful."

"It's a calcite crystal—it enhances what you have. The queen's necklace gives her powers. This one will strengthen yours and help you focus so you can use them faster." He lifted it from the box and held it out.

Alexandria looked at the councilmen to gauge their reactions. She knew Genesis would have talked to them before making such a big decision, but were they happy or upset with his choosing to give it to a Tolgarian? They were both smiling, so she figured they must have agreed with him.

Genesis clasped it around her neck.

She stroked the stone and was surprised by its warmth. "I don't feel anything."

"You won't. It doesn't take over like the other necklace."

"So what do I do?"

"Let's go back to the field and try it out."

The councilmen followed them to the training field. As other Amatarians noticed the necklace, they fell in step behind them, whispering amongst themselves.

Calum saw them approach and wondered why so many people were following them. "What's going on?" he asked.

Demetrius and Thaddeus stopped fighting and turned to see what Calum was referring to, immediately noticing the necklace.

Demetrius grinned and slapped Calum's shoulder. "You've just been given the key to winning."

Calum watched Alexandria, puzzled. When she raised a hand to her neck, he noticed the necklace and frowned. Was it like the queen's necklace? Given the way Alexandria felt about it, he couldn't image her wearing something similar.

Everyone created a circle around her as Calum approached.

"What's going on?" he asked again, frowning at the necklace and Genesis.

"It's alright," Alexandria said. Turning to Genesis, she asked, "What do I do?"

"Use your magick like you always do."

Someone placed a log in the center of the circle. When she moved towards it, Genesis held her back.

"From here," he said.

She nodded. Closing her eyes, she focused, and as the wind blew her hair, the red in it came alive. Feeling the power within her, she opened her eyes and stared at the log, and within seconds fire exploded and covered it.

Gasping, she stepped back while the Amatarians cheered. She'd never created fire from so far away before. She looked at Calum, who seemed as shocked as she, while Demetrius and Thaddeus grinned.

Genesis looked very proud as he motioned for more wood.

Soon there were three more logs. It took a few seconds for the first to light, but the other two burst into flames as soon as she looked at them.

The Amatarians continued to cheer, and for the first time Alexandria felt certain she would win. She was going to destroy the necklace, kill the queen, and go home. Turning to Calum, she saw the same thoughts in his eyes. *They* were going to win.

✠✠✠✠✠

Alva and Rufus had told no one of their plan to flee, and only spoke about it in hushed tones late at night while their children slept. During the day, they went about their work as always. Ever since the queen threatened to take her daughter, Alva hadn't had a moment's peace, terrified that anything she did might cost her her daughter's life.

They had even devised a story to tell the guards at the gate. They weren't planning on leaving during the night like the last family that had tried to flee.

Minerva sat on her throne, her head soldier at her side. Her dark gray dress complemented her necklace and crown.

Alva rushed into the throne room and curtsied before the queen. "You called for me, Your Majesty."

Tapping her fingers on a skull, Minerva said, "I've heard something very distressing."

Alva glanced at Brodrick. His stony expression was frightening. She didn't know what was going on. Facing the queen, she asked, "How can I help?"

Minerva raised a brow. "You can help by telling me it's not true."

"What have you heard?"

"That you and your husband are leaving the castle."

How does she know? Alva thought. Terror consumed her. "No, Your Majesty."

"Then you and your husband aren't planning to leave?" the queen asked, watching her closely.

Alva thought quickly, for the queen had obviously heard something. "We received word through a letter the other day that Rufus's mother is ill. She doesn't think she's going to make it and asked us to come see her, but I told Rufus I couldn't go, that I needed to stay and serve you."

"So Rufus is going?"

"Yes, Your Majesty, if it's okay with you."

"Are your children going with him?"

Swallowing loudly, she answered, "Yes, Your Majesty."

"That's nice. I'm sure she wants to see her grandchildren again before she dies," the queen responded with false sweetness.

Alva nodded, not sure whether to continue elaborating on the lie and say his mother had specifically asked to see the children.

"Where does she live?"

"In Maidstone, Your Majesty." Which was true, and she was sure the queen could easily find out. The plan had been to pick up Rufus's mother in Maidstone and take her north with them.

"How long will they be gone?" Minerva asked.

"Maybe two weeks," she answered. "It will take five days just to get there," Alva reminded the queen. When Minerva's eyes narrowed she thought she might have overstepped again.

Minerva stood and walked down the steps from her throne until she was standing in front of Alva. "You're not lying to me, are you, Alva?"

"N-no, Your Majesty," she stuttered.

"Because I would be very upset if I found out you were lying to me."

"I have the letter, if you'd like to see it," Alva said. She did have a letter—she'd written it herself.

After staring at her for another moment, Minerva replied, "No, I believe you." Her skirt swirled around her as she turned back towards her throne. "I'm fine with your husband and children leaving, but you're staying here."

Curtsying again, she said, "Yes, Your Majesty."

"When are they leaving?"

"He would like to leave tomorrow."

"Fine. We'll look forward to seeing them back in two weeks." She waved her hand, dismissing her, and watched Alva hurry from the room. "Brodrick."

He moved from her side to kneel in front of her. "Yes, Your Majesty."

"Find out what you can about her story, and have someone watch her. If she tries to leave with her family, I want to know."

"Yes, Your Majesty."

A few hours later, he returned to give his report.

"What did you find out?" Minerva demanded.

"They received a letter yesterday from Maidstone. Rufus spoke with some other blacksmiths and told them he's taking the children to see his mother."

"And Alva?"

"No one mentioned if she was going."

"Do you have someone watching her?"

"I have someone watching her and her cabin. She can't leave without our knowing. What about her husband? Are you going to let him leave?"

"Yes. He'll come back for his wife. Whether he comes back with his children or not is the question, but I'll know where to find them." Smiling evilly she added, "They can't hide from me."

✠✠✠✠✠

In their hut for the night, Alexandria and Calum sat on their pallets while she explained how the necklace worked and answered what questions she could.

"I don't know if I like this," Calum said, "but you were stronger this afternoon."

"I've never been that powerful before. It was a little scary," she admitted.

"How did it feel? When you were using your magick?"

"It didn't feel evil, if that's what you're really wondering. I felt a warmth spreading through me. I felt as if I could do anything." Looking him in the eyes, she said, "I know we'll win. If I can get to the queen, I can kill her."

"You're worried about getting to her?"

"Her necklace knows when someone's coming. How will I get past her soldiers?"

"We need an army," he told her.

"Where can we find one? How can I ask people to fight?"

"There's an army outside. They train every day and are ready to fight."

"No," she disagreed. "They train so they can protect themselves, but they aren't ready to fight."

"What do you mean? I watched them today—they have more skill than anyone I've seen. They can defeat the queen's soldiers no problem."

"No. I told you, the Amatar tribe is peaceful. Amatarians only fight when they have to, when they're being attacked. I would never ask them to fight for me. They don't get involved in the Tolgarians' problems."

"I'm sure they'd fight if you asked them," Calum said. He didn't understand her hesitance. They were fighting to save their country, and she wasn't willing to use everything at their disposal.

"They can't, remember? They have a truce."

"What's up with this truce?" he asked. "If they're such good people, why do they have a truce with the most evil witch alive?"

"I told you, they don't concern themselves with us as long as we don't do anything to hurt them."

"Then why do they train?"

"They only have a truce with the queen, not everyone else. Over the years they've defended themselves so vehemently they've earned the reputation of fierce warriors. When people started to believe this, they stopped attacking. The Amatarians continue to train to maintain that image, and to be ready should someone try to attack."

"So what is the truce?"

"After the queen took over Dorset, she wanted to rule the whole country and tried to take over the Amatarians. She could never find their villages, but she would try to kidnap any Amatarian she and her men did find. As you've seen, they aren't easy to defeat, and in fact they always ended up killing her soldiers. She was tired of losing men, and I think afraid that they could kill her, so she made a truce with them. Her soldiers wouldn't attack them, and they wouldn't kill her soldiers."

"That's it? What about everyone else?"

"She doesn't care about anyone else. The Amatarians just have to stay out of Dorset and leave her soldiers alone, which was fine with them, since they don't really travel that far south."

"Why did they agree to the truce? If they were winning why didn't they just end it?"

Softly she answered, "Just because they were winning doesn't mean they didn't lose anyone. They chose to do what was best for them. Besides, they can't destroy the necklace."

"How do you know? You said their magick is stronger than yours."

"It is, but when I was talking to Genesis he told me that when the necklace was first brought to them, many tried to destroy it but couldn't. That's why they hid it."

"But he thinks you can destroy it?"

"Yes, and with the help of this necklace, I know I can," she said, raising her hand to the necklace, which was still around her neck. She took it off and placed it on the table.

"So her necklace couldn't find the Amatarians?"

"I guess not," she said with a shrug as she sat back down on her pallet. "During their war, she sent soldiers and even went out herself and never found them. Their magick is very different from ours—maybe that's why she couldn't sense it."

"I'm just wondering because when we got here, you said you couldn't see their village but you could feel it. So why can't she feel it?"

"Oh, I see what you're thinking. Their magick repels evil—I think that's why she couldn't find it. Because I'm good, and a friend, I can sense it. I've been around them so long I feel the difference in the air when I'm close to their tribe."

"So if she can't find it, then she probably doesn't know what goes on here."

"I guess not," Alexandria said.

"Then, if we can't ask the Amatarians to fight with us—"

"We can't."

"Then maybe we can gather others and hide them here until we're ready to make our move." *And if men are willing to fight with us, maybe the Amatarians will help us train them*, he thought.

Biting her lip, she hesitated. "I don't know. They might consider it breaking their truce."

"Who would know?" Calum asked. He thought it was a great idea—the Amatarians wouldn't be fighting but they'd be helping the Tolgarians have a better chance of winning.

"They'd know," she answered. "The thing about being good is they don't break their word."

"This isn't breaking their word—they wouldn't be fighting."

"I don't know," she said with a sigh, looking at the necklace. "They've already done so much."

Watching her closely, he asked, "What's really stopping you?"

She sighed again. "I never planned on putting anyone but myself at risk. If anyone else helps us, how many will die before I reach her?"

Calum moved across the hut to sit beside her. Taking her hand, he said, "It's a risk I'm willing to take, and it's a risk I know many others will be willing to take to stop her. Even knowing everyone who has gone before them has died, men still gather and march on the castle because they hope one will get through and kill her."

"And you think men will come forward when they hear a woman is going after the queen?"

"Yes, and I'll prove it. There's a large field between the forest and Yarmouth. We'll set up camp there and send word that we're going after the queen. Men from all over the country will come to fight with us."

Resting her head on his shoulder, she said, "I don't want to be the cause of anyone's death, except for the queen's."

"You'll be the cause of their hope. You'll see."

CHAPTER TEN

Two days later, it was time to leave. Alexandria was dressed in her brown pants, her shortened white blouse, and her brown vest. Her belt held her knife on one side and a sword Genesis had given her on the other. Her satchel ran across her body and her bow and quiver were on her back.

When Alexandria stepped out of her hut, she was surprised to see Demetrius with his sword strapped to his waist and his bow and quiver full of arrows on his back.

"What are you doing?" she asked.

"I'm coming with you," he stated, ready for her argument.

"You can't," she countered. "The truce."

"Screw the truce. When we were young, I swore I'd never let anyone hurt you, and that includes the queen and her men."

"But what about your people?" Alexandria asked, desperate to get him to change his mind. "She could see this as a betrayal, a breaking of the truce. If we lose, she'll come after your tribe."

"She won't find us," he shrugged, not concerned. Before she could speak again, he added, "I've talked to Genesis and he agrees with me. We aren't breaking the truce. The Amatarians aren't fighting, but that doesn't stop one from seeing that his friend gets safely to the castle."

"Please Dem," she begged. "Reconsider. Stay here."

"Do you not want me with you?" Demetrius asked, wondering why she was arguing so much. "Would you rather go with Calum?"

Throwing her arms around him, she said, "I want you with me, but I wouldn't be able to bear it if you died."

Hugging her back, he said, "I have no plans of dying, only of helping you win."

She pulled back to look at him. "I can't talk you out of coming?"

"No." Looking over her shoulder, he saw Calum standing in the doorway. "Do you have a problem with me coming?"

"No problem at all. I'd actually prefer if more came with us," Calum answered, stepping forward. He adjusted the sword at his side. He'd decided to leave his coat and satchel behind so he'd have less to carry. He'd tried to convince Alexandria to leave her satchel behind as well, but she'd refused, saying she might need her supplies.

"Calum." She gave him a warning look, her tone indicating her displeasure.

"What?"

"Where's the necklace?" Demetrius asked, trying to change the subject.

"In my satchel," she said, placing her hand on it. "If she knows we're coming, I don't want her to know about the necklace until it's too late."

Having succeeded in distracting her, the men walked with Alexandria to the boundary of the village, where a few Amatarians were waiting to see them off. Genesis was there with his beautiful white stallion.

"Are you coming with us?" Alexandria asked.

Genesis shook his head. "No, I want you to take Stardust. You'll need a strong horse to lead your men."

With a slight smile she remarked, "If any men come."

"They'll come," Calum assured her.

Genesis nodded. "Listen to your friend. Men will come to fight with you." Motioning to Thaddeus, he said to Calum, "I hope you can ride bareback, horse breeder. We don't use saddles."

"I can ride bareback," he said, insulted.

Thaddeus stepped forward leading three brown horses. He also had a bow at his back and a sword at his side.

"Are you going somewhere?" Demetrius asked.

"You don't think you're going on this adventure without me, do you?" Thaddeus asked in return.

"We're going to war," Alexandria said. "Not on an adventure."

"War is the greatest adventure there is," Thaddeus told her.

She looked to Genesis for help, but he only shook his head.

"It's up to them. They must follow their own paths."

"When my brothers get here, will you send them home?"

"I'll pass on your message," he promised. "Where they go will be up to them."

Calum lifted Alexandria onto her horse before mounting his. Looking around, she saw Thaddeus embracing the woman he was interested in and realized she'd never gotten her name. Demetrius shook Genesis's hand before mounting his horse. Grinning, he winked at someone in the crowd. With one last farewell they rode out of the protected village and disappeared into the trees.

✠✠✠✠✠

They rode for six days before exiting the forest. A few hours afterward, they stopped.

"We should make camp here," Calum said.

"Where are we?" Alexandria asked, looking around. The land obviously wasn't traveled often, as the grass and wildflowers were untouched. The space around them was flat, but up ahead was a large hill, which explained why the land wasn't being used for farming.

"Yarmouth is a day's ride south, over that hill, Maidstone is two days west, and Guildford is two days east," Calum answered.

"If we're so far from another village, how will we spread the word that we're going after the queen?" Alexandria asked.

"Don't worry about that," Demetrius said, moving his horse beside hers. "Genesis will see to it."

After dismounting, Calum took Alexandria by the waist and lifted her off her horse.

"Why are we stopping here instead of closer to a village?" she asked him.

"It's easier to hunt in the forest," Calum answered. "And this field gives us plenty of room to train the men who'll come."

"If any come," she remarked again. She still wasn't as confident as her friends that men would come when they heard a woman was going after the queen.

He glanced at her. "What happened to your positive-thinking theory?"

Straightening, she said, "You're right. If I want something to happen, I have to believe it will. Men are going to come, and they're going to help me invade the castle, and I'm going to kill the queen."

Clapping her on the shoulder, he said, "That's the spirit."

That night they worked on her hand-to-hand combat skills, with Demetrius and Thaddeus calling out suggestions and teaching her a few moves. Alexandria didn't stop until she became too tired to continue. Stretching out by the fire, she fell asleep instantly. Calum kept an eye on her while Demetrius kept an eye on him. Having no interest in the triangle, Thaddeus lay down and went to sleep.

✠✠✠✠✠

Calum and Demetrius were hunting after filling their water canteens in one of the streams in Sedgemoor Forest.

"Have you slept with Alex?"

Surprised by the question, Calum stopped tracking and asked, "How is that your business?"

"Since her family isn't here, I'm making it my business."

"Have you slept with her?" Calum asked.

"For you to ask I know you haven't," Demetrius said with a grin before going back to his tracking.

"What a minute, you didn't answer my question."

He looked back. "You should know her well enough to know the answer yourself."

Falling in step beside him, Calum said, "She told me you haven't been together."

"Then why do you doubt her?"

"Because I've seen the way you look at her, and I know your reputation."

"My reputation?"

"Your tribe's reputation," he explained. "I can't see you denying yourself what you want."

Demetrius thought about it before answering honestly. "I do want her, but we aren't allowed to take Tolgarians as mates."

"What are you talking about? I hear about Amatarians with our women all the time."

Laughing he answered, "That's different. Our mating is what you call marriage. You know it wouldn't be appropriate for me to marry Alex, and I would never dishonor her by sleeping with her." Glancing at Calum, he asked, "What about you?"

"What about me?" Spotting some tracks, he veered to the left to follow them.

"You can marry her."

Stopping short, Calum exclaimed, "Where did that come from? I'm just helping her go after the queen."

"I can see you want her, and I don't see you denying yourself what you want."

They locked eyes for a few seconds without talking, understanding each other, before returning to their hunting.

✠✠✠✠

Minerva stood alone in front of a window in her private chamber. Her burgundy dress matched her dark lips, and a black ribbon was laced down the sleeves and back. Her long black hair was tied in an intricate braid that stopped at her shoulders. The arched windows that circled the round room let in the bright sun, though it did little to lighten the dark gray stone walls. In the center of the room was a large stone basin on a stone pedestal. Etched around the bowl were carvings of people cowering under cascading spiders.

Looking out of her window, Minerva watched people hurrying around her courtyard, going about their chores. There were also children running and playing. Some days their noise drove her mad, other days it made her sad. Today was one of those days, where all she could think about was what she'd missed out on with Henry. She didn't think about him often anymore, but sometimes his memory snuck up on her, and that had been happening a lot since she met a descendant of his family.

One of the mothers looked up and saw the queen in the window. Immediately she rounded up the children. Though the queen didn't take children from the castle, her subjects could never be sure how she would react. Sometimes she let them play, but most of the time she ordered them out of sight, somewhere she wouldn't have to see or hear them.

There are people coming to kill you, her necklace whispered, pulling her away from her thoughts.

Not in the mood to deal with it, she shrugged. "So? There are always people coming. My soldiers will take care of them."

This time it's different. A woman is coming, and she has powers.

Minerva paused. "What kind of powers?"

She's a healer, but this doesn't limit her. Word has gone out. Men are being called to join her.

Narrowing her dark blue eyes as anger filled her, she said, "She would dare to call for an army?"

You need to get rid of her before men join her.

She walked over to the stone pedestal and stared into the water. "Show me where she is."

The water shimmered then displayed a scene: Alexandria practicing with a sword.

"This is my opponent? She's a child," Minerva said with a laugh. "She'll never get past my soldiers. Why should I worry about her?"

She's stronger than you think, he whispered. *I can feel her power from here. She could be a danger to you. You need to kill her.*

Over the years, Minerva had learned to trust her necklace. He had never let her down. "What's her plan?"

I don't know.

"How do you not know?" she asked, frustrated. He always knew.

She hasn't voiced her plan. You know I can't read minds, and she must know I can hear her. I'm only hearing that men are traveling to join her.

"You can read mine," she reminded him.

That's different, we're connected. I've explained this before. I was able to call out to you because I didn't have a wearer. Now that we're connected I can't hear anyone else's thoughts.

Minerva was irritated by this limit to his powers but knew it didn't matter. Eventually he'd find out the girl's plan. "I'll send my soldiers to take care of her."

No, there's not enough time. You need to go.

Staring into the water, she didn't see anyone around Alexandria. "Who's she traveling with?"

I've only seen one man. You should take a few soldiers with you, in case there are more.

Nodding, she said, "I'll have Brodrick choose a few men." Turning away from the pedestal, she screamed, "Alva!"

Alva hurried into the room and curtsied before the queen, her tan skirt pooling around her. "What can I do for you, Your Majesty?"

"Find Brodrick and send him to me," Minerva demanded.

"Yes, Your Majesty." Alva curtsied again before hurrying from the room.

She searched the castle grounds and found him in the courtyard with several other soldiers. After delivering the message, she rushed back inside to stand outside the doors of the queen's chamber. Ever since Rufus left with the children, the queen had been keeping her busy—Alva assumed she was doing so to make sure she couldn't sneak off to meet her family.

Brodrick walked past her into the room and knelt before his queen, bowing his head. "You called for me."

"I want you to choose two or three men to travel with me."

"You're leaving the castle?" he asked. It was rare for the queen to leave the castle grounds.

"Yes." With a swirl of her skirt, she returned to the pedestal to watch Alexandria.

"You should have more than three men," he said. "There are bands of men out there who will attack if they see you."

"I know. There's a woman out there now who wants to attack me, and I want to meet her."

Brodrick looked up, surprised. She'd never gotten involved when she knew an attack was coming. She simply told him about the threat, and he would take care of it for her. Standing, he said, "If you know there's one coming, let me and my men take care of her for you."

"This one's different. I need to kill her myself."

Brodrick knew better than to argue with her. "Will I be going with you?"

"Yes." She'd never planned on leaving him behind. Like the necklace, he'd always protected her.

"When do you want to leave?"

"Now."

"I'll have your horse readied," he said with a bow.

"No. Go to the throne room when you're ready."

Bowing again, he left the room to gather a few of his most trusted men. They arrived in the throne room in their silver armor with the queen's spider emblem on the breastplate. Alva peeked around the corner, wondering what was going on.

On her throne, Minerva looked down, pleased at the sight of the three men Brodrick had chosen, confident they could handle any men traveling with the witch. She descended and joined them. "We're going to travel my way," she told them, raising her hands.

Black smoke started to swirl around them, and Brodrick's men shifted uneasily. Brodrick didn't move. He knew of this power, although he'd never experienced it before. Within seconds they couldn't see anything but smoke. Before the men could panic, the smoke started to fade, and they saw they were in a field.

Minerva immediately began walking, and they all followed, drawing their swords while glancing around, watching for signs of an attack. It wasn't long before they came upon a camp.

✠✠✠✠✠

Alexandria was practicing her sword maneuvers, remembering to constantly move, as if she were being attacked from all sides. As she turned she saw a woman approaching with four men in armor behind her. Her confusion only lasted a moment. Noticing the spider necklace, Alexandria froze, wishing for a moment that she weren't alone and then realizing it was better this way. The queen wouldn't know she had people helping her.

So the queen has come to check out her opponent. She must be feeling threatened, Alexandria thought when the shock wore off. She took in the queen's regal appearance as she and her soldiers drew nearer. Her eyes were as hard as the stone in her pendant, and her red lips were curved slightly in a menacing smirk.

She tightened her grasp on her sword, waiting for the men to charge when Minerva suddenly stopped a few yards away and her soldiers followed suit. Alexandria glanced at the four men with their swords drawn. She hadn't planned for this and didn't know what to do, but knew she needed to get rid of them first or they would kill her while she battled the queen. After a signal from one soldier, the other three fanned out, making it difficult for Alexandria to determine where they were while keeping her eyes on the queen.

"So you think you can kill me?" the queen asked mockingly.

Raising her chin, Alexandria answered, "I know I can."

With a scornful smile, Minerva spread her arms. "Then please, show me your awesome powers."

Hearing a noise behind her, Alexandria turned in time to block the sword coming towards her. The strength behind the blow vibrated through her body and sent her back a few feet. Glancing around, she saw one soldier beside the queen and the other two slowly approaching. *They probably think their friend won't need help killing me*, she thought.

The soldier swung again, and again she blocked before stumbling back, causing the two approaching soldiers to chuckle. She looked at the queen again, who wore an evil smile. The soldier beside her was like a statue with no expression.

"Is this how you planned to kill me?" Minerva laughed. "I've yet to see your powers." *This girl is weak*, she thought. *Why am I wasting my time?*

She has powers, the necklace whispered. *You need to be careful.*

Then why isn't she showing them?

I don't know, she must have a plan to trick you, to lead you into a false sense of winning.

I am winning.

Alexandria continued to defend herself, knowing the soldier was toying with her. She knew he could easily knock the sword from her hand if she fought back—instead, she wanted to find his weakness.

Thaddeus suddenly appeared and screamed when he saw Alexandria fighting. The sound distracted her opponent. Not sure she had the strength to pierce the soldier's armor, Alexandria swung her sword and sliced his neck. As he fell, she turned to the others.

Thaddeus was running towards her with his sword drawn when he suddenly stopped. His sword dropped to the ground as he gasped for air. Alexandria saw a faint wisp of black smoke around his neck and looked at the queen, who had a slight smile on her face as she watched Thaddeus.

"Stop!" she cried. "Leave him alone."

The queen turned to her as two of her soldiers approached Thaddeus. The other never left her side. "You would dare ask *them* to join you in your plot to kill me?"

"No. He only took me through the forest. He has nothing to do with this!" Alexandria exclaimed as she watched one soldier stop in front and the other move behind her friend. She glanced towards her satchel.

Minerva noticed her action. "There's something in your satchel that you want." Wondering what she had that she thought could possibly help her, Minerva said, "Go ahead and get it."

The flap of her satchel flipped open as she called her knife to her.

Laughing, Minerva asked, "Is that your big power? That's what's supposed to worry me?" Looking at her men, she called, "Kill him!"

"No!" Alexandria screamed as she began running towards Thaddeus.

Minerva threw out a hand, stopping Alexandria in her tracks as both soldiers raised their swords. Desperate to stop them Alexandria threw her knife, using her powers to keep it flying across the distance. But it was too late. As one, the soldiers embedded their swords in Thaddeus, and his body arched in agony before they pulled their weapons free. Alexandria's knife pierced the neck of the soldier in front, killing him as her friend fell.

With a cry of pain Alexandria fell to her knees as tears ran down her cheeks.

The queen turned back to Alexandria, and in a soft, almost pitying voice said, "Now I'm going to kill you."

Hatred filled Alexandria as she faced the queen. "Not before I kill you," she said clearly. Summoning her knife from the dead soldier, she sent it flying towards the queen.

Brodrick knocked it away with his sword at the same time as Alexandria summoned hers. Before she could throw it, an arrow shot through the air and embedded itself in the queen's shoulder. The soldier moved in front to guard her, waiting for the next attack. Alexandria gathered all her powers and sent her sword soaring, but black smoke suddenly surrounded the queen and her soldier, and they were gone. The sword flew through the fading smoke before crashing to the ground.

The last soldier saw Calum and Demetrius riding towards them and ran. Calum caught up to him and jumped from his horse, knocking the soldier to the ground. They both quickly got to their feet and started fighting. Calum managed to knock the soldier's shield out of his hand, and it landed several feet away from them. He then blocked a blow before striking back and sending the soldier to the ground. As his opponent started to rise, Calum thrust his sword through the soldier's breastplate. Calum then kicked the soldier back as he pulled his sword free. Racing back to the others, he found Demetrius and Alexandria kneeling beside Thaddeus.

Calum fell to his knees beside Alexandria and placed a hand on her shoulder in comfort. Weeping, she turned and pressed her face against his chest while he and Demetrius shared a look of grief.

✠✠✠✠✠

Minerva and Brodrick appeared in the throne room, startling some maids who were cleaning.

"Find Alva," Brodrick commanded as he helped his queen to her throne.

The maids scurried from the room and one quickly found Alva in the kitchen.

Alva made her way through the castle, grateful she hadn't decided to flee when the queen left. Rufus had told her how to get past the guards before he left, but she was afraid. She knew the queen would be able to find her, and she would then take her children. She prayed that since she had stayed behind, the queen would leave her children alone, even when she realized they weren't coming back.

Alva entered the hall just as the queen yelled, "Do it!" and saw Brodrick pull something from her shoulder. She sighed with disappointment, wishing the arrow had killed her, before rushing forward to offer her assistance.

The queen pushed Brodrick aside and gripped the arms of her throne, her fingers tight over the skulls as she gasped for air. Black smoke circled her shoulder, and when it was gone, so was the wound and hole in her dress. Breathing deeply, she said, "Leave me."

Alva curtsied but didn't move fast enough for the queen.

"Leave me!" she screamed.

Alva ran from the room with Brodrick striding out behind her.

Pacing in front of her throne, the queen said, "What are we going to do? She's gotten the Amatarians to join her. Can you see how many are with her?"

No, you know I can't see or hear them. I only see one man with her.

"Well there's obviously more than one. We need to get rid of her so there's no one for the Amatarians to follow."

You've dealt her a mighty blow. I can feel her pain from here. She's wishing she'd gone alone.

"Really? That's why the good are so weak. You don't see me crying for the men I lost."

She'll try to convince the others with her to leave.

"Will they?"

The one I see cares too much. He won't leave her. But don't worry, we can take care of him, and now she's not willing to let others join her.

✠✠✠✠✠

Alexandria stared into the fire as Calum sat down beside her.

"I was so stupid," she muttered. "I should have been wearing the necklace."

"You're not stupid. How were we supposed to know she would show up here?"

"I should have known. She always knows when there's a plot against her, but I didn't want her to know about the necklace, so I kept it in my satchel. But do I get it during the fight? No, I get my knife, and now Thad is dead."

"Hey," Calum said sharply, causing her to look up at him in surprise. "It's not your fault."

"It is," she insisted. "I let all this happen when I allowed you and Demetrius and Thaddeus to join me. The reason I was going it alone was so no one else got hurt." Waving her hand towards

Demetrius, who was praying over Thaddeus, she added, "Now look what's happened. Thad is dead. Who's to say it won't be you or Dem next."

"Like I said, it's the risk we're all willing to take. It's the risk many more will be willing to take to destroy the queen. You can't give up."

With tears in her eyes, Alexandria unfolded her legs and lay down, resting her head on Calum's lap. Watching Demetrius, she whispered, "I don't know if I can handle losing anyone else."

After a period of silence Calum said, "We need to move the soldiers from our camp. Will you light the fire?"

"Let them rot," she answered angrily. "They don't deserve the cleansing power of fire."

Calum didn't say anything and decided he could handle it by himself later, when she was sleeping. He knew she wasn't thinking clearly but was sure she knew what would happen in a few days if they left the bodies.

After a few minutes Demetrius stood and walked over to them. With grief still bright in his eyes, he said, "It's time."

Alexandria took his outstretched hand and stood, holding her other hand out for Calum. The three of them walked back to Thaddeus.

"Do you want to take him back to your tribe?" Calum asked.

Demetrius shook his head. "I've spoken to Genesis. We can have his burial here."

Releasing Alexandria's hand, Calum placed his on Demetrius's shoulder. "I'll help you bury him."

"They don't bury their dead," Alexandria said softly. Facing Demetrius, she said, "I'm going to pick some flowers."

Calum helped Demetrius carry their fallen friend away from camp. They positioned his sword between his hands on his chest. Alexandria placed her flowers on his hands and pressed a kiss to his forehead before moving to stand between the other two.

"Will you do the honors?" Demetrius asked Alexandria.

Nodding, she closed her eyes. When her hair started to darken and the wind picked up, Calum knew what she was going to do. The flowers were the first to catch fire, and she helped it spread until the body was completely engulfed.

Demetrius stepped forward and said one final prayer in Amatarian.

Alexandria stared at Thaddeus, offering a silent apology as her tears flowed.

Calum watched Alexandria, worried by how much she was letting Thaddeus's death affect her. He'd warned her that this was the cost of war. He'd liked Thaddeus and was saddened as well, but to win, they needed to put this behind them.

When Demetrius was done, she said, "I want you both to go home."

The Amatarian's eyes hardened. "Now more than ever I'm with you. We won't stop until she's dead."

"You can't do this alone, Alex. We're going with you," Calum stated as he moved to stand beside Demetrius.

Alexandria walked to her satchel, pulled out the necklace, and put it on before turning back to her friends. "Then let's get ready for war."

CHAPTER ELEVEN

Genesis called for a gathering of his people. The meeting hut was too small to hold them all, so he met them on the training field, where his people were talking amongst themselves, wondering what was going on. He raised a hand to quiet the whispers.

"The queen has broken our truce."

There was silence as shock moved through the crowd. The truce had been in effect for more than eighty years.

"She has murdered Thaddeus."

Women gasped as men roared with anger. One woman's eyes filled with tears as pain rolled through her, and she fell to her knees.

Genesis noticed the young woman and knew of her relationship with Thaddeus. He watched as another helped her back to her feet. Focusing again on the rest of his people, Genesis said, "I will be joining Alexandria. Any who wish to join me will be welcomed. I leave at first light."

He returned to his hut with his council. After much discussion it was decided that a few councilmen would stay to protect the women and children. Even though their magick kept the village hidden, and all the men wanted to go, most were in agreement that a few should stay behind in case anything happened.

As the sun was rising the next morning Genesis was pleased, but not surprised, to see thirty men ready to ride at the boundary.

They were armed with swords and bows and were standing beside their horses.

Stopping beside Cristian, he asked, "How did you decide who would stay?"

Grinning, Cristian answered, "Seniority. I'm making some of the younger and less experienced men stay, giving them the important task of protecting our women and children. Some of our elders are staying behind as well so they can continue training the younger ones."

"Are you ready to ride?" Genesis asked.

"We are."

"It's a six-day journey, but I want to get there as fast as we can."

"We can ride through the night," Cristian replied.

Nodding, Genesis took the reins of a horse from an Amatarian named Nestor and rode out of the village with his men falling in behind him. They traveled at a fast pace, only stopping to eat and rest. The sun had set on their fifth day when they came upon Alexandria's camp.

Relief flowed through her, and she welcomed Genesis with a hug.

"Look Genesis," she said, pointing to six tents pitched in the distance. "Men are coming."

Cupping her cheek, he said, "I told you they would."

She glanced at the men. "You look tired."

"We haven't slept much. We wanted to get here before the queen tried anything else."

Stepping back, she said, "You should get some sleep. We can talk in the morning."

He nodded towards her necklace. "I'm glad to see you wearing it."

As she rested her hand on the pendant, sadness filled her eyes. "I should have been the whole time."

Touching her cheek again, he waited until her eyes met his before saying, "What happened was not your fault. The queen killed him, and we'll see to it that she pays."

Alexandria nodded but inside she was still full of guilt.

Genesis patted her cheek before going back to his men.

Calum came up behind her. "Demetrius says now that the truce is broken, they've come to join us."

"Yes."

Glancing at her he added, "We can use them. We have a better chance with them here."

"Yes." Smiling softly, she touched his arm. "I'm okay. I don't like my friends being in danger, but nothing I say could stop them now." She returned to her fire and sat down, watching Demetrius greet some of his friends. By their grave expressions, she assumed they were talking about Thaddeus.

"Do you want me to find you a tent?" Calum asked, sitting beside her.

She shook her head. "I'm fine. I'm safe with them."

"I was thinking more for privacy."

Giving him a sidelong look, she remarked, "They'd wonder what I needed privacy for."

He understood her meaning but figured the Amatarians already believed that they were sleeping together—after all, they had stayed together in their village.

Alexandria yawned.

"You should get some rest."

Nodding, she lay down and let the noises of the camp lull her to sleep.

✠✠✠✠

The next day after breakfast, Alexandria noticed about twenty Tolgarians watching the Amatarians train, and they all looked wary. Knowing the two parties needed to work together if they were going to succeed, Alexandria shared her concern with Genesis. He agreed, and they came up with a plan.

First they asked Demetrius and Calum to fight, and as expected, all the men came over to watch, creating a circle around them with the Tolgarians on one side and the Amatarians on the other. The Tolgarians only cheered for Calum, while the Amatarians were split, some cheering for Demetrius and some cheering for Calum.

After several minutes of hand-to-hand combat they called it a draw, and the Amatarians surrounded them. The Tolgarians headed back to their tents. A few looked as though they wanted to talk to Calum, but none approached. Alexandria and Genesis knew they were going to have to devise another method to bring everyone together.

As she watched Calum talk to the Amatarians, Alexandria smiled, wondering if he even noticed he was now friends with people he hadn't trusted a couple of weeks ago.

As the group dispersed, Calum joined Alexandria.

"Well, this is different," he stated.

"What?"

"Last time we fought you weren't happy with us, and this time you're smiling."

Shaking her head, she replied, "I was thinking of something else."

Calum looked back at the field and noticed the Amatarians had separated into smaller groups. "What's going on? I've never seen them separate like this before."

"They're probably discussing battle strategies."

"I would have thought they'd do that together." From what he'd seen they seemed to discuss everything else together.

"The three men with Dem, they all have the same gift," she explained.

He looked at them with more interest. "They can all control vines?"

"Yes, and that group over there"—she pointed to five men standing together—"they can control water."

"What about them?" he asked, pointing to the four men Genesis and Cristian were approaching.

Taking a deep breath, she answered, "They can control the wind."

Remembering that wind control had been Thaddeus's power, Calum understood the sudden grief in her tone. "What's Genesis's power?"

"He and Cristian can both control the wind as well." Turning, she looked at the last group. "And those five men can control fire."

"Like you?" *That could really help during battle*, he thought.

"Not like me. They can't do mind tricks like I do and they can't make fire, but they can do some amazing things."

"Like what?" What was so amazing if they couldn't even make fire?

"Once a fire's been made they can hold it in the palm of their hand, shape it into a flaming ball, and send it flying into a target."

His brows shot up. *Now that would be a good weapon*, he thought. "I'd like to see that." Noticing several men walking around on their own he asked, "What about the others?"

"They have different gifts, not ones that can be used during a fight."

Demetrius joined them. "We need to see what the Tolgarians can do so we know what we're working with."

Nodding, Calum agreed. "Let's go talk to them."

Calum, Alexandria, and Demetrius walked across the training field to the tents where all the Tolgarians were residing. Seeing the three of them approach, the Tolgarians gathered around and looked to Calum.

"We need to see you fight so we can see where you're weak," Demetrius stated in a loud voice so they'd all hear him.

One man stepped forward and asked insolently, "Why do you need to see? We're not following you."

Before Demetrius could answer, Alexandria placed a hand on his arm and stepped forward. In a soft voice, she asked the man, "Why are you here?"

Another man stepped forward. "We heard there was a witch with the power to kill the queen."

"And you came to follow her?"

Several men nodded.

Looking at the first man who'd spoken, she said, "Well that's me, and if you're following me, then you're following them, because they're with me." Letting her eyes roam the crowd, she said, "I didn't ask any of you to come, and you can leave whenever you wish, but to defeat the queen, I need help getting past her soldiers. If you're going to help us, then you need to show us what you can do so we can teach you the things you can't do."

"Who will teach us?" the first man asked, eyeing Demetrius.

"We will," Demetrius answered.

Alexandria cut in before the Tolgarians could protest. "You couldn't ask for better teachers. I'm sure you all know of their skills."

"Any who brought swords can join us in the center," Calum called out. "We'll pair you off and see what you can do." His tone was stern—he'd leave the niceties to Alexandria. His job was seeing that they learned, so they could be of use during the battle, and he knew they didn't have much time.

Twelve men had brought swords, but it was soon apparent that only five were proficient with them. Each man who hadn't brought a sword was given one and paired with an Amatarian, who taught him how to use it. Next they worked on hand-to-hand combat, and the Amatarians were pleased to find that many of the Tolgarians were skilled in this area, though still not as skilled as they were.

More men arrived throughout the day and immediately joined the training. There were now thirty Tolgarians and thirty Amatarians.

Alexandria was thrilled to see everyone working together. While she could see that a few Tolgarians were still suspicious, most had accepted the Amatarians and were talking and laughing while they trained.

Moving to stand beside Cristian, she said, "I didn't think they'd get along so fast."

"We're not the enemies we used to be," he replied. "Some of these men have even dealt with us before, but this is the first time our people will fight together."

"I have to admit I'm surprised your people are so willing to train the other men."

Cristian grinned. "We're not showing them everything we know. Just a few moves."

"Oh." She grinned back. "So if you have to fight them in the future you'll still have an advantage?"

Still grinning, he didn't answer.

Shaking her head she looked for Demetrius and Calum. They were both working with other men and she didn't want to interrupt. "Since Dem and Calum are busy with the men, will you train with me?"

"It would be an honor."

They moved to an empty space to start practicing, and Cristian was impressed by how much she'd improved since he saw her two weeks ago. He offered several suggestions to help her improve even more.

When Calum saw her with Cristian, he stopped to watch, and several men on the field followed suit. Soon everyone was watching her and talking. Alexandria was so focused on her training that she didn't notice. Cristian did, however, and would occasionally throw in a trickier move to demonstrate how skilled she was. When he gave her direction, she picked up on it right away.

The Tolgarians hadn't expected her to fight, thinking she would simply battle the queen with magick. The fact that she was going to fight beside them made the men even more determined to improve so they could get her to the queen.

✠✠✠✠✠

The next afternoon, Alexandria rode into camp with a few Amatarians behind her. They had gone hunting in the forest a few hours away. Several rabbits were tied to her saddle, and a stag she had shot was draped over another horse. The Amatarians had also caught several rabbits and birds.

Genesis approached as she was dismounting. "You didn't have to go hunting," he told her. "We're happy to take care of that."

"I know, but you're already doing so much. Since I can't train the men, this is one thing I can do."

Looking at their bounty he replied, "And you've done an excellent job. The men will be well fed after their training tonight."

One of the Amatarians came forward and took her horse. She thanked him and turned to follow Genesis as he began walking along the field. Watching the men train, they discussed their improvement—the men were really working hard, and the difference was apparent. So far she'd only had to heal three injuries. A few of the Amatarians were healers, but she felt if they were going to fight for her, then she should do the healing.

Genesis suddenly stopped walking when he saw two riders in the distance. "Looks like we have some new arrivals."

Recognizing the men immediately, Alexandria gave a cry of joy, ran across the field, and threw herself into Finnean's arms while Niall dismounted. They were both looking a little scruffy and had bows strapped to their backs. Their faces looked tired and showed signs of stress. Alexandria felt a wave of guilt wash through her, knowing what she was putting her family through.

After hugging Niall, she said, "It's so good to see you, but you have to go home."

Finnean looked at her as though she were crazy. "We're not going anywhere. We're here to join you."

"That's not why you came," she replied.

"No, we came to take you home," Niall said. "But we found out what's going on, and now we're going to join you."

"What would Mum and Father think? Mum never told us the story because she didn't want you involved."

"And you think she wants you involved?" Finnean inquired with annoyance.

"They'll understand when they hear what's going on," Niall replied, once again proving to be the more levelheaded brother.

"What would your *wives* think?" she asked, thinking that would get them to think about what they were doing. "You have families to take care of."

"You're our family too," Finnean stated.

"Helen told me not to come home without you," Niall replied.

"Agnes added that you better be in one piece."

Smiling, Alexandria asked, "Was she worried you'd do something to me or that something would happen during my journey?"

"Probably both," he admitted.

With a softer smile she said, "I'm glad you want to help me, but I really think you should go home."

"How can you let these men fight with you but not your brothers?" Finnean asked, offended.

"I didn't ask them to fight," she explained. "They heard I was going after the queen and joined me."

"Can you get any of them to leave?" Niall asked.

"No, I've told them they don't have to follow me, but no one's leaving and more come every day."

"Then how do you expect to get us to leave?" Finnean asked.

She sighed. "Some of these men are going to die, and I don't want you to be included in those numbers."

Stroking her hair, Niall said, "There are no guarantees in life. As a healer you should know that."

Having no reply she made a face.

Laughing, Niall threw an arm around her, and the three started walking around the edge of the field.

"How'd you get the Amatarians to join you?" Finnean asked.

The laughter left her, and she said soberly, "The queen killed Thaddeus."

Her brothers stopped and cried "*What!*" in unison.

"How?" Niall asked.

Facing them, she answered, "The queen appeared here with a few soldiers and killed him while trying to kill me."

Demetrius appeared beside them. "Hey guys, what are you doing here?"

Giving his sister a look, Niall remarked, "What do you think?"

Demetrius laughed. "Your sister always was a troublemaker."

"I am not!" She glared at him.

"Yes, you are," Finnean stated with a grin.

"Speaking of which, we heard you were in Sevenoaks with a man," Niall said, watching her. "A husband. You didn't get married, did you?"

"No."

Frowning, Niall asked, "Then who were you traveling with?"

"Ahhh . . ." She didn't know how to answer, or what her brothers would do when she did answer.

"Why don't you guys come with me," Demetrius said, taking pity on his friend. They might take it better from him. "Calum's waiting for you to practice," he told Alexandria.

Sending him a grateful smile, she hurried off.

Her brothers watched her approach Calum, who was watching them.

"Do we have to kill him?" Niall asked.

"No."

"Can we kill him?" Finnean asked, frowning as he watched Calum talk to his sister.

"Only if you want to upset your sister."

"I'm not concerned with her feelings after everything she's put us through," Niall responded.

"She did what she did for all of us," Demetrius said as they walked back to their horses. Taking in their stunned expressions, he explained, "She didn't tell you because she was afraid you'd join her and die like all the other men who've gone against the queen, and she didn't tell me because she was afraid I'd go with her and die, as well as break the truce and thereby start another war."

"So she decided to go alone," Niall said with a nod. He could see his sister thinking that way. It was just like her to be more concerned about others than herself.

"I'm sorry to hear about Thad," Finnean said. He hadn't known him well but knew he and Demetrius had been close.

Nodding his thanks, Demetrius turned to watch Alexandria. "Alex is taking it hard. She thinks it's her fault."

Wanting to know how the Amatarians felt, Niall asked, "Is it?"

Demetrius shook his head. "No, I think the queen was trying to show off her power, trying to intimidate her, but if anything, the queen made a mistake, for it's made Alex more determined to kill her."

Seeing Demetrius was still mourning the loss of his friend, Finnean decided to change the subject to what was on his mind. "How'd she end up with this guy?" He frowned again at the man with his sister.

"Alex will get mad at me for telling you, but he saved her from some men."

Finnean looked at him sharply. "Did they . . . ?" He couldn't bring himself to finish his question.

"No, thanks to Calum."

Watching Calum, Niall asked his brother, "Does he look familiar to you, Finnean?"

"He does. What did you say his name was?"

"Calum," Demetrius answered. "He's a horse breeder from Thanet."

"That's it," Finnean said as it dawned on him.

"We bought horses from him last year," Niall said with a nod.

"We always get our horses from him. I like Calum."

"And if he's sleeping with our sister?"

Finnean's eyes narrowed as he said, "I'll kill him."

"He's not sleeping with your sister," Demetrius assured him.

"How do you know?"

"I asked him."

"And you believe him?" Niall asked.

"The things he said proved he hasn't been with her." Changing the subject he asked, "Do you need a tent, or did you bring one?"

"Which tent's Alexandria's?"

"She doesn't have one. She sleeps by the fire with me and Calum."

Niall stared at Demetrius sternly. He knew Demetrius and his sister were just friends, but he had always been suspicious of the time they spent together. His wife had told him he was crazy, but he couldn't help but worry, given the Amatarians' reputation. "She'll sleep with us from now on."

✠✠✠✠✠

Minerva stood by her pedestal and watched Alexandria in the water. She couldn't see the Amatarians but knew they were present based on the way the Tolgarians seemed to be fighting thin air.

"Her army grows every day," she said, her hands resting on the edge of the pedestal.

With weak men, not soldiers.

"Weak men can still fight."

Look at them, her necklace urged. *Most can barely hold a sword. They'll be no match for your men.*

Confidence filled her again. "That's true, my men will cut them down. Better yet, they should take them captive so they can watch while I kill their little witch."

Word will spread that even a large army led by a witch couldn't defeat you.

"And finally they will give up and accept my rule." Turning away from the pedestal, she asked about the one thing that truly worried her. "What about the Amatarians?"

Their magick is nothing compared to ours.

"But they could kill me. That's why we created the truce."

No, her necklace disagreed, *they killed your men but they never came close to you.*

Straightening, Minerva responded, "That's right. I only created that truce because I was tired of finding new men to fight for me."

That's right. If they could kill you they would have tried long ago. They would have destroyed me before we ever met.

"But they think their little witch can defeat us. Why?"

She has strong magick.

"She didn't show it," Minerva scoffed.

I can feel it. They probably can too.

"Then why didn't she try anything when we surprised her with a visit?"

She might not know how much power she has.

Pacing, she said, "The Amatarians will teach her."

It takes time. Even with years of training with the Amatarians, she still won't be as powerful as you.

✠✠✠✠✠

"Thank you for talking to my brothers," said Alexandria as she approached Demetrius, who was watching some men practice.

"I figured they'd take it better from me."

"And how did they take it?" she asked anxiously.

"Better than I thought." Grinning, he added, "I expected them to demand he marry you."

"Honestly, so did I." And she wasn't sure how she felt about that. She really liked Calum and wanted him to stay with her after this was all over, but she didn't want him forced to stay.

"I like Calum."

Smiling, she said, "I know. The two of you seem to have become good friends."

"We have, but I meant I like him for you."

She looked at him with interest.

"I told you I would give you my honest opinion next time, so I'm telling you I like him."

Blushing, she said, "Me too, but we have others things to think about right now."

Demetrius nodded. Spotting her brothers, he said, "Looks like your brothers might still force a marriage after all."

Following his gaze, she saw her brothers approaching Calum. "Oh no." She started moving forward.

Demetrius took her arm to stop her. "Let them talk."

She stood there watching nervously, wishing she could hear them.

Across the field, Finnean and Niall were seizing the opportunity to talk to Calum alone.

Niall held out his hand. "Hey, Calum. How are you?"

"What are you doing with our sister?" Finnean demanded before he could answer.

Calum had been expecting this. In fact, he was surprised it had taken so long for them to approach him. "I'm helping her go after the queen. What took you so long to find her?"

Finnean took a step forward. "Are you criticizing us?"

"You can bet one of my sisters wouldn't be able to sneak away like yours did."

"Your sisters are married," Niall reminded him.

"Even when they weren't they wouldn't have been able to sneak away like Alexandria."

While Finnean glared, Niall held up his hands in defeat. "Maybe you're right. You've spent enough time with our sister to realize she's not like anyone else."

"That's an understatement," Calum replied.

Getting defensive again, Finnean asked, "What do you mean by that?"

Calum shrugged. "Nothing bad. I've just never met anyone like her."

"And how well *do* you know her?" Finnean asked. He and his brother watched intently while they waited for his answer.

Looking back and forth between the brothers, he answered, "I'm not sleeping with your sister."

"Care to explain why people in Sevenoaks are saying you're married?" Niall asked.

This was a bit trickier to explain—he didn't want to tell them they'd shared a room at the inn, but he wasn't sure how much they knew. Instead he just said, "I thought it was safer. Nothing's happened between us."

Nodding, Niall said, "You don't have to explain it to us—you just have to tell our father."

Finnean grinned and slapped him on the back. "Welcome to the family."

As they started walking away, Finnean called back over his shoulder, "Our sister will be sleeping with us from now on, so you're free to join the other men."

Calum said nothing. He was going to stick close to Alexandria whether they liked it or not.

CHAPTER TWELVE

Alexandria stood with Genesis and Cristian on the edge of the training field. There were now about seventy men, including the Amatarians, training. The men moved off the field as five targets were brought out for archery practice. Alexandria watched her brothers proudly. They didn't have much skill with swords, but they hit the target dead center every time.

"So many Tolgarians couldn't use a sword when they got here, but most are very good with a bow," Cristian remarked, impressed.

"Many of them have had no need to fight, but use the bow to hunt," Alexandria explained.

Calum approached and said to Alexandria, "You need to practice your powers."

"Why? I thought we decided not to so the queen wouldn't know what I can do."

"I'm hearing whispers amongst the men. They don't think you're strong enough to kill her."

"Then why are they still here?" she asked, insulted. If they didn't believe in her why were they willing to follow her? It didn't make sense.

"Because you're going after the queen, and they're willing to die for even the slightest chance that you can kill her, but they're not putting all their efforts into training anymore. Show them your power. Show them that we have more than a slight chance of winning."

"But why? If they're going to fight anyway, why risk the queen seeing what I can do?"

"For morale," Genesis told her, joining the conversation. "They'll fight harder and with more conviction if they believe they can win."

Turning to Genesis, she asked, "You think I should do this?"

"Yes. They've seen you practice with the sword and they've seen you heal, so they know you have power. Now show them why we'll win."

She trusted Genesis implicitly, so if he felt this was important then she would do it. "What should I do?"

"Impress them."

Nodding, she walked forward, picked up a spare bow and quiver, and strapped it to her back. She then stopped behind all the men. When she caught Demetrius's attention, he understood what she wanted and started moving men out of the way. They all stood to the sides, waiting to see what she was going to do.

She knew it was showing off, but she'd been told to impress them. From where she stood she reached up, pulled an arrow from her quiver, and sent it flying. It hit its target in the center, and then she quickly fired four more shots, which hit the other four targets' centers.

After a few seconds of stunned silence, the men let out a cheer. Moving forward a few feet, Alexandria turned in a circle to look at everyone. "I know there's been some talk about my gifts. Even though you haven't seen these powers you've heard about, you're still willing to follow me, to train from sunup to sundown. So I think it's time for you to see who you're following."

Taking a deep breath to center herself, she dropped the bow and held her hands out at her sides. The arrows in her quiver rose up to hover above her head, and she rapidly shot one after the other at the targets. Each arrow hit the center circle. With an extra push, she sent her last arrow to the target directly in front of her, and it split the arrow that was already dead center.

Before the men could react they felt a change in the air. The wind picked up and her hair darkened, the red becoming brighter as it blew out behind her. She threw her hands out, and all five targets burst into flames as the men around her cheered. Then waving one hand in front of her, she dimmed the fires until they died.

Turning in another circle, she called out, "I'm not going to ask you to follow me, to fight with me—the choice is yours. Just know I can't win alone, so if you give it everything you've got, I promise to give her everything I've got, and together we'll defeat her."

The men cheered again, louder than before.

Walking back to Genesis, she asked, "How was that?"

Smiling, he answered, "Impressive," before remarking, "I don't remember you using your hands like that."

Shrugging, she said, "I don't normally but thought it would add a little flare."

Alexandria was suddenly lifted off her feet and swung around and around. When Finnean put her on the ground again he exclaimed, "That was awesome! How come you never told us you could do that?"

Laughing, she replied, "I didn't used to be able to. I've trained a lot since I left."

"Mum will be very proud of you," Niall told her seriously.

"After she's done being mad at me, you mean."

"When you come home a hero she won't be mad anymore."

"Our family may not have succeeded in the past," Finnean added, "but with you, this time we will."

✠✠✠✠✠

"That was impressive," a voice said behind Calum.

Calum turned to see his two brothers-in-law. He greeted them with hugs. "What are you doing here?"

"You didn't really think we'd let you do this alone?" Bran asked as his answer, shaking his head to get his chin-length red hair out of his eyes. He was a little shorter than Calum and not as muscular with a round face and a scar beside his left eye that he'd gotten in a fight when he was younger.

"How'd you know I was here?"

"The family was worried until they got word someone saw you in Sevenoaks with an armed wife wearing pants," Eadan answered. He was a tall, broad man with an oval face, a goatee, and long brown hair, which he wore pulled back. His blue eyes had once been full of life, but now they were always serious. He'd never forgiven himself for not protecting his daughter.

"Then the family was even more worried," Bran added. "Did you really marry her?"

"No, I was just trying to protect her," Calum said with a sigh. Did the whole country think they were married? What was he going to say to her father when they met? And he was sure they would meet after this was all over, especially if her brothers had anything to do with it.

"And then we heard that same woman was going after the queen and figured you were with her," Eadan said.

"I'm sorry I didn't send word . . ."

Eadan waved off his apology. "From the sounds of it, no one's heading north. They're all making their way here."

"How do Una and Clara feel about your being here?"

"Proud," Bran answered. "They wanted to come with us, but we weren't about to let our pregnant wives fight."

This didn't surprise Calum. His sisters were firecrackers with fierce tempers. He could remember a time when they'd put hot peppers in his soup, raw meat in his bed, and mud in his boots, all because he wouldn't let them ride one of the new horses that hadn't been trained yet.

"I think Clara will be happier about having her child with the queen dead," Eadan added when Calum didn't say anything.

"I think every woman would."

Bran and Eadan shared a grin.

"What?" Calum asked, clueless.

Slapping his arm, Bran said, "You're going to be an uncle again."

"I know. Una's due in a few months."

Laughing, Bran looked pointedly at Eadan, who was grinning.

"No! Really?" Grinning, Calum hugged his brother-in-law. "How's Clara?"

"Worried, afraid, but there was a spark of hope when we got word of this."

"Then we'd better win," Bran said.

"Let's get training," Calum said.

✠✠✠✠✠

"The men seem different," Alexandria told Genesis as they walked along the field a few hours later.

"That's what you get with renewed hope," he replied. "They now believe we're going to win, and each one is determined not to be the weak link."

"Even with all this training, many will die. They'll be no match for Minerva's soldiers."

"I've never heard you call her by name before," Genesis observed.

"She's not my queen, and I will no longer call her such."

"You can't think about the cost of war. We can only pray that whatever we do is enough to destroy her."

"What if we could even the odds?" she asked. "If we could give our men a better chance?"

Raising a brow, he said, "You have an idea."

She sighed. "Maybe, but I don't know how to implement it without her finding out."

Genesis stared off into the distance, deep in thought, as Calum walked over.

"We should practice," he said.

"Yes." She nodded. Turning to Genesis, she asked, "Will you excuse me?"

Still distracted he said, "Yes, yes. I need to speak to a few of my men."

"What was that about?" Calum asked as they watched him hurry off.

"I have no idea."

They moved to an empty spot and drew their swords. As they practiced, Niall and Finnean watched, impressed with her skills. They'd known she was good with a bow—after all, they had taught her—but they'd never seen her fight before. Though she wasn't strong, she was quick on her feet.

Finnean wanted to step forward when he saw Calum come close to striking his sister, but Niall held him back. Niall knew Calum wouldn't hurt her and could tell he was holding back his strength. A few other men joined Niall and Finnean on the sidelines to watch.

Calum suddenly knocked the sword from her hand, but it barely touched the ground before she brought it back to her with her powers. After a few more blocks she held out her left hand, and Calum's sword was ripped from his hand before flying into hers.

Extending both swords in front of her, she said with a grin, "I win."

Holding up his hands in defeat he replied, "Maybe we should teach you to fight with two swords next."

She used her magick to sheath his sword for him. "I think I'll stick with one."

Calum noticed the small crowd and raised a brow.

Turning to see what he was looking at, Alexandria noticed the crowd of men walking away. Her brothers were still standing there, Niall looking stunned and Finnean grinning.

Raising her sword, she asked, "Do one of you want to take me on?"

Holding his hands out defensively, Niall said, "I wouldn't dream of it."

"Then why are you two looking at me like that?"

"We're just impressed, little sister," Finnean said. "When you fought us before it consisted of hair pulling and biting."

She shot them a disgusted look and replied haughty, "I was a child, and if I remember correctly, it only took you a few seconds to throw me off." Grinning, she swung her sword a few times. "Want to try now and see how long it takes?"

Spotting something over her shoulder, Niall gestured with his head. "What's going on over there?"

"I'm not falling for that trick," she stated, keeping her sword up. It might have worked when she was a child but she could control her curiosity now.

Finnean looked behind her and said, "He's not joking, Alex. Look."

Alexandria narrowed her eyes. Her brothers had gotten better at keeping straight faces.

"They're not playing a trick," Calum said, placing a hand on her arm and lowering her sword.

Turning, she saw Genesis standing with several Amatarians around a tent with their arms out and their faces tilted towards the sky.

"What do you think they're doing?" Calum asked.

"I don't know," she answered, mystified. "I thought they didn't have any tents."

✠✠✠✠

Alexandria was eating supper around the fire with her brothers, Calum, and Demetrius. She found it funny that her brothers had situated themselves on either side of her. They'd never been this protective back home.

Cristian appeared before her and said, "Genesis would like you to join him in the tent."

She immediately stood, as did her friends and brothers. Glancing at Cristian, she waited for him to say whether they could join, but he remained silent as he turned and headed for the tent, knowing they would all follow.

Once there, he held open the flap and gestured for Alexandria to enter. After taking two steps, she disappeared. Demetrius followed while her brothers gasped.

"Haven't you visited their tribe before?" Calum asked.

"Only my mother and sister ever go to their villages," Niall said. He had known their villages were invisible, but seeing someone disappear right in front of him was a shock to the system.

"Are you joining us?" Cristian asked, still holding the tent open.

Calum immediately went inside. After a moment of hesitation, Niall and Finnean followed. They weren't about to be left out. Cristian let the flap close behind him as he entered. The tent had no furniture, for the Amatarians didn't travel with comforts, only necessities.

Genesis was sitting cross-legged on the ground, and Alexandria waited for permission to join him. He gestured for everyone to sit. No one spoke, waiting for Genesis to start.

"There are a few things we know about the queen's necklace," he started. "One is that it knows what people are doing. Whether it can read thoughts or hear people talk is unclear, but it always knows what's going on. Another is that it can't see or hear the Amatarians, nor can it hear anything inside our protective shield."

"How can you be sure?" Alexandria asked. "Maybe she can still hear me."

Genesis shook his head. "If that were true she would have known Thaddeus was traveling with you, and she would have known about the necklace."

She nodded, and waited for him to continue.

"We created this shield so we could talk without worrying that the queen might hear us," Genesis said.

"Can you create a bigger one in front of the castle?" Calum asked. "So we could sneak up on them?"

Cristian shook his head. "It doesn't work like that. To create a shield, we need to surround the area we want to protect. We'd be in the open for the queen's soldiers to attack."

Nodding, Calum understood. If it had been an easy thing, he was sure they would have suggested it.

Looking towards Alexandria, Genesis stated, "You have a different plan."

"Me?" Alexandria asked, surprised.

"This afternoon you told me you had an idea but didn't know how to implement it without her finding out." Lifting his hands, he added, "So we created this."

"Oh, well even if she can't hear, I don't know how we'd pull it off," she explained.

"Tell us anyways," Niall said.

"Yes," Genesis agreed. "By discussing it we might figure out a way to make it work."

She took a deep breath and told them her idea. "I was thinking about how no matter what we do, she'll know when we're coming and be ready. We'll be outnumbered and we're no match for her soldiers, but maybe we could lead them into a trap."

"How?" Calum asked, leaning forward.

"We get everyone to think and act as though we're leaving in a week. We pick a day and say that's when we're riding for Dorset. With everyone planning on leaving that day, Minerva will find out and send her soldiers here. They'll think they're taking us by surprise."

"How do you know she'll send soldiers?" Cristian asked.

"She's done it in the past," Niall answered, thinking Alexandria's idea was smart. "Most men who go after her never make it to the castle."

"That's brilliant," Finnean exclaimed. "We'll actually be ready for them and could take out half her soldiers before we attack the castle."

"There are a few problems with my idea," she warned.

"What? It sounds perfect," Finnean said.

"It's far from perfect. How do we get the men ready to surprise her soldiers when we need them to be thinking and acting as though we're leaving for Dorset?"

Genesis nodded thoughtfully. "If it can read minds it will know the truth and that it's all a trap."

"And how do we get her to send half her men?" Alexandria asked next. "We need her to send enough to leave the castle in danger."

"We lie," Calum said. He turned to Genesis. "You said she can't see you, so she doesn't know how many are here."

"That's right."

"So we tell them that when we're leaving we're going with over a hundred men."

"But the men will know we're lying," she said. "And then Minerva will know we're lying."

"They're not going to count how many are here," Calum told her.

"We could always say men from our tribe up north will be joining us," Demetrius suggested.

"That's good," Finnean said. "She'll want to send men to take us out before they join us."

As they discussed this plan Alexandria cut in, "But there's still the big problem—how do we get the men ready to surprise her soldiers without her finding out?"

"We don't tell them," Niall said, looking at Demetrius. "We only tell a few."

Catching on, Demetrius grinned. "Since she can't see us, we tell only the Amatarians. We'll keep watch and surprise the soldiers."

"Once the fight starts, we can join in," Calum said.

"Do you think this will work?" Alexandria asked Genesis somberly as the other men talked.

"Yes, but you'll have to be careful with your thoughts. If she's watching anyone it will be you."

Nodding, she said, "I can do that."

"Where do we set the trap?" Calum asked.

"It needs to be close to camp so it won't take long for us to join you," Finnean said.

"We also need somewhere for the Amatarians to hide so the soldiers don't see them as they ride towards us," Alexandria added.

"We'd better take a ride tomorrow," Genesis replied.

Everyone agreed that only Amatarians would ride out, in case the queen was watching.

"I just had a thought," Alexandria said as the men started to rise.

They sat back down.

"The soldiers will be riding here, won't they?"

"Most likely. It will take too long to march," Calum answered.

Looking at Genesis, she said, "We need Nestor."

Demetrius and Cristian grinned.

"Who's Nestor?" Calum asked.

"He's our horse breeder," Demetrius said, still grinning.

"How will that help?" Finnean asked, confused by their enthusiasm.

"His talent is talking to horses," Genesis answered.

"He can talk to horses?" Calum asked. He'd thought the Amatarians' horses were just impeccably trained, and had been hoping to learn a few of their tricks to take home. "I'd like to meet this man," he said.

"He could ask the horses to help," Alexandria replied.

"Then we'd have more horses for our journey," Niall added, thinking of the men who'd arrived on foot.

As everyone rose to leave again, Genesis stopped Alexandria. "This tent is yours now. You can sleep here."

"What about you?"

"I'll be sleeping with my men, as always."

"I have no problem with sleeping outside."

"I know, but the queen can't see you when you're inside. This tent will protect you if she's watching."

He made a good point and she nodded. Maybe it would be smarter to sleep inside.

Glaring at Calum, Finnean said, "We'll be staying here with her."

Slapping Calum on the back, Demetrius said, "Come with me. I'll introduce you to Nestor."

The next day, word spread that the army would be leaving for Dorset in a week. The men talked amongst themselves as they prepared to travel.

Genesis, Cristian, and Demetrius rode out to look for a place to lay their trap. On the other side of the hill they found a large flat plain—a perfect spot. The hill would obscure the soldiers' view of their camp, and the grass was tall enough to hide in. Nestor would hide on the hill and send word to the camp when the soldiers arrived. Now they just had to wait for the soldiers to take the bait.

✠✠✠✠✠

Minerva took a sip of wine and looked down from her throne at Alva, who was curtseying before her. "Have you heard from your husband?" she asked in an almost concerned tone.

"No, Your Majesty," Alva answered.

"I hope nothing's happened."

"So do I." She wondered how long it would take for the queen to figure out that he wasn't coming back. Or maybe she already knew and was just playing with her.

Minerva did in fact know he wasn't coming back. She also knew he'd taken his children and mother up north. The question was whether or not he was coming back for his wife. Either way, she hadn't decided what she was going to do about it yet.

They've planned their move, her necklace whispered.

Seeing the queen's eyes harden, Alva shrank in fear. But all Minerva said was, "Leave."

Alva rushed from the room and pressed her back to the wall a few feet from the door, not knowing how much more she could take.

"What are they planning?" Minerva asked, her fingers gripping the skulls.

They're going to leave their camp next week and march here.

"How many?"

I see only fifty or sixty, but they say they have more.

She relaxed into her throne. "Then they're lying."

I don't think so. The Amatarians have joined them.

"How many?"

I can't see them, he reminded her.

Not noticing Alva huddled against the wall, Minerva stalked out of the throne room, down a long hall, and then up a spiral staircase to her private chamber. As she approached her pedestal, she demanded, "Show me their camp."

The water glowed and a picture shimmered to life in the center. She could almost feel the excitement. The water zoomed in on Alexandria, who was walking amongst the men, confirming when they were to ride out. The scene changed to two men talking.

"We don't have enough men," one said.

"More Amatarians are coming from the north," the other answered. "They'll catch up to us in time."

Minerva slapped her hand against the water before turning away. "She's built an army of Amatarians!" she shrieked as she paced the room.

Forget them. Look at the other men. Your soldiers will kill them easily.

"But what about the Amatarians? They're strong."

And not all of them are there. Kill the men before they arrive, kill the witch before they arrive, and they'll have no one to follow.

With an evil smile, she said, "Yes. I'll be ready for her this time. I'll kill her in front of all her men."

No, it's too risky. You need to stay here.

"You've assured me I have nothing to worry about," Minerva said, annoyed. "Now you're telling me to be careful. Which is it?"

You have nothing to worry about when it comes to her men, but I've told you she's strong. Let your soldiers deal with her.

"Fine." Her skirt swirled around her as she spun and yelled, "Brodrick!"

Not a patient woman, she called for him again before screaming, "*Alva!*"

Alva had followed the queen to wait outside her chamber, and hurried in. She curtsied low before asking, "What can I do for you?"

"Find Brodrick."

"Yes, Your Majesty." She scurried from the room in search of Brodrick. He was never in the same place, so finding him was always difficult.

CHAPTER THIRTEEN

Brodrick strode into the queen's chambers and knelt before her. "You called for me, Your Majesty."

"Yes. That little witch has created an army. I want you to take some soldiers and kill them."

Standing, he nodded his agreement and asked, "Where am I going?" Even if they were going to the same place they'd met the witch last time, since they'd gone there by magick, he didn't know where they'd actually been.

"Come here and I'll show you." She motioned for him to join her.

When he was standing beside her at the pedestal, she waved her hand over the water, and for the first time, its magick was revealed to him. He could see men training with swords.

"They're in the fields between Sedgemoor Forest and Yarmouth. About sixty men."

Watching them in the water, he scoffed. "That's not a problem."

"There are also Amatarians. I don't know how many."

"We can handle it."

She smiled. "Good. I know I can trust you, so I'm going to tell you a secret."

He stared at her intently while she leaned forward.

"Their witch can hurt me," she whispered. "You *must* kill her first. Her men will try to protect her above all else."

"I won't let her near you," he promised.

"I believe you." Leaning back, she said, "Now, you need to ride fast. In six days' time they'll be joined by more Amatarians and begin their journey here. They need to be dead before the others arrive."

"How many men do you want me to take?"

"As many as you need to kill them all."

Bowing again Brodrick said, "We'll leave immediately."

✠✠✠✠✠

Calum entered the tent. "They're almost here." Glancing around, he saw Alexandria was alone, which was rare—one of her brothers always seemed to be with her.

Alexandria turned around, and Calum could see the worry in her eyes. "Are they ready?" she asked.

"Yes. Don't worry, we'll know when the soldiers arrive, and we'll be ready to join our army," he said. "Are you staying here?"

"Just until the fight starts. I don't want to risk Minerva being able to warn her soldiers."

He knew how she was going to feel about his suggestion but decided to make it anyway. "Maybe you should stay inside until it's over."

She looked at him, speechless for a moment. "How can you say that?"

"Because the soldiers' main goal will be to kill you."

"They're here to kill us all," she reminded him.

"If I were the queen, I'd make you the main target. Without you, there's no one to follow. We need you for the big battle, not this one."

"I understand what you're saying, but how would the men feel if I didn't join them? I promised them we were in this together."

"They'll understand, Alex. We need you to kill the queen."

"And I will, after we defeat her soldiers."

Knowing her well enough to know she wouldn't listen, he gave up. "Fine, I'll come get you when it's time."

She narrowed her eyes suspiciously, wondering if she should believe him.

"I will come for you," he promised. "That way I can keep an eye on you. God only knows what you'll do if I'm not with you."

Smiling smugly, she nodded, glad to see he knew her.

Calum left the tent to wait for the signal.

Not far away, the Amatarians were lying low on both sides of the field, shielded by the tall grass. Amongst them were the vine controllers, with Demetrius and another on one side and two more on the other side.

The soldiers rode right into their trap. When the lookout gave the signal, men lit bonfires on either side of the field to give the fire controllers something to control. A wall of fire rose before the riders, blocking their path. Their horses reared, but most of the soldiers stayed mounted. Nestor, who was hiding in the grass with several fire controllers at the base of the hill, began calling to the horses. Like all animals, the horses listened to him and began trying to buck off their riders.

This was their signal. Each vine controller placed a hand on the ground and called forth his power. The vines burst from the soil, wrapped themselves around the soldiers' waists, and pulled them from their horses, which then rode off towards Nestor.

The vines disappeared and the soldiers scrambled to their feet. Drawing their swords they looked around for the source of the attack, but no one was in sight.

"It's the witch!" cried Brodrick. "Find her! Kill her!"

As the soldiers started to spread out, more vines rose from the ground and ensnared them, and the men desperately chopped each other free.

While his men struggled with the vines, Brodrick searched for the witch, certain that if he killed her, the magick would stop and they could take care of her pitiful army. When he reached the spot where the fire wall had been, a gust of wind threw him back several feet.

At that moment Nestor rode into camp with the horses behind him, and Calum knew it was time.

He called out to the confused men, "We're under attack. The queen's soldiers are just over the hill."

The men rushed for their swords while Calum ran to fetch Alexandria. She was ready, her sword strapped to her side.

"Stay close to me," he said, holding the flap open for her.

Alexandria neither agreed nor disagreed for she knew it was impossible to promise. She had no idea what would happen during battle.

They mounted their horses and joined the others before riding to the top of the hill. Some men had mounts, the rest were on foot. Looking down, they could see the Amatarians hiding in the tall grass while the soldiers fought their magick. Though impressive, none of their powers, other than the fire, were able to kill the soldiers. It was time to join the fight.

Raising his sword over his head, Calum let out a battle cry before charging down the hill. The members of his army echoed his cry and followed, swords raised. Just as the Tolgarians reached the soldiers, the Amatarians leapt from the grass, and the battle began.

Alexandria was in the thick of it, and it wasn't long before she was separated from Calum. A soldier charged her, and while she managed to raise her sword in time, he struck with such force she was sent flying from her horse. On her feet, she fought with all the skills Calum had taught her, but she wasn't as strong as the queen's soldier and was soon knocked to the ground. She quickly used her magick to send her sword into the soldier as he raised his above her. Back on her feet, she pulled it from his dead body and turned just in time to block another blow.

Brodrick saw her fighting and raced towards her, knocking men out of his way, even his own soldiers, determined to kill her for his queen. Calum also saw her and called to Finnean, who was closest to him. Together they fought their way to Alexandria.

She lost her sword and was immediately surrounded by four men. They didn't strike but grinned smugly, chuckling as they closed in on her.

"Kill her!" Brodrick screamed as he struggled to reach them.

With her eyes closed, her hands slightly raised at her sides, she called on her powers. The wind blew and her hair darkened, and when she opened her eyes the soldier in front of her was instantly hypnotized by the flames he saw in them. As he leaned forward he burst into flames, and the two closest to him jumped back only to be engulfed themselves.

Finally, she turned her gaze to the one behind her, and he stumbled back, thinking he was on fire. She knew she could have made the fire real but couldn't bring herself to torture anyone like that. Just then one of her men killed him, and she turned back to the other three as Calum and Finnean arrived. They quickly cut down the soldiers.

"Are you alright?" Finnean asked, looking her over.

Holding out her hand, she called her sword to her, saying, "I'm fine." She looked at Calum. "Let's finish this."

Turning, they rejoined the fight, and Calum noticed Brodrick. He recognized him as the soldier who'd been standing with the queen when Thaddeus had been killed. Raising his sword he charged, and the two fought as men continued to fall around them. Soon they were the only two left, and men gathered to watch. Calum found his opening and stabbed him through the chest. As Brodrick fell to his knees, Calum swung his sword wide and decapitated him.

✠✠✠✠

"*No!*" Minerva screamed as she watched Brodrick's death through the stone basin. "We lost! How could we lose?"

She had more Amatarians than we thought.

"How does that help us now?" she asked angrily. "They've killed my men and are coming here."

She lost a lot of men today. It won't be easy for her to recover.

"They won't need to recover if they have more Amatarians on the way."

You still have more men, and you have me.

"My men are no match against the Amatarians' powers."

Their powers are no match for us.

"You have a plan," she said, smiling wickedly.

They may kill more men, they may even breach your walls, her necklace whispered, *but they are no match for our powers. We will destroy them all.*

"Yes," Minerva hissed. "And I will personally kill the little witch. She will wither and fall before me."

✠✠✠✠

Calum raised his sword in victory, and the men surrounding him cheered.

After mounting the injured on horses, the army headed back to camp, where Alexandria was kept busy healing. Her necklace allowed her to heal faster than she ever had before. After each healing, she made the wounded drink a potion the Amatarians had prepared to ward off infection. When she had done all she could, she joined Genesis, Demetrius, Cristian, Calum, and her brothers in her tent.

As soon as she entered, Genesis handed her a goblet. "Drink this," he instructed.

"You're tired," Demetrius said when she was done drinking. "You should rest."

Alexandria shook her head. "How many?"

They knew what she was asking but no one wanted to answer her—they didn't want to add to the pain they saw in her eyes.

Looking at Niall, she asked again, "How many?"

Placing a hand on her shoulder, he replied, "Twenty-seven."

She bowed her head as tears spilled down her cheeks. Niall wrapped his arms around her and ran a hand up and down her back in comfort. Sniffing, she pulled back.

"You must think I'm foolish for crying. You've all told me time and again the cost of war."

Wiping away her tears, Niall said, "You're not foolish."

"You've always felt things more strongly than we have," Finnean added.

"The gift of healing also has a price," Genesis said. "You feel pain and loss more so than others."

"Were your men part of the twenty-seven?" she asked.

"I didn't lose any men." Genesis didn't want to sound superior, but his men were better trained and had come through with minimal injuries.

She turned to Calum. "What about your brothers?"

"They're fine. I saw them a few minutes ago."

Looking around, she asked with sorrow in her eyes, "After today, how can I ask anyone to ride with me?"

"The men see this as a victory, not a loss," Calum said.

"Don't they know how many men we've lost?"

"Yes, but we won," Finnean said.

Nodding, she understood. The men had known some would die. They'd understood the cost even when she hadn't wanted to accept it.

"Where are they?" she asked.

"The men?" Calum asked, confused. She'd just been with them.

Demetrius knew her better. "The fallen men," he explained. "We've brought them in from the field, and they've been laid out past the tents."

"What will happen to them?"

When no one answered, Calum said, "We'll leave them and ride for the castle."

She didn't like the sound of that. Glancing around at the men, she asked, "Can't we give them a proper burial?"

"It will take too long to dig graves," Niall explained. "Not to mention the men are too tired and hurt. They need to rest before we leave."

Alexandria thought they deserved more respect and honor but understood the reasoning.

Seeing how upset she was, Genesis said, "We'll give them an Amatarian burial."

Grateful, she said softly, "Thank you."

"I'll see to it," Cristian said. He left the tent with Demetrius behind him.

"I'm going to pick flowers for them," Alexandria said.

When she left Niall jerked his head, motioning Finnean to follow. In the fields Alexandria picked twenty-seven flowers. Everyone was standing in a circle around the fallen when she returned. She moved down the line and one by one placed a flower on each man's chest while saying a silent prayer for him. When she was done she stood beside Genesis.

He said a prayer in Amatarian before explaining, "We don't bury our dead. We burn them so they can be reborn from the earth. Tonight we will mourn our friends, tomorrow we will plan our next victory." Turning, he stepped aside for Alexandria.

Moving forward she closed her eyes to gather her powers. As a breeze blew, and the red in her hair brightened, she opened her eyes. Moving her gaze over each man, she set the fallen on fire. Her brothers moved to her side as she watched them burn. In the glow of the fire, everyone could see the tears on her cheeks.

✠✠✠✠✠

The next day Alexandria walked amongst the men as they prepared to leave and was surprised by how ready they were for the next fight. She had thought they'd be having second thoughts after losing so many men, but they were ready, even eager, to go after the queen.

Seeing Calum and Cristian riding back from the field, she stopped to wait for them. They dismounted and Nestor stepped forward to take the horses.

"Is something wrong?" she asked, taking in their grave expressions.

"Let's talk in the tent," Calum said as Cristian walked away.

"What's wrong?" she asked when they were alone in the tent.

"Nothing. Cristian has an idea," he answered. "He's going to get the others."

Niall and Finnean burst through the tent's flap.

"What's going on?" Finnean asked.

"You saw Cristian," she said.

"No, we saw you coming here and figured something was up," Finnean answered.

Looking at them suspiciously, she said, "You guys were on the other side of camp. What are you doing, watching my every move?"

"Yes," Finnean stated, frowning at Calum.

"We saw Calum come back, so we started over," Niall responded more reasonably. "When you entered the tent we figured something was up."

Genesis, Cristian, and Demetrius entered before she could say anything else.

"You have an idea," Genesis said, looking at Calum.

"Actually it's Cristian's idea."

"We went to the battlefield to see what weapons we could take from the queen's soldiers," Cristian said. "And I thought we might be able to use their armor as well."

Alexandria wrinkled her nose at the thought of wearing a dead man's armor, but the men didn't seem to mind.

"And that's when it occurred to us—how are we going to breach the castle?" Calum asked.

"I thought I'd use fire," Alexandria told them.

Calum nodded. "That's great if it's made of wood, but what if it's made of iron?"

She didn't have an answer, having never thought of that.

"Has anyone in camp been to the castle?" Niall asked.

"I don't know," Calum answered. "We can ask, but we need to be careful about what we say."

"What happens if it's iron?" Niall inquired.

"If we could get some men in armor into the castle before we get there, they could open the gate for us," Cristian said.

"But how do we get them in the castle?" Alexandria asked.

"If they're in armor, they could ride right in," Finnean stated, liking the idea.

"But what if her soldiers know they're not from the castle?" She felt they could be sending men to their death this way. They needed a better plan.

"We'll figure something out," Genesis said, understanding her feelings.

"We need to ride soon," Calum insisted. "While our men are still high on their victory, and before she can summon more men."

Another Amatarian entered the tent. "There's a man here insisting on seeing Alexandria."

"Did he know her name?" Genesis asked.

He shook his head. "No. He demanded to see the witch in charge."

Turning to Alexandria, Genesis raised a brow. "Do you wish to see him?"

She looked around the tent, confused by the expressions of apprehension. "Why wouldn't I?"

"It could be a trap," Finnean said.

"He could have news," she countered. Waving a hand in dismissal, she added, "Besides, what could he do with all of you here?"

"Bring him in," Genesis instructed.

A muscular man entered unarmed. He glanced around warily at the armed men in front of him. When he spotted Alexandria he took another step forward. "You're the witch going after the queen?"

Raising her chin, she answered, "I am. My name is Alexandria."

"I'm from the castle."

All the men except for Genesis placed their hands on the hilts of their swords.

"You bring a message from the queen?"

"No. I've come to join you."

"Why should we believe you?" Calum asked, moving protectively in front of Alexandria.

"Because I want the queen dead."

"Why?" Demetrius asked, also moving closer to Alexandria, his hand still on his sword.

"She has my wife," he said, his eyes flashing.

Placing a hand on Demetrius's arm, Alexandria stepped around him and stood beside Calum. With a reassuring smile, she asked the man, "What's your name?"

"Rufus."

"And your wife?"

"Her name is Alva."

"How did the queen take her?"

With a deep breath he explained, "I work on the castle grounds. My wife is one of the queen's servants."

Alexandria raised a hand when she saw the men were about to speak. "They why do you say she has your wife?"

"Because she can't leave. I'm not even sure she's still alive."

She could feel his pain, knew it was genuine, but couldn't let that sway her. "Explain."

"My wife displeased the queen, and if she displeases her again, the queen will take our children."

This surprised everyone, for it was known that the queen didn't take children from the castle. People assumed she ensured her subjects' loyalty this way.

"What does your wife do for the queen?" Niall asked.

"It doesn't matter," Alexandria answered before Rufus could. And it didn't. She knew that many served the queen out of fear, not loyalty. "Please continue."

"We made a plan to leave, saying my mother was ill and wanted to see her family before she died. The queen must have suspected we were lying and made Alva stay behind. My wife thinks when the queen realizes we're not coming back, she'll kill her."

"Then why'd you leave her?" Finnean wasn't sure they should believe him—he wouldn't have left Agnes behind for anything.

Alexandria raised her hand again, this time to stop Rufus. She could tell by his red face he was about to shout. Looking at her brother, she said, "He left to save his children." Turning back to Rufus she asked, "If you think your wife is dead, why do you want to go back?"

"She might not be dead. She told me not to come back for her, but when I heard you were going after the queen, I decided to join you."

"Where are your children?" she asked.

"They're with my mother, heading north."

"You realize by joining us you could make your children orphans."

"Yes, but if there's any chance Alva's alive, I will find her and get her out."

Now it made sense to Alexandria. "So while we're fighting you'll be looking for your wife."

Answering honestly Rufus said, "Yes. But I can help you. I can give you the layout of the castle. I can help you get inside."

The men shared a look before Calum said, "Wait outside while we talk."

"He can't leave," Alexandria interjected. "If Alva is alive and Minerva sees him here, she'll kill her."

"We need to discuss this," Calum insisted.

"Yes," she agreed.

"I know what to do," Finnean stated. Without warning he punched Rufus, knocking him unconscious.

"*Finn!*" Alexandria knelt beside Rufus.

"What?" He lifted his hands defensively. "Now he can't hear us and he didn't have to leave. Problem solved."

Shaking her head in disgust, she turned to Genesis. "What do you think?"

"There are ways we can handle this. We can question him about the castle, on how to get in, and we don't have to tell him our plan."

"What is our plan?" Demetrius asked.

"We'll figure that out after we question him."

"He can't leave the tent," Alexandria said. "How do we plan without Minerva and him hearing?"

"I'll knock him out again," Finnean answered flippantly.

"No." She didn't want him to hit Rufus again, but the men all looked as though they liked Finnean's idea, even Genesis.

"Do you trust him?" Demetrius asked Alexandria.

"I don't know."

"Then you can't have it both ways. Either he hears, or the queen hears."

"Or we knock him out," Finnean added a little too eagerly.

CHAPTER FOURTEEN

Rufus woke to three men standing over him—one Tolgarian and two Amatarians. Rubbing his jaw as he sat up, he asked, "Did you have to do that?"

"Yes." Calum held out a hand to help Rufus to his feet. "I'm Calum, this is Genesis and Cristian. We want you to tell us everything about the castle."

"Jeez, Calum, did you wait for him to wake up before you started questioning him?" Alexandria asked as she entered the tent.

"He's up," Calum replied.

"Here." Alexandria smiled softly and handed Rufus a goblet of water and a plate of food before sitting cross-legged on the ground.

"Thanks." He sat down across from her. Eating some meat he watched her and asked, "Are you always this nice, or is this just to gain my cooperation?"

She threw her hand up and hit Calum's thigh when he took a step forward. "It's alright." Looking Rufus in the eyes, she replied, "No, I'm not always this nice, but I am a healer. It's my job to take care of people."

"I've already said I'll tell you whatever I can."

Alexandria laughed. "So what? You think I should starve you and be mean until you do?"

That's what the queen would have done, he thought. *And she would have tortured me for the fun of it.* He knew that coming here had been the right decision. "What do you want to know?"

The men sat down and Calum asked, "How many soldiers does she have?"

"Around two hundred."

Calum and Genesis shared a look. They had faced sixty-two men in the field. That left about a hundred and forty to deal with at the castle.

"Is the gate wood or iron?"

"Iron."

Great, Alexandria thought, *there goes my plan of burning it down.*

"How many men control the gate?"

Rufus shrugged. "Three or four, I'm not sure. You need to get some men inside to open the gates," he realized. "I can sneak you in."

"How?" Alexandria asked, ignoring Calum's look of annoyance. They had agreed that he would do the questioning, but that didn't mean she couldn't ask anything.

"There's a secret passageway leading to Lake Lewes."

"Does the queen know about it?" Calum asked, taking charge of the interrogation again.

"Probably, but she won't expect you to know about it." Setting his empty plate aside, he drank his goblet of water. "I can get you in."

"What about Dorset?" Alexandria asked. "What's it like?"

"There aren't many people left in Dorset. The queen didn't extend her generosity to the village when it came to the children. All the young families have left, only single men and the elderly live there now."

"Will the men give us any trouble when we ride through?" Calum asked.

"I don't know," Rufus answered honestly. "Many of the soldiers spend time in Dorset when off duty and have friends there, but at the same time many hate the queen."

"What about Yarmouth?"

"They won't give you any trouble. Most of the men have probably already joined you."

Wondering how well he knew the castle itself, Alexandria asked, "What do you do at the castle?"

"I'm a blacksmith. I mainly make armor for the soldiers."

"Have you been inside the castle?"

"Only a few times," Rufus answered, beginning to understand where she was going with the questions.

"Can you get me to Minerva?"

"I have to find my wife."

"Won't she be wherever Minerva is?" Alexandria asked with a raised brow.

"You're right. I'll take you to the queen."

Nodding, she stood, and the men followed. She began moving towards the flap of the tent but then stopped and turned around. "You're not a prisoner here, but I would ask you to stay inside the tent. Minerva is watching us, and if she sees you here, she will kill your wife." Watching him intently, she added, "And then she'll take your children."

"But they're safe. They're heading north," he said, scrambling to his feet as panic filled him. Had he made a mistake by leaving them?

Shaking her head sadly, she said softly, "There's nowhere you can go that she can't find you. She found me here. She can appear before you out of smoke, as she did here when she tried to kill me."

"But she can't see me here?"

"In the tent, you're protected by the Amatarians' magick."

He nodded, but his mind was still on his children. Was he doing the right thing by going after Alva? Had he put his mother and children in danger? It was too late to change things now. He'd just have to do his part and hope Alexandria killed the queen.

Alexandria left the tent with the men right behind her. Outside, she turned to Genesis. "Should we trust him?"

He already had an opinion but wanted to know what her instincts were telling her. "What do you think?"

"His fear for his family is real. I think we should trust him."

Nodding, he said, "I agree."

Turning to Calum she asked, "What do you think?"

"I'm not as trusting, but I don't have your gift of feeling. If the two of you think we can trust him, then we will." But he planned on keeping an eye on Rufus, and would talk to her brothers and Demetrius to get their points of view.

✠✠✠✠✠

As the sun rose, the camp prepared to leave. Thanks to the queen's soldiers, there were enough horses for all the men, as well as a few extra to use as packhorses. Many men also wore the soldiers' armor and swords—including Rufus, to hide from the queen—and rode the soldiers' horses. More men from the north had joined them over the past two days, and they now journeyed with over eighty men.

While the army rode through the battlefield, Alexandria did her best not to look at the queen's dead soldiers, the sight filling her with conflicting emotions. The men had a different reaction. They sat straighter, prouder, on their horses, their faces showing their confidence as they were reminded of their victory.

Riding hard, they reached Yarmouth just after sunset. The villagers cheered as they traveled to the other side, closer to Dorset, which was still a day's ride away. Sharing their firewood, the locals helped make several fires on the outskirts of town, where a few tents had been set up. Villagers from all over town brought food for the men to cook over the fires.

Genesis found an empty cabin, where he and several of his men created a protective shield around it. Rufus hid inside.

Alexandria was walking around making sure everyone had something to eat when she saw Calum across the fire. He motioned towards the cabin and she knew it was time.

Entering, she saw only a chair and small table, where Rufus was sitting with an empty plate.

When he saw her he stood and offered her the chair.

She shook her head. "Rest, you'll be leaving soon."

The door opened and Niall and Finnean entered holding their helmets under their arms. Their breastplates displayed the queen's spider emblem, and their sword sheaths were engraved with spiders.

Putting his helmet on, Rufus left to wait outside, wanting to give them some privacy for their goodbyes.

"It's time," Niall said.

Swallowing, Alexandria tried to hide her fear and nodded.

"Hey," Finnean said with a smile, "we'll be okay."

She smiled weakly and remarked, "You promised to bring me home safe, but did you promise your wives you would come home too?"

Cupping her face in his hands, Niall said, "We will be going home. We're going to win." He pressed a kiss to her forehead before hugging her. In truth he didn't fully believe his own words but didn't want to worry his sister. She needed to mentally prepare for her battle ahead.

Finnean wasn't as worried and continued to grin. "Don't worry about us. We'll get that gate opened for you."

She hugged her brother tightly and said a silent prayer for their safety.

Outside, Calum was saying goodbye to his brothers, who all looked somber. Eadan and Bran were also wearing the queen's soldiers' armor and swords. They'd left their swords behind for others to use.

"Don't trust him," Calum warned. "He might try to find his wife as soon as you're inside."

Bran nodded. "We'll keep him in line."

Calum left it at that—they knew the plan, and he knew they would see it happen. Giving them each a hug, he said, "Be safe. My sisters will kill me if anything happens to you."

Niall and Finnean joined them and both shook Calum's hand.

"Take care of our sister," Niall requested firmly.

"I will."

Before anyone could say anything else, Nestor arrived with five of the soldiers' horses and Rufus joined them.

As the men prepared to mount, Calum joined Alexandria in the cabin. Seeing her tear-stricken face, he took her into his arms, offering silent comfort.

A few minutes later Demetrius entered and said, "They're gone." He could see the fear in his friend's expression and wanted to comfort her but felt it would be better to leave that to Calum. He left and closed the door behind him.

Calum led her to the chair and said, "You should sit down."

Shaking her head, Alexandria wiped her tears away. "No, I need to be out there where the men can see me. I don't want them thinking I'm hiding in the cabin crying."

"You are in the cabin crying."

Fury entered her eyes as she glared at him. "So I had a moment of weakness. I'm worried about my brothers, and yours too."

He cupped her face and looked into her eyes. "I'm worried too, but it's not a weakness. Let them see you're worried but still ready and willing to fight."

Nodding, she straightened her spine and left the cabin with Calum. After confirming with Genesis and Cristian when she and the rest of the men would ride, she went to one of the fires and took off her satchel and bow and quiver.

"I'll find you something to eat," Calum said from behind her as she sat down.

Shaking her head, she answered, "I can't eat anything." Thinking about her brothers and the fight ahead was making her stomach jump, and she wasn't sure she'd be able to keep any food down.

An elderly woman came forward, her gray hair curling around her face, and knelt beside Alexandria with a plate of food. "I've saved some food for you." Her blue eyes were tired and her smile sweet.

Alexandria couldn't deny her kind gesture. "Thank you," she said, taking the plate. Since the woman didn't leave her side, she took a few bites, praying her stomach could handle it.

"It's us who should thank you," the woman said.

"What's your name?"

"Lottie."

"Why should you thank me, Lottie?"

"You've brought hope back to us—hope that we'll be free again."

Alexandria asked her the question she was still struggling with. "Is that hope worth the lives lost?"

With a sad smile, Lottie said, "Freedom always comes with a cost. My boys went to join you a week ago, and I haven't found them here."

Sorrow filled Alexandria's eyes as she guessed what had happened to them.

Lottie continued. "Even knowing they're gone, my James would join you if he could."

"Who's James?"

"My husband. He was hurt a few days past."

Alexandria straightened. "He's hurt?"

"Our horse stomped on him while he was working in the fields."

Standing, she picked up her satchel and said, "Take me to your husband."

Lottie led Alexandria and Calum to her cabin, which was not far from the fire. Inside, James lay on a bed with a lit candle on a table beside him. Lottie rushed to his side and took his hand while saying his name.

When he didn't answer, she turned to Alexandria with fear in her eyes. "He's been getting worse. I don't know what to do."

"Has a healer been here?" she asked, placing her satchel on the table.

Lottie shook her head. "We don't have a healer here."

Alexandria crossed the room and placed a hand on his forehead. He was covered in sweat and burning hot. Pulling the blanket back, she lifted his shirt. His bruised, swollen stomach indicated that he was bleeding internally. Without a healer's help he would be dead in a day's time.

She'd never healed anything this bad before, having always gotten to people before too much time had passed. Praying her necklace could boost her healing power, she placed both hands on his stomach and closed her eyes. Opening herself up, she felt her way through his wound and mended it as she went.

Lottie gasped as she watched the swelling go down and the bruise fade.

As she pulled back, Alexandria felt that something else was wrong. She dragged the blanket the rest of the way off him and saw that his leg was bent unnaturally. Placing her hand on his leg she helped the bone straighten and mend until it was healed. She kept her hand on him and searched the rest of his body for injuries but found only bruises, which she healed until he was no longer in pain.

His eyes blinked open and Lottie cried in relief, resting her head on his chest. Raising a hand to his wife's hair, James stared at Alexandria, confused, and she smiled reassuringly.

She retrieved some herbs from her satchel and added them to a goblet of water Calum handed her. After stirring them in, she turned back to the couple at the bed.

"Lottie," she called.

Lottie sat up, tears streaming down her cheeks. "Thank you, thank you, thank you."

Feeling Lottie needed something to do to help steady herself, Alexandria held out the goblet. "He needs to drink this."

Lottie rushed forward to take it from her.

"Every drop," she told her.

Nodding, Lottie turned back to her husband. He was still too weak to sit up, so she held his head while helping him drink.

Wanting to give them some privacy, Alexandria packed her satchel and left with Calum. Outside, she went to one of the fires and asked a villager to take Lottie and James some food.

It didn't take long for word of her healing to spread through the village, and the news reassured everyone of her power and kindness. Hours later, when the sun started to rise, it was time to leave. Her satchel was loaded onto one of the packhorses, as it would be impractical to wear while fighting.

Calum walked with Alexandria to her horse. She put her foot in the stirrup and started to mount but after a slight pause stepped back down, turned to Calum, leaned in and kissed him. Before he had a chance to react, she pulled away and said, "For luck," then turned back to Stardust and mounted.

He stood there stunned as her horse trotted over to Genesis. With a shake of his head Calum turned to mount his horse. He didn't have time to think about what had just happened, but they would talk about it when this was all over.

While she waited for the others to mount their horses, she saw Lottie and James standing off to the side, calling out their farewells. James was still pale, and leaning on his wife, but Alexandria was pleased to see him up.

They rode through the day and night, needing to reach the castle gates by sunrise the next day.

✠✠✠✠✠

The men reached the secret passageway by the lake as the sun was setting. Rufus led them and their horses, which they had dismounted, through the tunnel.

"We have to hide the horses," Niall said.

Rufus shook his head. "There's nowhere to hide them. We need to get them to the stable. There are lots of horses on the grounds, so hopefully no one will notice these are the ones the soldiers took."

"How do you suggest we get them to the stables?" Bran asked.

"Soldiers go riding every day. No one's going to look twice at us for taking them back. As long as they don't recognize the horses, we're fine. We just need to wait until it's dark so no one sees us coming out of the tunnel."

"What about us?" Bran asked.

"We don't have to worry about that. The stable boys don't know every soldier."

In the tunnel they couldn't tell how dark it was outside, so Rufus waited an hour before opening the secret door a crack. Greeted by darkness, he opened the door the rest of the way to let the other men out.

After closing the door, he mounted his horse and said, "Follow me and act like you belong."

They rode to the stables and sure enough, the stable boys didn't even look at the riders as they hurried forward to lead the horses away.

"Now we just have to hide out until sunrise," Finnean said as they left the stable.

"We could stay at my cabin," Rufus suggested. In truth he just wanted to see if his wife was there, and safe.

"No, it's too risky," Bran answered. He knew what Rufus was thinking, but they still needed his help. What if he decided to take off with his wife?

"Trust me," Rufus said. "I'll get you to the gate."

"And Alexandria?" Finnean asked, stepping forward aggressively. "Are you going to help her like you promised?"

"My wife knows the castle better than I do. If she's alive, she'll help," Rufus promised.

Before anyone could answer, a soldier approached and asked them, "Who are you? I haven't seen you before."

Staying calm, Eadan stepped forward. "We're new."

Looking them over, the soldier asked, "Where are you from?"

"Guildford and Exeter."

The soldier nodded, not doubting their story. Since the queen's men hadn't come back from the battle on the plain, she had sent soldiers out to find more to join them. "What's your first duty?"

"Guarding the gatehouse. We're due there at dawn."

"Then you better get some rest. The shifts are long."

As the soldier walked away, Rufus let out the breath he'd been holding, relieved that he hadn't been recognized.

The others were also glad to once again be alone.

"We need to get out of here before someone else stops us," Niall said, sharing a look with the others.

Bran turned to Rufus, deciding to trust him. "Okay, take us to your cabin."

They walked with purpose across the field behind the castle, and no one paid them any mind. Entering the cabin, the men stayed by the door while Rufus looked for his wife.

He moved behind a screen to their bed and was heartened to see a body under the covers. Sitting on the edge of the bed, he touched her shoulder. "Alva."

Rolling onto her back, she said groggily, "Rufus?" When her eyes focused on him, she shouted, "Rufus!" and threw herself at him.

Hugging his wife tightly he whispered, "Shhhh."

Pulling back, she asked in a hushed voice, "What are you doing here? Where are the children?"

Brushing her hair off her face, he said, "They're fine. We're not alone. You need to get dressed."

After putting on her robe, she emerged from behind the screen and immediately clutched her husband's arm. "What's going on?"

Her frightened expression reminded Niall that he was dressed as a soldier, so he took off his helmet and said, "We didn't mean to scare you."

Still clutching her husband, she asked, "Are you here to take me to the queen?"

"No," Niall answered. "We're here to kill the queen."

"You're with the witch," she said with a gasp.

"She's my sister."

Alva's fear was replaced by hope. She knew the queen was worried about Alexandria, and that told her this witch had the power to defeat her. "Please, sit down. How can we help?"

The others took off their helmets as they sat at her table.

Rufus turned to his wife, and for the first time she noticed he was also in armor.

"At sunrise I'm taking them to the gatehouse," he said. "When the witch enters, we need to take her to the queen."

Nodding, Alva said, "I can do that. She's usually on her throne at sunrise."

"We just need to avoid Brodrick," Rufus said. "He'll know we're not soldiers."

"Who's Brodrick?" Bran asked.

"The queen's head soldier. When the battle starts, he'll be in control, and probably with the queen. He's always by her side to protect her."

Touching his arm, Alva said, "Brodrick's dead. He was with the men who went to attack the witch last week."

Rufus looked at the men.

Finnean shrugged. "We killed many. We didn't know who they were."

"This is good for us. Without him, there will be chaos."

CHAPTER FIFTEEN

Alexandria and her men rode through Dorset, and she couldn't believe how barren the land was, with no flower or vegetable gardens anywhere. There were no children running around—in fact, there was no one around. She'd always thought of Dorset as a bustling village but instead it was empty, with cabins that looked abandoned.

They stopped as the castle came into view. Even with the distance they could see the battlements full of soldiers and weren't surprised, knowing the queen would be prepared for their arrival.

Sensing something, Alexandria turned to Genesis, who was next to her.

"Yes," he said. "I feel it too."

"What?" Calum asked from the other side of Alexandria.

"Those soldiers, they're not real." Turning, she called for Demetrius. "When we're riding we need to shoot them, all at the same time."

Nodding, he rode off to spread the word.

"Are you ready?" Calum asked.

Looking him dead in the eyes, she answered, "Yes. Let's finish this." Holding her bow high, she yelled, *"Charge!"*

The horses' hooves rumbled like thunder. Pulling an arrow from her quiver, she called, "Now, Demetrius!"

He gave the order, and dozens of arrows shot towards the men on the battlements. Just before they struck Alexandria used her magick to light them on fire, and the men who were hit burst into smoke. The remaining soldiers fired arrows back.

✠✠✠✠✠

Inside the castle, Minerva watched the scene in her basin.

"So she recognized my trick," she said with surprise.

You have many more.

"Yes, and she won't be prepared for them."

✠✠✠✠✠

Rufus and the others waited by the gatehouse. They didn't want to attack too early. When they heard the cries of their army in the distance, they knew it was time. Slipping into the gatehouse, they saw four men shooting through arrowslits, and pulled their swords.

Hearing a noise, one of the queen's soldiers turned and realized they were under attack. With a yell he charged, causing the others to stop shooting and turn. The soldiers also pulled their swords, and fought the intruders. The room was small, making maneuvering difficult, but it wasn't long before the last soldier fell. Eadan ran to an arrowslit and looked out to see that Alexandria and her army were closer than he'd expected.

"Raise the gate," he called.

As it rose, several of the queen's soldiers ran for the gatehouse to stop them. Hearing their footsteps, Eadan turned to face them, ready to fight. He kicked the first man in the chest, and as he flew backward, he took a few more soldiers down with him. Three soldiers climbed over the fallen with their swords raised. Niall rushed to Eaden's side to help, seeing more soldiers storming towards them. With the gate secured, the others joined the fight to keep the gate open.

Alexandria and her men rode through the open gate, swords ready to fight the men in front of them. As the battle began raging around her, she dismounted and sprinted for the castle. Along the way she fought soldiers, some real, some smoke. Seeing her intentions, three soldiers moved to guard the main entrance. Alexandria raised her sword as she ran, preparing to fight, but just as she reached them an Amatarian called forth a gust and sent them flying, clearing the doorway. Inside, she looked for Rufus as planned but didn't see him.

✠✠✠✠✠

Minerva's hands clutched the edge of her pedestal as she watched her soldiers die.

"How did they get in?" she hissed.

You have traitors in the castle.

"Who?" she demanded, vowing to take care of them when this was over. She still had no doubt she would be victorious.

In the water a new picture glowed, showing her the men in the gatehouse fighting her soldiers.

"Rufus," she snarled, recognizing one of them. "Where's Alva?"

With the witch. She's taking her to the throne room, looking for you.

Straightening, Minerva said, "Then I better not disappoint her." She stalked from the chamber.

✠✠✠✠✠

Thinking Rufus had betrayed her, Alexandria rushed through the halls alone in search of the queen.

"Psst."

Glancing around, Alexandria heard the noise again.

"Psst."

Then she saw a woman hiding behind a column, waving her over. She was obviously a servant, dressed in all beige except for her white blouse, her hair pulled back in a bun with a few pieces around her face. As Alexandria approached the woman's eyes widened, and she pointed behind her.

"Look out!"

Alexandria turned just as a soldier reached her. Blocking his blow she struck back. He was too skilled for her to fight, so she used her powers to take his sword from him as she struck again, this time killing him.

The woman rushed to her side and took her arm. "Follow me. I'll take you to the queen."

"Who are you?" Alexandria asked as they hurried down the long hall.

"I'm Alva. Rufus is with your brothers."

After turning a few corners, Alva stopped and pointed. "That's her throne room."

"Thank you," Alexandria whispered. "Now run, so no one knows you helped me."

With a curtsy Alva rushed off, and Alexandria headed for the opening. Taking a deep breath, she held up her sword and entered.

At the end of the long hall, Minerva sat on her throne as though she had nothing to worry about, as though there weren't a war going on outside the walls of her castle. She wore a black dress with silver spiders embroidered along the neckline, and a silver band around her waist. Her hair was pulled back and up, and her lips were painted her signature dark red.

Alexandria stared at the spider necklace around her neck. As Minerva tapped her fingers on one of the skulls, horror filled Alexandria, for she knew they were real—she could feel it. Feeling the anger rise up in her, she started forward.

All of a sudden Minerva smiled wickedly and soldiers filed out from behind her throne on both sides. They moved down the stairs towards Alexandria. Raising her sword, she charged forward, blocking a blow before slicing her sword through the soldier's middle. He burst into black smoke before becoming a man again.

Alexandria took a step back in shock while Minerva laughed.

"Did you really believe you could defeat me?" she called from her throne.

The men surrounded Alexandria but didn't attack. Holding her sword in front of her she slowly turned in a circle, trying to figure out which one was going to attack first.

"Well, little witch, let's see what you can do." With a wave of her hand she ordered her creations, "Kill her," and sat back to watch the show.

As the circle tightened around her, Alexandria summoned the swords from their hands. She then dropped to the ground just before sending the weapons flying across the circle and into the opposite soldiers' chests. As they burst into smoke she rolled away, out of the circle.

Minerva clapped slowly. "Impressive, but you didn't destroy them."

The smoke once again became men, this time holding new swords. The old ones lay on the floor behind them. They turned as one to face her. She didn't know how she was going to get past them. Hearing thundering feet behind her, Alexandria braced for more soldiers.

But it was Calum, Demetrius, Niall, Finnean, Genesis, and Cristian who entered the room, along with more of their men behind them. Her confidence back, she moved to stand with them.

"They're not real," she told them. "They're just smoke."

A line of smoke began to shimmer down the middle of each soldier's body. As the smoke faded all the soldiers stepped to the right; there were now two in the place of each one—they had doubled their numbers.

"I can see that," Calum answered. Sharing a look, he and Alexandria raised their swords together, and with a scream they charged, the others right behind them.

Alexandria's only goal was to reach the queen. She fought with all her strength, blocking one blow while ducking another, moving through the creations towards the throne.

Her hands gripping the skulls, Minerva watched the fight through narrow eyes.

Bursting through the final soldiers, Alexandria finally stood before Minerva.

Breathing heavily, she raised her sword. "Are you ready to fight me, or do you have more smoke to throw my way?"

Minerva stood and descended the stairs, then moved to her right. Alexandria turned to face her. "I've never been afraid to fight you," said Minerva. "I've just been enjoying your little rebellion."

Alexandria ran towards her. Throwing out her hand, Minerva sent her spinning backward into the wall. Her head smacked the concrete before she fell to the ground. Dazed, Alexandria lifted her hand to her forehead and felt blood.

Laughing, Minerva asked, "Is this how you planned to kill me? And here I thought you had powers."

Alexandria got to her knees, and her eyes hardened. "You want power? You got it." Throwing both hands out, she sent Minerva flying back. She crashed into the table along the wall launching the goblets, jugs, and platters into the air before they clattered to the ground around her.

Minerva sat there, stunned, as the pool of water and wine slowly crept towards her. She'd never come across someone with this much power before.

I told you, her necklace whispered. *You have to kill her now.*

She threw out her hands again, and black smoke surrounded Alexandria, lifting her off her feet. Standing, Minerva smiled wickedly, her eyes dark as night. Alexandria began to choke, and her hands flew to her throat. With a laugh Minerva stepped closer, closing her fingers to tighten the grip.

Alexandria closed her eyes and relaxed, not fighting Minerva's magick.

Don't let go, her necklace told her. *She's not dead.*

And she wasn't. Alexandria gathered all the power she had within her, and when she felt the full force of her strength, she opened her eyes and threw out her hands, sending Minerva's magick back at her.

Free, she fell to her knees, gasping, and saw Minerva on the ground.

Realizing this was her chance, Alexandria grabbed her bow and an arrow from the quiver on her back. As Minerva was getting up she aimed her arrow and, saying a prayer, sent it flying, using her magick to help it find its target.

Nooo! the necklace screamed as Minerva stood.

She saw the arrow too late. The stone shattered into a million pieces.

Minerva fell to her knees, screaming with rage as she felt the necklace's power drain out of her.

Her soldiers turned back to smoke before fading away, and the other men turned to see Alexandria and the queen facing off.

Alexandria quickly picked up her sword and ran forward. It appeared as if Minerva had lost most of her power, but not all of it. A sword appeared in her hand, and she blocked Alexandria's first swing. As they fought a dagger appeared in Minerva's other hand, and she plunged it into Alexandria's leg. Minerva then twisted the dagger before ripping it out and kicking her backward.

Holding her injury, Alexandria crawled back a few feet.

Laughing, Minerva stepped forward. "Even without the necklace I'm stronger than you."

When the men started forward, Genesis held up his hand. "No. This is for Alexandria to finish."

With her hand still on her leg, Alexandria stood and said, "You're wrong." Spreading both hands at her sides, she called for all the fallen weapons. One by one the swords rose from the floor and circled Alexandria. Her hair blew around her in the strong wind. Throwing her hands out she sent all the weapons flying towards Minerva.

Minerva used her sword and dagger to block and dodge the weapons, but for every one she blocked another came. Alexandria picked up her sword and ran at her. Ducking under a flying sword, she thrust hers forward. Minerva gasped as the blade pierced her heart. She fell back, her hand on the sword, her eyes locked on Alexandria's as she struggled for her final breath.

Alexandria fell to one knee. Breathing heavily, she placed her hand over her injury again and healed it.

The men rushed to her side. As she stood back up, Calum wrapped her in his arms and kissed her in a long, intimate embrace.

After a few seconds Finnean cleared his throat loudly.

Pulling away, Calum said, "It was my turn to kiss you."

Alexandria answered in a whisper, "I didn't kiss you in front of my brothers."

"You kissed him?" Finnean asked in a loud voice, stepping forward.

Niall put a hand on his brother's shoulder to keep him in place.

She ignored Demetrius's grin and said to her brothers with her hands on her hips, "I kissed him for luck. You got a problem with that?"

"No," Niall answered. "But Father might."

A grin slowly spread across Finnean's face at the thought. "I look forward to that conversation."

Not ready to think about it, Calum turned back to the dead queen and said, "I always thought she'd turn to dust when she was killed."

"Why?" Alexandria asked.

Calum shrugged. "Because she was so old."

Shaking her head, she turned to focus on her brothers, searching for any signs of injury. Alexandria let out a sigh of relief that all three were in one piece before she looked over the others.

Finnean laughed and said, "I thought the same."

Niall nodded. "Me too."

Thinking that was the most ridiculous thing she'd ever heard, she started to laugh, and hugged her brothers.

Niall touched her forehead. "You should heal this."

"Soon," she answered, looking around sadly at her fallen men, feeling guilty that she was so happy her friends and family weren't amongst them.

Men swept the castle to confirm all the queen's soldiers were dead. Though most of them had been smoke, many had been real. A few Tolgarians and Amatarians searched for survivors. Men entered the throne room and cheered when they saw the queen dead. The sounds of their cheers told the people outside that Alexandria had won, and the cheers echoed.

Turning to Genesis, Alexandria took off the necklace and held it out to him.

"Don't you want to keep it?" he asked, not taking it from her. "You've earned it."

She shook her head and continued to hold it out. "No, I don't need it anymore."

Nodding, he took the necklace back, very proud of her.

Calum went to one knee before her and bowed his head.

"What are you doing?" she asked, perplexed.

Looking at her, he answered, "I'm pledging my allegiance to the new queen."

While she stared at him in stunned silence, her brothers immediately went to one knee as well.

"I can't be queen," she told them. "I'm not of the royal line."

"There's no one left of the royal line," Genesis told her. "Minerva destroyed it long ago."

Thinking of the throne behind her, she knew that was true.

"The Tolgarians couldn't do better than to have you as their new queen," Genesis added.

The other Tolgarians in the room knelt and bowed their heads.

She turned to Genesis. "I don't know anything about leading."

Waving his hand, he said, "Look around you. What do you think you've been doing these past weeks? These men followed you, rode into war with you, because they believed in you. You'll be a great queen, and by giving the necklace back you proved it."

"How?" she asked, not understanding.

"You proved you're not hungry for power, and that's the kind of ruler the people need."

Looking at the men still on their knees, she said, "I'm just a healer."

"Then heal the land, and all the people within it." With that, Genesis went to one knee.

The Amatarians in the room followed suit, including Demetrius, who had been grinning the whole time.

Finnean rose and walked over to Minerva. He took her crown and placed it on his sister's head before kneeling before her again.

Overwhelmed, Alexandria looked at Genesis.

He stood and said, "There will be time to celebrate later, but now we need to tend to our injured."

Everyone left the room except for Alexandria's friends and brothers.

Turning to Calum, she asked, "Are you going home now?"

"And miss my chance to dance with the queen?" Calum grinned. "You promised me a party when this was over," he reminded her.

"I never said *I* was going to throw a party. We said there would be a huge party."

"Well, now that you're queen, you can do whatever you want."

"Then my first order of business is to give them a proper burial," she said, pointing to the throne behind her.

"Do you think the bones are real?" Finnean asked, staring at the throne.

"I know they are. They belonged to the last king and queen."

"We'll take care of it," Niall promised her.

"I'm going to see who's hurt."

Alexandria took off the crown and left it behind as she went outside to join the Amatarians, who were healing the injured. They dealt with the serious injuries first—thankfully there weren't many. Even without the necklace, she could feel her gift was stronger. When they were done she walked amongst the men to see how many they had lost, and was grateful there weren't as many dead as there had been after the last battle.

That night Alexandria led a procession of men carrying the fallen to the lake. They laid them out in two rows by the peaceful blue water. She placed a flower on each man's chest and said a prayer for him, thanking him for his sacrifice, just as she had after the last battle. Then standing beside Genesis, she lit the bodies on fire with ease that surprised her.

Word of the queen's death spread quickly throughout the country. As joy filled the air, people began traveling to the castle for the big celebration that would happen in a month's time. Her friends were surprised she was waiting so long, but this celebration was for the whole country, and she wanted to give everyone enough time to make the journey. She especially wanted her parents there and knew their trip would take several weeks. During that time, she wiped Minerva from the castle.

✠✠✠✠✠

On the day of the celebration, Alexandria's parents still hadn't arrived. Genesis had told her they were traveling with some Amatarians, so she knew they were on their way. She prayed everything was okay. Standing on the balcony of the throne room, she watched people setting up tables for food and drinks beside the lake.

Closing her eyes, she enjoyed the breeze as it blew her hair off her face, and thought of how much things had changed in only a month. The hall looked and felt much brighter. Stands decorated with tall, colorful flowers had been placed in front of the columns of the arches. The throne and small platform had been removed, and the royal platform currently housed a long table with several chairs. The setup was similar to that of Genesis's hut.

After the battle, she'd asked the female servants if anyone had a skirt to spare, and a couple of days later, she was presented the most beautiful dress she'd ever seen, followed by more throughout the week. They had been sewn by Minerva's dressmakers. Though Alexandria had told them many times she didn't need anything so fancy, no one would listen. It seemed the dressmakers enjoyed creating these new dresses for her.

Inhaling another breath of fresh air, she looked down at the exquisite dress she was wearing. It was the color of cream and adorned with beautiful gold embroidery. The neckline swooped across her chest, a little lower than she would have liked, but the dressmakers had ignored her protests about that too. The soft material made her feel like a queen.

"If I had known this was all it would take to get you to dress like a lady, I would have made you queen long ago," a woman said.

Grinning, Alexandria spun around and saw her parents standing in the doorway. Her father's hair was down, and he looked as though he hadn't shaved in weeks—since he'd been traveling, she assumed he probably hadn't. He was wearing brown pants and a beige shirt. Her mother was wearing a green skirt and tan vest over her blouse. Her hair was pulled back in a bun, but as usual the wind had pulled a few pieces loose to lay against her cheeks.

She laughed as she ran towards them. "I'm so glad you came," she said, throwing her arms around them.

"Of course we came," Alpin said. "Where else would we be?"

Looking at her mother, Alexandria could see how worried she'd been in the form of new wrinkles. "Are you still mad at me?"

With tears in her eyes, Adella cupped her daughter's face in her hands. "Yes. But I'm more proud of you."

Her father patted her shoulder. "We're both proud of you, but I'm more interested in meeting this man you were traveling with."

Smiling, Alexandria said, "You can meet him later. Just remember, he did save my life and help me kill Minerva, so go easy on him, okay?"

Kissing his daughter's cheek, he told her, "I make no promises."

She laughed again, wrapped an arm around each of their waists, and led them to the drawing room, where the rest of her family was waiting. Niall was holding his little girl.

Alexandria ran across the room to hug her sisters-in-law. "I'm so glad you're here."

Helen hugged her tightly. "We're happy to see you too."

When it was Agnes's turn, her sister-in-law whispered, "We'll be happy to meet your man too."

She gave Agnes a "behave" look before going to her brother. "She's gotten so big," she said, looking down at her niece.

Niall handed his daughter over, and then wrapped an arm around his wife. They smiled watching Alexandria cuddle her niece.

Looking around, she noticed one person was missing. "Where's Grandmother?"

"She's checking out her new home," Agnes answered with a smile as she leaned against her husband.

Calum walked into the room with Genesis.

"Everyone, this is Calum."

Agnes snuck to Alexandria's side and whispered, "Good job."

Alexandria elbowed her and sent Calum an apologetic smile.

Stepping forward, Alpin said, "So you're Calum."

He glanced at Alexandria before answering, "Yes, sir."

"I believe we need to have a talk."

"Yes, sir."

"Father—"

Alpin held up his hand to stop his daughter. "Let's take a walk."

As they left the room Niall and Finnean followed, leaving a worried sister behind.

✠✠✠✠✠

A few hours later, Alexandria walked with her family to the lake, where a crowd was already gathered. She greeted each person as she made her way through and was pleased to see the Tolgarians and Amatarians mingling—the party was for them all. Seeing Genesis, she headed towards him. He was dressed more regally than she'd ever seen him, in an intricately woven robe he only wore on special occasions. This garment was the only item Genesis owned that displayed his status.

"Why aren't the musicians playing?" she asked when she reached him.

"We have something to do first." He moved aside and gestured for her to walk ahead of him.

After taking a few steps, she saw a platform. Demetrius was standing beside it holding a box.

Confused, she climbed the few steps to the top of the platform with Genesis and Demetrius behind her. When she faced the crowd she saw her family up front, all dressed in the fancy new clothes that had been prepared for their arrival. Seeing the pride on her parents' faces, and on the faces of her brothers and their wives, put her at ease. Her grandmother stared at her with tears in her eyes and a huge smile on her face.

She saw Calum standing with them and smiled. Her dressmakers had also created a new wardrobe for him, and she was enjoying seeing him in nicer clothing. She hadn't seen him since he left with her father and really wanted to know how the conversation had gone. Her brothers had refused to tell her anything.

Calum's family was only a few feet away from hers. She'd met his father and sisters when they arrived a few days before, and felt grateful to have witnessed Clara's and Una's joyful reunions with their husbands.

Looking around, she spotted Rufus and Alva with their two children and an older woman, who Alexandria assumed was Rufus's mother. Lottie and James were also in the crowd smiling up at her. In fact, everyone was smiling at her except for two people: Michael and his bride, who had married shortly after Alexandria left the village.

Seeing him now, she wondered what it had been about him that she'd been so interested in. He seemed so small and ordinary and, she was sorry to say, lacking in comparison to Calum. She harbored no bad feelings towards him and wished him nothing but happiness with his bride—she was just glad that bride wasn't her.

A hush fell over the crowd as everyone turned to watch her. Alexandria glanced at Genesis, hoping he would let her know what to do.

He smiled and looked at the people. In a loud voice that carried across the gathering, he said, "It's time to celebrate a new era, and a new queen to lead the way." Turning to Demetrius, he opened the box and pulled out the crown his people had created— ropes of gold woven in a beautiful, intricate design. Lifting it high, he moved behind Alexandria and lowered it until it rested on her head.

Finnean yelled, "Long live the queen!"

The crowd chanted, "Long live the queen! Long live the queen!"

Genesis moved to her side and went to one knee before her, bowing his head.

Then Demetrius, her family, and Calum knelt, and everyone followed like a wave. Alexandria looked around, wondering what she should do. Going with her instincts, she held out the sides of her skirt and curtsied low, bowing her head as well. After a moment everyone rose together. Genesis took her hand and led her down the stairs.

Phoebe stepped forward and wrapped her granddaughter in a hug. "I told you your day would come."

Pulling back she asked, "My day of what? Did you know I was going to go after Minerva?"

"No. I knew you'd find love on a journey, but I didn't know what the journey looked like."

Alexandria lowered her eyes. She was in love with Calum but didn't know if he felt the same. They hadn't really spent any time together over the last month. He'd been with the men and the horses, while she'd been meeting everyone in the castle, and everyone who'd traveled to Dorset for the party. Calum had joined her for supper every night, but so had her brothers. So they'd never talked about what would happen next. For all she knew, he could be planning to go home with his family.

Phoebe placed a finger under her granddaughter's chin and tilted her face back up. "I don't see a broken heart in your future."

A smile spread across Alexandria's face. She might not know what was going to happen next, but now she had faith everything would work out.

Calum joined them and Phoebe gave him a hug. She patted his cheek as she stepped back. "It's nice to see you again."

"You say that as though you knew this day would come," Calum said with a smile.

"I always knew our paths would cross once more." Running a hand down her granddaughter's arm she added, "And I'm very happy with this path."

The music started and Calum held out his hand. Smiling, Alexandria placed her hand in his, and the crowd parted before them as they walked. When they reached an empty piece of land beside the lake, Alexandria turned to face her partner. She rested her free hand on his shoulder as his went to her waist, and they started to dance.

Genesis and his wife joined them, and then Alexandria's parents and siblings. Calum's sisters joined next, and then the land was full of dancers.

Spinning her around, Calum said, "There seems to be one unhappy couple."

Glancing to her right, she saw Michael frowning at her while his wife frowned at him.

"That's Michael and his wife," she told him.

Raising a brow he asked, "The Michael you thought you were going to marry?"

"Yes."

"I guess he's seeing what a mistake he made."

She shook her head. "No, if we had married, I probably wouldn't have gone after the queen."

"And then you wouldn't be queen."

"And I wouldn't have met you," she added softly.

Their eyes locked, and he lowered his head and kissed her. The people around them cheered, and they danced the night away.

EPILOGUE

The old woman smiled at her enthralled grandchildren, who were all watching her with wide eyes. If only all histories were such good stories. Finishing, she said, "For the first time, there was true peace in Tolgaria. The Tolgarians and Amatarians even grew to become friends. Alexandria's whole family moved to the castle, which gave her a sense of security in her new life. She appointed Genesis a member of her council and always spoke with him before making big decisions to ensure that whatever she did was right for her people and his. She was a kind ruler, and loved by all. It's said her servants were eager to do anything she asked, and even things she didn't ask. Fun returned to the castle grounds, and the children ran free, their laughter filling the air. Their parents no longer worried about the noise upsetting the queen since Alexandria loved to watch them play, and would even join them. Everyone was welcome in the castle, whether Tolgarian or Amatarian."

"What happened with Alexandria and Calum?" one granddaughter asked.

"And Demetrius?" another piped up.

"Alexandria and Calum married in a simple wedding surrounded by people on the shore of Lake Lewes, and afterward, Calum's family moved to the castle and continued their business. With Nestor's help, theirs became the number one horse breeding business in the land, and still is to this day. Alexandria loved to go riding and hunting with Calum, and when she did she wore pants, to her mother's dismay."

The girls giggled as they tugged on their pants.

"Demetrius visited often and one day showed up with Talora, his wife. Alexandria was upset she hadn't been invited to their wedding, but he explained that they had married quickly, before Talora could change her mind. Alexandria was nothing but happy for them, and even though Talora had shown interest in Calum, she knew there was nothing to worry about now. The years passed and families moved back to the southern villages, which doubled in size. The Tolgarians and Amatarians shared their knowledge and worked together to help the land flourish. As Alexandria watched her children grow, she continued to use her gifts to heal, and helped deliver many new babies into a world of peace."

Amanda Simoni and her family moved around often when she was younger, which sparked her passion for traveling. She loves visiting other countries and would eventually like to visit every continent.

Amanda has worked at Banff and Jasper National Parks in Canada. Currently she lives in Calgary, Alberta, and owns a bookkeeping business there with her mother.

When she is writing, Amanda likes to bounce ideas for stories off her older brother, with whom she is very close. In addition to writing and travel, she enjoys photography and watching TV and movies.